J. H. Brennan is a professional writer whose work has been published in over fifty countries. His books include *An Occult History of the World, Nostradamus – Visions of the Future, Experimental Magic, Understanding Reincarnation* and *The Aquarian Guide to the New Age* (with Eileen Campbell). He lives in County Wicklow in the Republic of Ireland.

ANCIENT SPIRIT

AN EXPLORATION OF MAGIC

J. H. Brennan

WARNER BOOKS

A *Warner* Book

First published in Great Britain by Warner Books in 1993

A CIP catalogue record for this book
is available from the British Library.

ISBN 0 7515 0182 4

Typeset in Trump Mediaeval by 📐 Tek-Art,
Addiscombe, Croydon, Surrey

Printed and bound in Great Britain by
Richard Clay Ltd, Bungay, Suffolk

Warner Books
A Division of
Little, Brown and Company (UK) Limited
165 Great Dover Street
London SE1 4YA

CONTENTS

PREFACE

Just a few weeks ago, I was involved – along with more than thirty others – in an unusual experiment. We were attempting to evoke a spirit to visible appearance.

The techniques used were fundamentally those of the medieval magicians. A circle was drawn on the floor and beyond it, in the east, an equilateral triangle was marked out. Both were 'fortified' by divine and angelic names. Candles were lit and incense burned.

There were, however, departures from tradition. The ancient grimoires specify that the operator and all others present should remain within the circle. The triangle is set to contain the manifesting spirit.

In this instance, by contrast, there were only two people within the circle: myself and the woman who habitually channelled the entity we were attempting to evoke. Three others of those present were stationed at the points of the triangle. Five more stood in a bow formation to the south, outside the circle. The remainder were ranged in two groups to the north and south, again outside the circle.

There were reasons for each of these departures, all of them encompassed by traditional magical postulates, and safeguards were built in to reassure the more conservative elements among those present.

The theory of the operation was that an aspect of the

entity evoked would pass from the medium through whom he habitually communicated and enter a specially constructed 'astral vehicle' within the triangle. An astral vehicle is a suitable body for the entity, created by collective visualization – a body, in other words, that those present *imagine* to be there.

From one viewpoint, the experiment was a failure. If anyone present saw the entity materialize, even briefly, they did not report it. From another viewpoint, however, it was an extraordinary success. At the point of transfer – that is, the point at which the entity was supposed to enter the astral vehicle – one of those standing at a point of the triangle was slammed back violently against the wall and began to emit guttural, animalistic sounds. It took him some twenty minutes to return to normal.

The channeller within the circle was even more profoundly affected. She went into a trance state that resisted all attempts to break for more than an hour. The reason given for these unexpected effects was that too much 'power' had been generated.

The interesting thing about all this is not what happened, but the fact that magic is still practised in our civilized world – and still capable of producing unpredictable results. That they were, in this instance, interior results is hardly surprising for it is clear to any dispassionate investigation that magic is an aspect of depth psychology, dealing with the same forces in the unconscious that are the concern of psychoanalysis.

What has not been generally realized, however, is that depth psychology is also an aspect of magic. For magical theory is quite capable of clarifying – in some instances explaining – many of the mysteries of depth psychology while magical practice goes far beyond the phenomena of the consulting room.

In short, it is not just the magicians who have something to learn from the psychologists. The psychologists could usefully study the work and findings of the magicians – based literally on millennia of experience – in order to enlarge their own system.

If magic and psychology are two aspects of a single whole, it would be a great mistake to assume that knowledge of psychology will somehow help 'explain away' magic. Quite the reverse is the case. The discoveries of the magicians not only enrich our knowledge of psychology, but positively force acceptance of a new and different viewpoint of the human mind – particularly of the way it interacts with what we think of as physical reality.

This book is an examination of evidence which points to the conclusion that magic works, although often in a different way and for different reasons than magicians themselves believe. It is also a plea for the dispassionate evaluation of magical phenomena (long considered far too disreputable for scientific interest) and a fervent hope that the disciplines of magic and depth psychology may someday draw close to one another. Both have much to gain from a cross-pollination.*

J. H. Brennan
Ireland
August, 1992

---

*Those who agree may be interested in the study course based on an integration of the two disciplines. Details of the course are available from: Sacred Science, Stratford Lodge, Raheen, Baltinglass, County Wicklow, Republic of Ireland.

CHAPTER

1

THE CAVE-ART MYSTERY

On a chill day more than twenty thousand years ago, in what is now North-Eastern Spain, a solitary figure crawled along a narrow corridor in the dark, inaccessible depths of a rambling cavern complex. She was smallish in stature, stockily built and plump, heavily wrapped in animal skins and furs.[1] Her face was pale and flat, with narrow eyes like those of the modern Eskimo. She lit her way in the darkness with a shallow stone saucer-lamp burning animal fat.

There was a medicine bag strung round her neck with a length of sinew-gut cord drawn perhaps from an ibex. In it were sticks of charcoal and mineral pencils of yellow ochre, red ochre, manganese and iron oxide, along with damp clay, some tuberous roots and several twigs chewed at one end to produce a collection of fibrous brushes. In another pouch, much more heavily wrapped in insulating skins, was water, in the form of a small block of ice.

The woman reached the end of the corridor, now tapered to such narrow confines that it was little larger than a crack in the surrounding rock. She placed her stone lamp on a convenient ledge and began to extract the brushes and the pigments from her bag. One imagines she may have hesitated, perhaps even voiced a prayer, but eventually she began to paint. Her picture, outlined in black and red on the cavern wall, was drawn from memory and imagination. It was a picture of a hind.

Millennia later, in 1879, Don Marcelino de Sautuola raised his torch to examine the same hind and a veritable gallery of prehistoric art so sophisticated in its execution, so technically advanced in style, that experts of his day were universal in their condemnation of the whole find as a modern fake. Then other, similar painted caverns were discovered and opinions had to be revised. To date, about 230 caves containing art are known. The great majority are in France and Spain, but additional examples have been found in Italy, Portugal and the former Soviet Union.

The paintings in these caverns exhibit various techniques. Some are done in outline only. Others are filled in with a flat wash, or shaded in colours. Drawings can be seen, made by dipping the fingers in wet clay or paint. Hand imprints are also featured. These seem to have been made by applying a paint-daubed hand against the wall, or placing a clean hand flat then spraying around it a mouthful of pigment, usually a solution of white clay. The colours used were ground from natural deposits of mineral ore and mixed with animal fat, vegetable juices, water or blood, then applied with a stick or brush.

Prehistoric art first appeared during the Upper Palaeolithic, the final division of the Old Stone Age, and was almost exclusively associated with Cro-Magnon humanity *(Homo sapiens sapiens)*, who appeared in Europe about 35,000 years ago. Animals were the favourite subject-matter. Those artists who followed our cave woman into the Altamira cavern depicted bison, ibex, stags, chamois, aurochs, horses and one example of what appears to be a large feline.

But many symbols – lines, spirals, zig-zag abstractions – and some masked human figures have also been found.

The earliest known style was developed in the Aurignacian culture around 30,000 BC. These paintings, primitive though they were, show the familiar gamut of prehistoric art – animals engraved in rigid outline or painted black or red, finger drawings on clay, imprints of hands, and engravings on slabs. From c. 29,000 to c. 20,000 BC the quality of work improved, and the animals were sometimes shaded. Symbols became numerous and complicated.

There are two problems with all of this. One is what those symbols represented. The other is why the people of the Palaeolithic bothered to paint caves in the first place.

Today, of course, art is used to decorate our homes and, more formally, as a display designed to elevate the human spirit.[2] This cannot have been the case in prehistory. Painted caverns like those at Altamira give no indication of having ever been used as habitations. Even the notion of a primitive art gallery does not bear examination. While sculpted cave art is generally found in shallow rock shelters or near cavern entrances, most paintings are found deep inside. At Niaux in France, for example, the first paintings are about 600 yards from the entrance. From cave mouth to the great fish at La Pileta cave, Spain, is even further – about 1,300 yards. A major feature of another cavern is so inaccessible that it requires you to risk life and limb swinging out from a natural window with one foot on a tall rock spur before it can be seen at all. Manifestly, these artworks were not meant for general viewing.

Yet they were not casual creations either. An enormous amount of effort went into their composition.

The Cro-Magnon artists often – indeed usually – worked in cramped, difficult conditions. Some paintings are so high that ladders or scaffolding obviously had to be used; no mean feat in a pre-technical culture. The paints were applied in gloom and semi-darkness, by the flickering of torchlight or animal-fat lamps. Smoke smudges can still be seen on the walls.

The artworks themselves are intricate. They might be carved in high or low relief, modelled in clay, or engraved deeply or finely and then hatched. The animals depicted – mammoths, bison, horses, deer, cattle, goats and wild boars; with woolly rhinoceros, antelopes, cave lions, wolves, cave bears, birds and fish more rarely shown – were executed with a skill and grace that suggests a substantial investment of time. A writer on prehistoric art in the *Grolier Electronic Encyclopedia* goes so far as to say, 'Often ... these artworks are masterpieces of their kind, rivalling the finest art of any later age in force, splendor, and elegance.'

One wonders where the artists found the leisure to produce such masterpieces. They lived in interesting times, the heart of the Pleistocene Ice Age. The whole of Scandinavia lay beneath a single ice sheet, like much of today's Arctic. Almost all of northern Europe was devoid of woodland, chill wastes of tundra broken only rarely in the most sheltered spots by a straggle of pinewood. The Baltic Sea was cut off from the North Sea and existed as little more than a deep, brackish lake. The Gulf Stream was diverted south. The area where London now stands was an open steppe, inhabited by mammoth, bison, woolly rhino, lion and hyena. So much water was locked up in glaciers that sea levels were substantially lowered – the British Isles were joined to Continental Europe, Australia linked with New Guinea, Sumatra, Borneo, Java and the Philippines attached to South-East Asia, and a land bridge was created across the Bering Strait, allowing the colonization of the Americas.

For our cave artist, the immediate environment was harsh, similar in many respects to semi-glacial Siberia today. Great herds of bison and reindeer roamed through the plains of central and western Europe, as did now-extinct species like the mammoth and the woolly rhinoceros. Small, nomadic bands of Cro-Magnon hunter-gatherers, moving with the herds, lived in open-air encampments of tents and huts, often using mammoth bones to build their shelters since wood was near-impossible to find.

Archaeological excavation of their sites show these people lived on venison, fish and eggs. They used bone and flint spears for hunting, bone harpoons for fishing, and bone needles to sew together the furs and skins that kept them warm. They were few in number. Tribal communities were small. Nature was unforgiving. If the hunting and the foraging were poor, they starved. If they entered a cavern occupied by a lion or a bear, they died. If they were careless in an attempt to hunt elephant or mammoth, the creatures gored them and they died. If they slipped and broke a bone, they died. If they fell ill, they died. If they were too weak to keep pace with the tribal migrations, they died. Even when health and strength and hunting skills and luck were with them all their days, conditions were so extreme they still died long before they reached what we would now call middle age.

Yet against these pitiless conditions, Cro-Magnon people found something so important in art that they took time to paint the insides of several hundred caves. To date, there is no satisfactory explanation.

For more than a century now, since Marcelino de Sautuola's dramatic find, experts have voiced their guesses. Footprints around the clay bison at the French cave site of Tuc d'Audoubert indicate a tribal gathering, possibly an initiation rite. At the same time, as we have already noted, much cave art is hidden in gloomy, inaccessible depths where it never could have been seen by more than one or two people at a time. Whatever has been said about Tuc d'Audoubert, initiation ceremonies cannot have been a general explanation.

Religion has also been put forward. There is a strong inference, largely from burial sites, that the people of prehistory did practise a religion. Female figurines, such as the rotund little Venus of Willendorf found near Vienna, suggest a belief system associated with the Great Goddess. But while the Neolithic settlement of Catal Huyuk (c. 7,000 BC) in Anatolia provides evidence that such a belief experienced long continuity, it is far less certain that She was celebrated in cave art. The problem is that both cave paintings and cave engravings were often executed on top of other work, obliterating or at least defacing it. This is hardly the act of someone honouring a religious figure.

Many anthropologists consider that the artworks were an act of magic, specifically hunting magic. Belief in sympathetic magic is widespread in primitive communities today, so it seems reasonable to assume it was equally widespread in prehistory. The theory of sympathetic magic suggests that if you create a representation of a thing, you can use the representation to influence the thing itself. The notorious Voodoo doll of Haiti, the moppet of medieval European witchcraft and the fetish of tribal Africa are all examples of sympathetic magic.

On this basis, the theory is put forward that the

paintings were created to influence the success of the hunt. Although few human figures are portrayed, many of the animals are shown transfixed by arrows or spears, which would seem to support the idea. The fact that old artworks were painted over would support it too: fresh magic would have to be made if not for each hunt, at least for each hunting season.

But there are problems with this theory too. The first, surprisingly, is that the hunt was probably not all that important to Cro-Magnon people. Studies of modern Stone Age cultures, like the !Kung Bushmen of Botswana, indicate that hunting will typically account for only 20 per cent of tribal food. The remaining four-fifths result from foraging. Contrary to the commonplace picture of hunters tracking game herds every day, !Kung tribesmen hunt strenuously for a week, then put their feet up, metaphorically speaking, for the rest of the month. It is the !Kung tribeswomen who put most of the food on the table.

The second problem is that even if we ignore the relative unimportance of hunting, the artworks do not entirely work as sympathetic magic. The reindeer is known to have been an important food source, for example, yet it is very seldom pictured. If the paintings were conceived as magical aids to hunting, one would expect reindeer to have been the most prominently featured animal of all.

Then there is the fact that some of the representations are composites. At Pindal, in Northern Spain, for example, there is a painting of a trout with the tail of a tuna. Not even the most enthusiastic magician will bother to cast a spell on a creature that does not exist.

But the composites, like the abstract shapes and symbols found in much cave art, generate their own mystery. Prehistoric rock art is not limited to Europe and in some areas there is a continuity of the tradition carried through into modern, or relatively modern times. Any study of the continuity clearly indicates that the art was meant to be representational – the artists painted what they saw, what was important to them, what most influenced their lives. At Tassili N'Ajjer in the Algerian Sahara, there are scenes that include hunters and the herdspeople, while paintings of charioteers and horses, dating to 500 BC, may indicate the influence of dynastic Egypt. The nomadic San people of Tanzania, Zimbabwe, South Africa and South-West Africa have a Pleistocene art tradition that has actually been carried through, uninterrupted, well into modern times. Among their more recent paintings are those which show European traders with stove-pipe hats.

In view of this evidence, it is tempting to consider rock art as a sort of pictorial history of the tribe, a representation for posterity of life as it used to be, with highlights like the appearance of Victorian tradesmen faithfully recorded. But for all its representational thrust, there are still the abstract elements; and, oddly, these elements seem to be near universal.

Large areas of the Americas contain rock art, which is as often symbolic or schematic as naturalistic. The intricate, maze-like Chibcha drawings from Colombia reflect the elaborate whorls and spirals carved into the world's most ancient monument at Newgrange in Ireland. The geometric zig-zags and mythic (spirit) elements found in the Ice Age caverns of Europe show a striking similarity to elements in the rock art tradition of the Australian Aborigine.

There can only be a limited number of explanations for similarities of this sort. One, obviously, is migration, carrying a particular tradition of abstract art from one place to another as humanity spreads itself into new territories. But unless we postulate that abstract art began with the primeval Eve and spread with her descendants out of Africa, the notion of a migratory answer will not do. The similarities appear in diverse cultures, some of which have been isolated for hundreds of thousands of years.

If we rule out migration, the next most likely explanation must be common experience. San Bushmen produced drawings of men in stovepipe hats precisely because they met up with men in stovepipe hats. The fact that artists in Victorian Britain drew similar images, means only that stovepipe hats were prevalent in London too at the time.

The notion of a shared experience has taken some of our more eccentric modern commentators into strange by-ways. Faced with widespread cross-cultural evidence for a belief in flying humans and animals that talk, they postulated human contact with aliens from Outer Space at some stage in prehistory. The idea met with considerable public interest, generated by several popular books on the subject, but ignored the fact that shared experience does not have to have a physical reality. The experience is just as valid if it is psychological.

It was this very point which gave rise to one of the most recent – and in many ways most interesting – explanations of the cave-art mystery. A group of anthropologists went beyond the evidence of the artworks themselves, even went beyond the study of such 'living fossils' as the Bushmen and the Aborigines. In doing so, they turned their attention to the experiences of those engaged in personal experimentation with psychedelic drugs. They quickly discovered that the visionary drug trips of the modern user contained precisely those 'mythic' elements – including the experience of abstract geometric patterns – which had for so long been a puzzle in cave art.

From this they concluded that the ancient artists were moved to paint what they saw not in their normal waking state, but in trance.

CHAPTER

2

TRANCE

Trance is an umbrella term referring to aspects of what are now commonly called 'altered states of consciousness' – a range of experiences in which mental functioning and outward behaviour may be impaired, improved, or simply changed.

A common example of trance is the hypnagogic state which occurs – in everyone – during the process of falling asleep. It is marked by a shift from abstract thought to visual imagery, sometimes of a bizarre nature, and accompanied by brain wave changes.

About 20 per cent of sleep is spent in a brain wave pattern known as Stage 1-REM. REM is an acronym for Rapid Eye Movement and the presence of rapid eye movement is an indication that we are dreaming. Our eyes move with the imagery of the dream, and our bodies would move too if a special mechanism did not paralyse the muscles. Dreaming is not generally considered a trance state, but there is ample reason to believe it should be. Certainly it fulfils the criteria by which trance is usually judged.

After dreaming, hypnosis is the most widely investigated altered state. A majority of people respond to induction techniques to some extent and some subjects achieve a level in which they are extremely suggestible, following instructions in an uncritical fashion and paying attention only to those aspects of the environment made relevant by the hypnotist.

In deep hypnotic trance, the subject hears, sees, feels, smells and tastes in accordance with what he or she is told to experience, even though the suggestions may be in direct contradiction to actual stimuli. Memory and awareness can both be altered through hypnosis, as if suggestions given during trance come to define the individual's perception of the real world.

Although the hypnotized individual may at times appear superficially asleep, he or she is actually awake at all times. In contrast to sleep-walkers, the subject's brain waves are those of a waking individual. Similarly, although the hypnotized subject may be instructed to ignore surrounding events and will apparently be unaware of them, the events actually do register and can be shown to exert an effect.

Another very common form of trance is that achieved in meditation where a variety of procedures are used to concentrate awareness and achieve states of consciousness in which direct insight into reality may (reportedly) be attained.

Many drugs, including marijuana, alcohol, mescaline, LSD and heroin, induce altered states. People tend to be very suggestible in drug-induced states, so it is difficult to determine what effects are due to the drug itself and what to suggestion or expectation.

In one sense, trance is among the most widespread of human experiences. This is not to say it is commonplace (apart from dreaming and the hypnagogic state), but it would be difficult to find a single example in the multiplicity of human cultures where it has not played a part. In many, the part played has been major, even central: so much so, indeed, that the experience has, from the earliest times, supported specialists.

Anthropologist John Stewart[3] gives the following interesting description of a skeleton discovered in the Shanidar caves of Iraq:

> The man ... had been crippled by a useless right arm, which had been amputated in life just above the elbow. He was old, perhaps forty ... which might be the equivalent of eighty today, and he suffered from arthritis. He was also blind in the left eye, as indicated by the bone scar tissue on the left side of the face. It is obvious that such a cripple must have been extensively helped by his companions. . .

The conclusion (that he must have been extensively helped by his companions) is inescapable. But Stewart then goes on to say, 'The fact that his family had both the will and the ability to support a technically useless member of the society says much for their highly developed social sense.'

Although the skeletal remains were at least 30,000 years old, it is possible that this gravely handicapped man did indeed come from a society with a highly developed social sense. But in describing him as 'technically useless', Stewart has forgotten that not all human talents require 20/20 vision, two sound arms and a body free from arthritis. In one ancient profession, the forty-year-old's injuries and ailments might even have been considered an advantage. The profession was that of tribal shaman.

There is little doubt that shamanism has been a feature of primitive societies since the Ice Age.[4] It still exists today among many peoples (the Australian Aborigines are a well-studied example) who have a cultural tradition reaching back to Palaeolithic times. Besides, there are several cave paintings like that of the famous antlered figure at Ariège in France, which are universally interpreted as depicting shamans at work.

It seems to have been important work. According to the *Grolier Electronic Encyclopedia:*

> It is the shaman's function to regulate the relations between spirits and the community in order to ensure the community's well-being. Shamans concern themselves with such communal matters as locating and attracting game or fish, finding lost animals or tools, controlling the weather, detecting broken taboos that bring sickness or misfortune, expelling harmful spirits, and planning community activity. In some instances, as among the Eskimo, a shaman may use spirits aggressively, causing injury or death for revenge or in competition with other shamans. Because of such special powers, a shaman can gain considerable political influence in his or her group.

In order to achieve these ends, the shaman must be chosen by the spirits. To attract spirit attention, he[5] needs to exhibit some physical or mental peculiarity, such as epilepsy, an additional finger, more teeth than usual or, like our Shanidar skeleton, a missing arm.

Modern studies of shamanism indicate that the choice – frequently expressed when the candidate reaches adolescence – is not always welcome. Some candidates show a capacity to resist, even for years. But the spirits are persistent and will torture the candidate with visions, pains and chronic illness until such time as he accepts his destiny. 'Had I not become a shaman I would have died,' a Siberian shaman is quoted as saying and the sentiment is echoed by his fellows down the centuries.

Scholars consider nineteenth-century Northern Asiatic practice the classic expression of shamanism. This belief system included a view of the Earth as disc-shaped, floating on water supported by the back of a gigantic creature, variously considered as a turtle, a fish, a bull, or even a mammoth. But shamanic beliefs are unimportant when set beside shamanic practice, for the differing mythic systems evolved in various cultures are little more than local interpretation of the essential shamanic experience. There is substantial evidence to suggest that the experience – and much of the methodology which produces it – is similar whatever culture we happen to be examining.

This is quite remarkable. Although the term shaman derives from the Tungus word saman ('he or she who knows'), shamanism is confined neither to this Manchurian tribe nor to the peoples of Northern Asia. It appears among the Indians of North America, the jungle peoples of South America, the Aborigines of Australia, the Eskimos of Alaska, the tribal communities of Africa. It is present in the Bön religion of Tibet (where many of its elements have been absorbed into Buddhism) and among the Ainu of Japan. There are clear traces of its practice among early Celtic peoples and in the cunning man and wise woman traditions of Western European witchcraft.

Across this whole broad spectrum of peoples, widely separated by geography, environment and culture, shamans practise techniques which enable them to share a common experience. At the heart of that experience is a very unusual journey.

CHAPTER

3

SHAMANIC JOURNEY

A candidate for shamanic initiation among the Warao peoples of Venezuela is required to undergo a stringent test of suitability. He must find and travel to the manaca palm, a tree that holds a special power and promise for all shamans.

This journey is not easy. Typically it begins in a wasteland, where the candidate must use his skill and intuition to discover a series of water-holes which are his only guarantee of survival. The water-holes have religious as well as mundane significance: they are used for ritual purification.

Somewhere beyond the water-holes, the candidate is likely to reach a fearsome abyss at the bottom of which runs a river infested by alligators and dangerous fish. The area around this chasm is a favourite hunting ground for jaguars and the Warao firmly believe it is also the haunt of demons who attack anyone attempting to cross.

Should the candidate navigate the abyss safely, he will encounter a number of strikingly attractive women who will try to tempt him from his path with promises of sexual favours. If he resists the women, he may rest assured that he is nearing his goal, but there remains a further guardian to overcome before he reaches it – a giant, aggressive hawk.

Even when he reaches the tree, his troubles are not over. Doors set in the massive trunk open and close so rapidly that anyone attempting to enter runs a severe risk of being crushed. Nonetheless, the candidate will hear the voice of his guide inside the tree encouraging him to take the chance. If he does so, he will find himself within the hollow trunk facing a huge serpent with four colourful horns and a luminous ball on the tip of its protruding tongue. The serpent is served by a second creature, human-headed but with a distinctly reptilian body, which carries away the bones of novices who have failed to clear the doors. . .

Should you find the latter stages of this journey have begun to stretch your credulity, you will not, perhaps, be surprised to learn that the candidate prepares for his ordeal by fasting and smoking large, foul-smelling cigars of a native tobacco known to have narcotic properties. Given this information, you might be forgiven for concluding that he never really went anywhere, that his test had no more substance than the LSD 'trips' of the Flower Power Sixties, characterized by inward visions which, while vivid, were no more than eruptions of unconcious contents.

Nonetheless, the shamanic journey is a central aspect not only of shamanic initiation, but of shamanic practice. Black Elk, the Sioux holy man who lived through some of the most turbulent days of the Old West, including the massacre at Wounded Knee, recounted many of his own shamanic journeys before his death in 1950. Like the Warao, several of these involved a holy tree, surrounded by a lush, green landscape. During one of them. . .

> I was standing on the highest mountain of them all and round about beneath me was the whole hoop of the world. And while I stood there, I saw more than I can tell and I

understood more than I saw; for I was seeing in a sacred manner the shapes of all things in the spirit and the shape of all shapes as they must live together like one being. And I saw that the sacred hoop of my people was one of many hoops that made one circle, wide as daylight and as starlight, and in the centre grew one mighty flowering tree to shelter all the children of one mother and one father. And I saw that it was holy.[6]

Such visions seem to reflect the culture of the individual who experiences them. Bhirendra, a Tamang shaman from Nepal, gave this description to Larry G. Peters of his journey to meet with the supreme shamanic deity, Ghesar Gyalpo:

I walked into a beautiful garden with flowers of many different colours. There was also a pond and golden, glimmery trees. Next to the pond was a very tall building which reached up to the sky. It had a golden staircase of nine steps leading to the top. I climbed the nine steps and saw Ghesar Gyalpo at the top, sitting on his white throne which was covered with soul flowers. He was dressed in white and his face was all white. He had long hair and a white crown. He gave me milk to drink and told me that I would attain much shakti [power] to be used for the good of my people.[7]

The journey can even be undertaken by those whose cultural background includes no shamanic practice whatsoever. The following account was given by a contemporary middle-class North American, journeying for the first time:

It's in a wooded forest and the entrance is about four feet in diameter. You go down into a large room with several passages. It continues down into a mountain. I had to go over some crevices that were pretty deep and there was one spot where I got to a place where you literally have to squirm your way through – very difficult to do it just by yourself.

> I went on down to the deepest part of the cave that I've
> been in. I had never really been any farther than that. But
> I just kind of went even further and came out at another
> entrance or, in this case, an exit and I came out onto a
> tropical island with a nice big shore, just tropical birds and
> a lot of tropical vegetation.[8]

The subjective nature of the journey and its linkage
with the experience of prehistoric shamans as
expressed through Palaeolithic cave art is underlined
by the experience of Gordon Wasson. A banker by
profession, Wasson was interested in anthropological
reports of secret 'sacred mushroom' ceremonies carried
out by the Mazatec Indians of Mexico. Since the
interest was shared by Wasson's wife Valentina, the
couple made three field trips between 1953 and 1955.

On the last of these, in the summer of 1955, an
official in the town of Huautla not only showed them
where to gather the mushrooms, but also introduced
them to Maria Sabina, a shaman held in high regard by
the Mazatec community. In company with Sabina, a
colleague named Allan Richardson, the town official
and several other locals, Wasson ate a number of the
mushrooms during a magico-religious ceremony in the
official's home. They had an unpleasant, acrid taste
and undoubted mind-altering properties. By midnight,
Wasson was feeling the effects. 'We saw,' he wrote
afterwards, 'geometric patterns, angular not circular,
in richest colours, such as might adorn textiles
or carpets.'

Those angular geometric patterns are precisely the
representations seen in so much cave art, while the
vivid colours became a commonplace in psychedelic
drug trip reports a decade later. But unlike the shifting
perceptions of reality brought on by LSD, Wasson's trip
solidified into something at least comprehensible:

... the patterns grew into architectural structures, with colonnades and architraves, patios of regal splendour, the stone-work all in brilliant colours, gold and onyx and ebony, all most harmoniously and ingeniously contrived in richest magnificence extending beyond the reach of sight. For some reason these architectural visions seemed oriental though ... they could not be identified with any specific oriental country. They seemed [like] ... architecture described by visionaries of the Bible.

However fantastic the journeys themselves appear, shamans undertake them for a purpose – and that purpose is the acquisition of power. The precise nature of the power differs from individual to individual. In one it might be healing ability, in another a talent for precognition. A third might seek the ability to blight crops, generate good luck, even kill at a distance. As we noted earlier, shamans concern themselves with such matters as locating and attracting game or fish, finding lost animals or tools, controlling the weather, detecting broken taboos that bring sickness or misfortune, expelling harmful spirits and planning community activity. The power to do all these things is drawn from and maintained by their 'journeys'. One wonders how they manage it if the journeys are no more substantial than dreams.

This difficulty has failed to exercise the mind of the average anthropologist who does not, by and large, accept there is any reality to the shaman's claims of power ... or indeed to his journeys. Although it is an academic convention to report the assertions of the shamans without comment, it is not particularly difficult to determine where scholarly sympathies lie.

Descriptions of the lower world are principally obtained from shamans who *believe* they have visited that country during a trance. According to the statement of an old

woman who *believed* that as a little girl she had visited
the lower world during a trance, the entrance is through
a hole situated in each house between the doorway and
the fireplace.

I have added the italics to this typical extract from *The
Mythology of the Bella Colla Indians*, published in the
Memoirs of the American Museum of Natural History.
But even without them, it is plain that the author,
Franz Boas, is unimpressed by what he has been told.

In the entry on shamanism in the *Grolier Electronic
Encyclopedia*, the author almost falls over himself to ensure the reader will not suspect he might
actually accept any of the nonsense swallowed by
primitives. Once again, the italics are mine:

> A shaman is a religious or ritual specialist, man or
> woman, *believed* capable of communicating directly with
> spirit powers . . . Shamanic power *is said* to come directly
> from a supernatural source . . . A shaman *is said* to be
> chosen by the spirits . . . The person *believed* chosen for
> this calling must undergo an initiatory ordeal . . . In many
> cultures the candidate *is believed* to receive during this
> ordeal a mystical light that enables him or her to see far-
> off things and to discover the secret places to which lost
> souls have been taken.

Essentially the same attitude is reflected in the
prestigious *Encyclopaedia Britannica*:

> The belief that he [the shaman] communicates with the
> spirits gives him authority. Furthermore, the belief that
> his actions may not only bring benefit but also harm
> makes him feared.

It would seem our most respected anthropologists are
too sophisticated to take seriously the convictions of
the peoples they study. Yet if this attitude represents a
valid stance, it also creates a problem. The *Britannica*

reference ably describes the reality of the shaman:

> In consequence of his profession, the shaman cannot go
> hunting and fishing and cannot participate in productive
> work; therefore, he must be supported by the community,
> which considers his professional activity necessary.

The problem that arises is why, if the shaman's abilities are fictitious, the community should consider his professional activities of any value whatsoever. Yet shamanic prestige is typically so high that far more than minimal support is offered. Among the Evenki, for example, the shaman is automatically awarded the best stretch of river fishing, is helped with reindeer herding and is given frequent gifts of food and furs. It is the absolute duty of every tribal member to aid him economically. For many peoples – among them the Tungus, the Samoyed and the Eskimo – the post of shaman and tribal chieftain are one and the same.

The mystery deepens when we recall the history of shamanism. The practice flourished in the bitter extremes of the Ice Age when the borderline between survival and extinction was often razor thin. Tribes living in such conditions can afford to carry no passengers.

Our contemporary world is warmer, but it is still noteworthy that, in many cultures where the shaman is revered, the living is far from easy. Conditions in the Kalahari desert, the Australian outback, the Siberian steppe and the Alaskan Arctic are so hostile that civilized whites find it impossible to survive at all without supply lines and substantial back-up. Yet here, as in many other harsh environments, the shaman practises his craft as he has done for 40,000 years. If he really is a charlatan, one would have thought somebody would have found him out by now.

CHAPTER

4

SHAMANIC SORCERY

Magic, declared Weston La Barre resoundingly, is a 'self-delusory fixation at the oral–anal phases of adaptation, with purely fantasied operation of the omnipotent will'. In an earlier age, Sir J. G. Frazer put it more succinctly: 'Magic,' he said, 'pulls strings to which nothing is attached.'

For all this, there have always been individual anthropologists prepared to report honestly on the results of shamanic sorcery, even where these appear to run contrary to conventional wisdom.

Waldemar Bogoraz, for example, writing on the Chukchee in volume three of *The Jessup North Pacific Expedition* recounts how a shaman, naked to the waist, performed an apparent feat of teleportation. Possessed by the *ke'le* (spirits), she took a round rock about the size of a man's fist and set it on the surface of a drum. She then blew on it from all sides, snorting and muttering in the manner of the spirits, before taking the rock into her hands and rubbing it vigorously.

At once a stream of tiny pebbles began to pour from her hands and continued to do so for fully five minutes until there was a substantial heap of them on the drumhead. The larger rock, however, remained undiminished.

Suspecting trickery, Bogoraz moved closer to the

woman, but could not discover how the effect was produced. Later he abruptly asked her to repeat the trick, hoping to catch her unprepared. She 'immediately took up her stone, and without more ado wrung out of it a stream of small pebbles still larger than the first'.

U'pune, the Chukchee sorceress, was not the only shaman to play with pebbles. In his *Die Feuerland-Indianer*, M. Gusinde reports watching a Selk'nam witch-doctor, also naked to the waist, make three small stones disappear.

> He fixed his eyes upon them and then blew violently: the pebbles disappeared, although his hand had not made the slightest movement. He repeated the trick: this time I paid more attention. I chose the three pebbles myself and placed them on his palm; once more he made them disappear. There was no possibility of conjuring or illusion.[9]

Was there really no possibility of conjuring or illusion? Although Gusinde concluded that the powers of the shamans he studied were 'undeniably real', it is probably true to say that any competent stage magician could duplicate such feats with little difficulty, including the 'nothing up my sleeve' undressing to the waist.

But what is one to make of Father R. G. Trilles' report of a ritual used by the Fang pygmies of Equatorial Africa to admit novices into the ranks of their shamanic brotherhood? Trilles, who witnessed the ceremony personally, described the erection of a sort of giant see-saw using a thick plank set on a fulcrum more than six feet above the ground. Experienced members of the shamanic brotherhood then circled the structure, clapping their hands and singing a hymn of evocation to the sound of loud, rhythmic drumming.

The novices, who had undergone various ordeals, were brought into the clearing to straddle one end of the high see-saw. This naturally tilted the apparatus so that the end on which they sat came down to the ground. An experienced shaman then came to stand underneath the other end, arms stretched up above his head and hands cupped. In this position, he was still some feet from the underneath of the plank.

As Trilles watched, the see-saw slowly began to swing. Although there was no weight at all on the side nearest the shaman, that end came down towards him, carrying the novices off the ground. When the plank was level, the movement stopped. The novices were now more than six feet above ground and the plank to which they clung was approximately one and a half feet above the shaman's outstretched hands.

As the tribespeople circled the see-saw, chanting, the shaman slowly knelt. The plank above him continued to dip, carrying the novices even higher into the air. The shaman then lay down and folded his hands across his chest. The plank followed his movement.

The ritual concluded with the shaman, apparently in trance, climbing once more to his feet and raising his arms above his head. This had the effect of returning the see-saw to its natural position with the novices back on the ground at the other end of the fulcrum. The shaman who had performed the feat then collapsed and had to be revived with water.[10]

It seems fairly obvious that sleight of hand was not the explanation here, although it is just possible that trickery of some sort may have been used since Trilles does not record having examined the apparatus. What

Trilles has recorded, however, are several other examples of shamanic sorcery where mechanical trickery was definitely out of the question. Among them was this fascinating example of magical healing:

> One of our catechism instructors was struck by an algid fever and was gravely ill. Quinine was of no use. The witch-doctor had him carried to a mpala tree, one that had particularly large leaves, then he went through his ritual, first over the sick man, then near the tree. The leaves soon began to move and then turn black and fall to the ground. The patient sweated a great deal and, the next day, was completely cured.[11]

This was not an isolated incident. Trilles witnessed other healing demonstrations in which the 'spirit of sickness' was sent into kid goats and occasionally dogs. Typically the fevered human would sweat profusely, then fall quietly asleep. The unfortunate animal, by contrast, would begin to shiver and sink to the ground. This was followed by convulsions, sudden stiffness and usually death.

Arthur Grimble tells an even more remarkable story following his visit to the Gilbert Islands. There he watched a shaman sink into trance and call porpoises. The mammals duly swam ashore in such a passive state that the natives were able to club them to death, for food, without the slightest difficulty.[12]

Porpoises are not the only things capable of being called. S. M. Shirokogoroff credits V. K. Arseniev with the story of a Tungus shaman who, when faced with the sudden illness of a young tribesman, mentally 'called' two other shamans to help. Although they were a considerable distance away and no other means of communication was apparently used, they arrived far more quickly than they could have done had they been summoned by a physical messenger.

Shirokogoroff credits this account[13] without hesit-ation, largely because he had experienced similar abilities among the Tungus people at first hand:

> The following occurrence may be taken as proof: a small boy 'saw' his uncle commit patricide and he predicted that the murderer would return three days later with the antlers of a deer that had been killed by the father. The man returned as foreseen and was led immediately in front of the boy who repeated his accusation. The man confessed and was condemned to death.

Shirokogoroff speculated that the mechanism which permitted such phenomena was the same as telepathy.

Telepathy may well have been involved in several jungle experiences of Trilles. In one of these he and his party arrived by canoe at a remote village to be greeted by the local shaman who described in detail the route they had taken, the stops they had made, various meetings and the food they had eaten. He was even able to repeat, word perfect, details of conversations they had had among themselves, despite the fact that they had spoken in French, a language unknown to the shaman. The shaman himself claimed he had simply seen (and heard) them in his magic mirror.

The facts of this case might be explained by an elaborate fraud. The shaman might have sent out spies to keep watch on the whites unobserved and report back to him everything they did. But even this unlikely explanation has to be ruled out in a second, similar case which also involved Trilles.

> One day I was talking to a negrillo witch-doctor. I was waiting for my paddlers to bring provisions and I spoke of this to the fellow while wondering aloud if they were far away and if they would bring me the things I'd asked for.
>
> 'Nothing could be easier to find out!' he cried. Then he took his magic mirror and with great concentration

pronounced some incantation. Then he said, 'At this moment the men are rounding this bend in the river (it was more than a day's paddling away), the tallest man has just shot a large bird, it falls into the water and the men are paddling hard towards it. They've caught it. They're bringing you back what you asked for.'

In fact everything was true; the provisions, the shooting, the bird and, as I said, they were a day away.

Trilles was impressed – as was D. Leslie when he came across something very similar while travelling through Zulu territory. Leslie had arranged to meet up with eight Kafir hunters and consulted with a Zulu shaman when they did not turn up. The shaman set eight small fires which he fed with roots until they gave out a thick, odorous smoke. Then he threw a small stone into each, shouting out the name of a particular Kafir as he did so. Finally he ate something which caused him to fall into a shaking trance for about ten minutes.

When he awoke from trance, he raked the ashes from each fire and studied the stones intently. In each case he gave a physical description of the Kafir, then went on to describe what had happened to them in considerable detail. One, he said, had died of a fever. Another had killed four elephants. Another had himself been killed by an elephant. And so on.

I took particular note of all this information at the time and to my utter amazement it turned out correct in every particular. It was scarcely within the bounds of possibility that this man could have had ordinary intelligence of the hunters; they were scattered about in a country two hundred miles away.[14]

There is evidence that shamanic sorcery includes the ability not merely to see at a distance, but to see through time – in other words, to predict the future. Trilles witnessed a spectacular performance by a negrillo shaman who correctly forecast the outcome of a hunt in substantial detail, including the number of elephants which would be killed, how many of these would be males, and the fact that one of the hunters would himself be killed.[15]

The shamans themselves insist they manage feats of this type with the aid of spirits ... and are quite prepared to substantiate their claims by producing the spirits themselves. Bogoraz gave the following account of phenomena he witnessed:

> The separate voices of their calling came from all sides of the room ... Some voices are at first faint, as if coming from afar; as they gradually approach, they increase in volume and at last they rush into the room, pass through it and out, decreasing, and dying away in the remote distance. Other voices come from above, pass through the room and seem to go underground, where they are heard as if from the depths of the earth ... I heard ... the spirit of a grasshopper, horsefly and mosquito, who imitated exceedingly well the sounds produced by the real insects.
>
> In proof of the accuracy as to the location of the sounds, the shaman, Qorawge ... made one of his spirits shout, talk and whisper directly in my ear ... involuntarily I put my hand to my ear to catch the spirit. After that he made the spirit enter the ground under me and talk right in between my legs. All the time that he is conversing with the separate voices, the shaman beats his drum without interruption in order to prove that his force and attention are otherwise occupied.
>
> The spirits will scratch from the outside at the walls of the sleeping room, running around it in all directions so that the clattering of their feet is quite audible. In contrast to this, the motion of the ke'le inside the room produces but slight noise.
>
> Often, however, a mischievous spirit suddenly tugs at the skin spread in the centre of the room with such force that things lying on it fly about in all directions ... Sometimes an invisible hand seizes the whole sleeping-room by its top and shakes it with wonderful strength, or

even lifts it up high, letting in for a moment the twilight
from the outer tent . . . Other invisible hands toss about
lumps of snow, spill cold water and urine and even throw
blocks of wood or stones at the imminent risk of hurting
some of the listeners.

All these things happened several times in my
presence. . .[16]

Despite this intimate personal experience, Bogoraz
was not convinced.[17] He believed he was watching a
display of ventriloquism and though he allowed that
'the Chukchee ventriloquists display great skill' felt no
more was involved than that. As a test, he persuaded
the shaman Scratching-Woman – a male sorcerer
despite his name – to call up spirits for the purpose of
recording their voices on a phonograph. The shaman
complied. 'The records,' Bogoraz wrote later, 'show a
very marked difference between the voice of the
shaman himself, which sounds from afar, and the
voices of the spirits, who seemed to be talking directly
into the funnel.'

The scientific detachment shown by Bogoraz is
creditable, but it would be a mistake to assume that
such an attitude is the exclusive prerogative of European anthropologists. In his book *The Religious
System of the Amazula*,[18] R. P. Callaway describes
how the Zulu he studied differentiated between individuals who had Itongo (spirit power) in them and
those who were simply mad or fakes. It was their
practice to hide various objects – sticks, pots, orna-
ments, baskets, kilts, etc. – and challenge the shaman
to find them. Only if he succeeded quickly in doing so
was he adjudged genuine.

But for all the evidence that something very odd is
going on, the scientific establishment continues to
deny – or at least ignore – the possibility that there

might be any reality to shamanic sorcery. Those who examine the evidence explain it away by reference to the fact that we are dealing, by and large, with primitive peoples. Primitives, so the unstated theory goes, are far more easily hoodwinked than civilized humanity. They lack discernment and sharp powers of observation.[19] The (rare) Western observer who claims there might be more to shamanism than has been generally supposed, is assumed to have succumbed to the ambience of the environment, to have been sucked into some sort of communal delusion.

There has even been a suggestion put forward in anthropological circles that the initiatory rites of primitive tribes work as a sort of accelerated Darwinian selection, weeding out those members who are naturally resistant to suggestion. According to this theory, the initiatory ordeals are structured to favour easily hypnotizable individuals. Those who fail either die in the attempt or are accorded such a low social status that they experience substantial difficulties in finding mates, and hence in reproducing. The end result, over generations, is the creation of a culture easily bamboozled by its shamanic leaders.

Unfortunately for this comfortable notion, shamanic methods are still in use today among people whose culture could scarcely be described as primitive and who abandoned initiatory ordeals millennia ago.

CHAPTER

5

MODERN MAGIC

Almost all children are interested in magic, their perception of which is conditioned by the fairy tale. They are also prone to what psychologists call 'magical thinking'.

According to Christian Clerk,[20] the concept of magical thinking was first proposed by the anthropologists Sir Edward Tylor and Sir James Frazer, who advanced influential theories of magic in the late nineteenth and early twentieth centuries. Tylor proposed that magic was based in the (erroneous) equation of physical causality with associated ideas. This notion was elaborated by Frazer, who saw as the basic principles in magical thought that:

a) Like produces like.

b) An effect resembles its cause.

c) Things formerly in contact continue to act on one another.

Frazer termed the magic based on similarity homoeopathic, and that based on contact contagious. Together, these two categories form sympathetic magic, a term which has achieved widespread usage since it was first coined.

Children work sympathetic magic all the time . . . or
at least are heavily influenced by it. They see linkages
between, for example, stepping on pavement cracks
and the wellbeing of their parents,[21] or their own
survival, marriage prospects, etc. These are only semi-
serious linkages for many children, but nonetheless
powerful for all that. The reason, according to anthropologist Bronislaw Malinowski, is that magical
thought has psychological value. Where there is uncertainty of practical success, or the outcome of events is
uncontrollable, magical acts, he suggests, reduce
anxieties, thus widening the apparent range of an
individual's ability to deal with the environment.

Malinowski's theories arose out of a four-year study
of the Trobriand Islanders, a tribal community which,
lacking a sophisticated understanding of the laws of
nature, might be expected to become prey to anxieties.
Children, who have not yet learned the way of the
world, fall into essentially the same category and, like
the primitive, seek to ease their feelings of helplessness by magical thinking. They believe that wishing
will make it so; and if wishing fails, it is only because
they did not wish hard enough. Many children, to the
relief of their parents, grow out of magical thinking at
puberty, a period of life when they realize they know
all there is to know about everything and feelings of
helplessness recede.

For most people a small, unimportant residue of
magical thinking remains. It is this which prevents our
walking under ladders and persuades us, against all
experience, that we really do have lucky numbers
when entering a lottery. But for some people, magical
thinking is never abandoned. Rather it is expanded and
systemized until it becomes an important – possibly
even central – aspect of life. The largest category of

such people are those we would term 'religious'.

Nineteenth-century anthropologists were particularly concerned with distinguishing between magical and religious activity. Frazer, for example, saw magic in an evolutionary context and argued that, as its techniques were found unproductive, it would typically be succeeded by religion, which in turn would be followed by scientific enlightenment. Thus magic and religion belonged to different stages of cultural development, with magic as the earlier, more primitive form. Other anthropologists suggested that whereas religious acts generally involved a personal approach to spiritual powers, magical activity was largely impersonal.

The sociologist Emile Durkheim, however, stressed the dependence of magic on collective religious belief and ritual. Magic contrasted with religion in that it did not involve a church, or a moral community, but its powers were derived from notions of the sacred established within such a community.

Whatever about this academic controversy, there is a clear example of magical thought in the act of prayer, particularly when prayer is aimed at influencing personal circumstances or the course of physical events. The individual praying for the sick, for a better job, for a loyal spouse, for a safe landing of an aeroplane, is engaged in an activity with which the Neolithic shaman would have felt entirely comfortable. The parallel is even closer in those religions like Roman Catholicism where prayer is often directed not to God, but to the saints – i.e. selected spirits of the dead.

While many, indeed most, who practise magic in this way remain quite unaware of what they are doing, a minority grouping in every modern culture engages in magical acts quite consciously. This grouping includes wiccans, Qabalists, ritualists and various others, all loosely covered by the umbrella term occultists. Minority though it is, the category seems to be expanding, to judge from the phenomenal increase in the sales of 'occult' books, literature and equipment throughout the Western world since the 1960s. The really remarkable thing about this development is that the methodology of modern occultism is virtually identical to that of the primitive shaman.

This is not always – indeed not usually – recognized by the occultists themselves, largely because serious shamanic study has, until very recently indeed, been confined to a small band of specialists whose reports attracted only an academic audience. But the fact remains that modern magical practice, exactly like its Palaeolithic counterpart, proceeds from the inside outwards. The witch's spell, the magician's ritual are no more than physical reflections of the real work, which goes on inside the practitioner's head. There is even an exact parallel to the shamanic journey. It is referred to as a pathworking.

Dolores Ashcroft-Nowicki, a leading contemporary exponent of the practice, defines pathworking as follows:

> A pathworking is a journey between this side of the mental worlds and the other side. One of the most exciting journeys mankind can take because it offers a path, a map through the landscapes of the mind, landscapes that are as yet barely explored and offer one of the last great frontiers. They are Doorways between the known and the physical and the unknown and the non-corporeal. They accomplish their work through the medium of the creative imagination, which ability is the seed from which everything made and produced by mankind has sprung. . .
> . . . Pathworking is a term used to describe the trained

use of the creative imagination and ... such journeys within the mind can inform, calm, heal, relax and train the mind and its tool, the brain.[22]

Like her ancient counterparts in the Ice Age caverns, Ashcroft-Nowicki is convinced such mental exercises are a source of power. She writes:

They [pathworkings] can and do cause actual physical effects in the everyday world in which we live, which is one of the reasons why they have been held in secret for so long.[23]

And again, only two pages later:

We know that it [pathworking] can cause events to happen in accordance with the will, not always as precisely as we could perhaps wish but, given training, time and the all-important mental discipline, an occultist can expect a reasonable amount of success.

These are uncompromising statements and the question naturally arises as to whether we should take them seriously; whether, that is, they represent an accurate perception of reality. Certainly Ashcroft-Nowicki does not stand alone in her assertions. One has to assume that those who engage in prayerful supplication – and they are legion – do so because they believe it will work, even if only sometimes. There has actually grown up in America what I can only describe as a technology of prayer, which differs radically from the traditional Christian reliance on God's will. It teaches that when one learns to pray 'correctly', results inevitably follow – and these results are measurable, having more to do with the achievement of mundane success than spiritual evolution. This development, whether its followers realize it or not, is a magical movement by any rational definition.

Another, and in many ways very similar, example of magical thinking is the substantial sub-culture devoted to what is usually categorized as 'self-help' or 'self-improvement'. If the technology of prayer is largely an American phenomenon, the methods of the self-help movement have attracted a much more international audience. A glance at any one of the (literally) thousands of textbooks[24] is enough to indicate that the underlying thinking is esoteric, even though the terminology tends to be severely psychological. Fundamentally, the message of these books is that if you are prepared to visualize something long enough and hard enough, it will eventually come true. Again, one has to ask whether such claims should be taken seriously.

This is an extraordinarily difficult area to examine dispassionately. The claims of the prayer technologists ('God wants you to have a Cadillac'), the positive thinkers ('My system made me a multi-millionaire while I slept'), and the magicians ('Spirits help me achieve my ends') appear so ridiculous that scientific inquiry into their validity seems almost disreputable – which is probably the reason why any such inquiry has yet to be carried out. The only really respectable 'magicians' bred by our Western culture appear to be the Jesuits, whose famous 'spiritual exercises' are classical examples of occult visualization. But the Society of Jesus, while attracting some of the finest and most subtle minds of the age, has been careful to claim only spiritual benefits from the legacy of St Ignatius.

But disreputable or not the sheer persistence of the magical method throughout human history suggests such an inquiry might be useful, if for no better reason than to consign magic once and for all to the dustbin of outmoded ideas.

One problem, perhaps the central problem in this whole field, is the lack of any rational theory to explain how subjective gymnastics could influence objective reality. Such a theory is lacking even within occultism itself. The closest one comes to it is the Qabalistic notion of Yesod, the sphere of imagination, as the foundation of physical manifestation. But until supported by evidence, this remains no more than a religious statement about the nature of reality.

This problem is itself compounded by another factor. If a child's perception of magic is conditioned by fairy tales, that same perception is shared by a great many adults. This is, of course, the result of thoughtlessness. Since the study of the occult arts was banned from the universities of Europe, few educated individuals[25] give them more than a passing thought.

Thus if the topic ever arises at all, there is an unthinking reversion to childhood prejudice. The magical method is seen as a matter of peep and mutter, the waving of wands and the chanting of spells that have power in their own right. Magical results are expected to follow at least a metaphorical thunderclap. When nothing of the sort occurs, magical thinking is dismissed as superstition.

Against such an unpromising background, a good starting-point for our inquiry might be to find out what it is magicians really do.

CHAPTER

6

OCCULT PRACTICE

One of the most detailed historical accounts of magical practice – and its results – is contained in the private papers of Benvenuto Cellini, Italy's Renaissance master painter.

In 1533 or 1534 (the exact date is uncertain), Cellini met with a Sicilian priest versed in the art of ritual magic. In the course of their conversation, Cellini, an outgoing, adventurous character, remarked that he had always wanted to see a magical operation. The priest agreed to show him, having voiced a few dire warnings about the dangers.

The site chosen for their experiment was the imposing ruins of the Roman Colosseum. With Cellini came his friend Vincentio Romoli, while the priest was accompanied by a second magician from Pistoia. The equipment laid out included ceremonial robes, a wand several grimoires,[26] a pentacle,[27] incense, kindling and a supply of assafœtida grass, a plant that burns with such an abominable smell that even demons are unable to stand it.

While the others watched, the Sicilian drew circles on the Colosseum floor and fortified them by means of some impressive ceremonial. One of the circles was left incomplete. The magician led his companions through the gap before closing it and concluding his ritual preparations.

Cellini and Romoli were given the job of lighting a fire in the circle. When they got it going, they were instructed to burn quantities of incense. While the man from Pistoia held the pentacle, the priest began a lengthy ritual of evocation. An hour and a half later it bore fruit. According to Cellini's own account, the Colosseum was filled with 'several legions', presumably of spirits.

Never one to miss an opportunity, Cellini promptly asked that these entities should bring him a young woman named Angelica, with whom he was in love. Unsympathetic with this untimely exhibition of lust, the spirits ignored him.

Despite his disappointment, Cellini expressed himself well enough satisfied with the demonstration. But the Sicilian seems to have been something of a perfectionist, for he undertook to perform the ceremony again in the hope of obtaining more spectacular results. To this end, he made a fresh stipulation: he wanted a virgin boy to attend. Cellini brought a young servant with him, a twelve-year-old named Cenci.

Romoli returned to the Colosseum for the second operation, but the magician from Pistoia did not. His place was taken by another of Cellini's friends, Agnolino Gaddi. Once again the circles were drawn and consecrated, the fire lit and the incense burned. Cellini himself held the pentacle this time as the Sicilian priest began the evocation.

The conjuration, it is plain from Cellini's account, was directed towards those demons who controlled legions of infernal spirits. It was spoken in a mixture of Hebrew, Greek and Latin not uncommon in the grimoires and seems to have been a remarkable success. Much sooner than before, the Colosseum was packed tight with entities whom Cellini again asked for the miraculous transportation of his lady-love. The spirits replied through the mouth of the magician that Cellini and she would be together within a month.

Although all seemed well at this point, the operation quickly began to go wrong. The magician himself was the first to notice. There were, he said, too many spirits present – possibly as many as a thousand times more than he had called up. Worse, they had begun to misbehave. Twelve-year-old Cenci screamed that they were all being menaced by a million of the fiercest 'men' he had ever seen. Four giants, fully armed, were trying to enter the fortified circle.

The priest launched into a formula of dismissal. The little boy began to moan and buried his head between his knees, convinced they were all as good as dead. Cellini tried to reassure him but failed, possibly because he himself was shaking like a leaf. The child cried out that the Colosseum was on fire and that flames were rolling towards them. He covered his eyes with his hands in a paroxysm of terror.

The magician broke off his chanted licence to depart in favour of stronger means. He instructed Cellini to have his assistants pile assafœtida on the fire. But Cellini's assistants were by now too paralysed with terror to comply. Cellini lost his temper and shouted at them. It had the desired effect and soon the foul-smelling grass was burning merrily. The spirits began to depart 'in great fury'.

None of the experimenters felt like leaving the protection of their magic circle. They stayed huddled together until morning when only a few spirits remained 'and these at a distance'. With the sound of Matins bells ringing in their ears, the sorry group left the circle and headed home, with little Cenci clinging desperately to Cellini and the Sicilian. Two spirits accompanied them, racing over the rooftops and along the road.

What are we to make of all this? Cellini's account, so vivid in many respects, is frustratingly vague in others. Who actually saw the spirits on the first occasion, for example? Despite Cellini's insistence that there were several legions of them, one is tempted to infer they were visible only to the Sicilian priest, although it is possible Cellini and his friend thought they sensed them also. On the second occasion, the frightened boy certainly believed he saw something and his fear communicated itself to the others. There is more than a passing hint of hysteria in Cellini's story at this point. But was it justified? Were the demonic spirits ever really there? Even the promise of Angelica's favours was delivered by the Sicilian, rather in the manner of a Spiritualist medium. But unlike Spiritualist mediums, the magician offered no proof that the supposed communication was genuine.

Three hundred years after the incident at the Colosseum, another spectacular – if rather more solitary – magical operation was carried out in London. Once again it took the form of a spirit evocation. The man who carried it out was the son of a Parisian shoemaker. His name was Alphonse Louis Constant.

In 1854, Constant – better known to generations of occultists by his Hebraic *nom de plume* Éliphas Lévi – was forty-four years old and at the height of his reputation as a magician. He had been educated at Saint-Sulpice with a view to taking up the Roman Catholic priesthood, but proceeded no further than Minor Orders. He was a deacon when expulsion from the seminary cut short his religious career. The expulsion was for heresy.

Lévi had a mystical streak in his nature even then, but the real problem was his civic conscience. He embarked on a mission to help the poor and published several pamphlets of a socialistic nature. Neither activity endeared him to the authorities, who saw to it that he was fined and jailed.

Lévi's marriage was another mistake. He elected to wed Noemi Cadot who, at sixteen, was substantially younger than himself. She bore him two children, but walked out when they died. The marriage was anulled on the curious grounds that Lévi had been pledged to celibacy when he contracted it.[28] Noemi remarried and went on to achieve fame as a sculptress. Lévi plunged headlong into the troubled waters of occultism.

His major study was Qabalah,[29] an ancient Hebrew mystical system which underpins much modern magical practice. He published a number of books, none of which sold well enough to keep him,[30] so that he was forced to supplement his income by giving lessons in Tarot and other aspects of the occult.

He did, however, manage to achieve something of a cult following and a substantial reputation in his chosen field, despite the fact that his knowledge was entirely theoretical. This was not something he sought to conceal. In an Appendix to his substantial *History of Magic*, he wrote:

> Once and for all, he [the writer] desires to forewarn his readers that he tells no fortunes, does not teach divination, makes no predictions, composes no philtres and lends himself to no sorcery and no evocation.

But the *History of Magic* was not yet in print when Lévi was invited to London in 1854. His host was Baron Lytton of Knebworth, the novelist Bulwer Lytton who was himself an occultist. Lévi had scarcely

time to step off the ship before Lytton and his friends
were pleading with him to demonstrate his powers.
Unlike Cellini's Sicilian priest, Lévi refused to do so.
He withdrew from his new acquaintances and im-
mersed himself in study.

But if Lévi had withdrawn from England's fashionable occultists, not all of England's occultists had
withdrawn from him. Before long, he found himself
involved in an adventure which would have done
justice to Lytton's most romantic novels.

It began when he returned to his hotel to find an odd
message awaiting him. It comprised part of a card and
a pencilled note stating, 'Tomorrow at three o'clock,
in front of Westminster Abbey, the second half of this
card will be given to you.' Lévi examined the portion
of the card in his possession and discovered it featured
a section of the Seal of Solomon, a magical sygil
believed by (some) occultists to have been used by the
biblical King Solomon to seal djinn in bottles of brass
before casting them into the sea.[31]

His curiosity aroused, Lévi presented himself before
Westminster Abbey at three o'clock the following
afternoon. A carriage drew up and a footman emerged.
After signalling Lévi to approach, he opened the
carriage door to reveal a heavily veiled lady entirely
dressed in black. She motioned Lévi to enter the
carriage and showed him the other half of the card.

As the carriage drew away, the woman removed her
veil to reveal grey hair, black eyes and a strangely fixed
expression. She told Lévi that a friend of Lytton's had
informed her of his reluctance to produce phenomena
and assumed this was because he did not have the
requisite magical equipment. She then proposed to
show him a complete magical cabinet, providing he
would promise to remain silent about the whole affair.

Lévi, by now convinced the woman was a high initiate, agreed. They drove to the woman's home where she loaned him several rare books, showed him an impressive collection of magical robes and implements, and prevailed on him to undertake a magical operation. Lévi agreed. The proposed operation was the evocation of Apollonius of Tyana,[32] using a ritual drawn from the *Magical Philosophy* of Patricius.

Following the instructions embodied in the ritual, Lévi spent twenty-one days in intense meditation. For fourteen of them, he held to a vegetarian diet; for the final seven he fasted. On 24 July, he bathed, put on a white robe and crown of vervain leaves intertwined with a gold chain, took up sword and book, then entered the turret room where the experiment in evocation was to be carried out.

The woman in black had done a remarkable job in furnishing the room. It was equipped with four massive concave mirrors and a spectacular altar surrounded by a chain of magnetic iron. The altar top was white marble, engraved with a pentagram – the five-pointed star of ritual magic that signifies the dominion of spirit over the four Elements. There was a new white lambskin, also bearing a pentagram, on the floor. Beside it was a copper chafing dish on a tripod. A second chafing dish was on the altar itself, filled with charcoal.

Lévi lit fires in both dishes, burned incense and began to read the invocation 'in a voice at first low, but rising by degrees'. Eventually . . .

I seemed to feel a quaking of the earth, my ears tingled, my heart beat quickly. I heaped more twigs and perfumes on the chafing dishes and as the flame again burst up, I beheld distinctly, before the altar, the figure of a man of more than normal size, which dissolved and vanished away.[33]

Lévi quickly stepped into a protective circle he had drawn on the floor and continued with the evocation. A 'wan form' appeared in the mirror behind the altar, then:

> When I again looked forth, there was a man in front of me, wrapped from head to foot in a species of shroud, which seemed more grey than white. He was lean, melancholy and beardless and did not altogether correspond to my preconceived notion of Apollonius. I experienced an abnormally cold sensation.

Finding it difficult to speak, Lévi placed one hand on the pentagram and pointed his sword at the figure. It vanished. He called on it to return and felt a breath on his cheek. Something touched his sword-hand and his arm went numb to the elbow. He put the sword down and the figure reappeared at once. It seems Lévi was so frightened at this stage that he fainted. When he came to, the figure had gone.

Lévi's account of the experience is convincing in that he does not seek to dramatize his role or conceal his weakness. One is left with the conviction that he was recording faithfully what happened . . . or what he thought happened. But the question is, did Apollonius really appear?

So far, there is very little in these two well-known reports of esoteric practice to suggest that magic is capable of producing anything more than subjective effects. Cellini's account reads like a case-study of collective hysteria. Lévi inclined to the belief that his own experience resulted from a 'drunkenness of the imagination'.

But in dealing with magic, it does not do to jump to quick conclusions. There is one further historical case-study, rather less widely known, where end results seem to have passed well beyond hysteria or imagination. This study concerns the murderous ritual at Jena in 1715.

CHAPTER

7

RITUAL AT JENA

In 1716, a judicial inquiry in Germany issued a report of recent findings under the title *A True Account of the Jena Tragedy of Christmas Eve*. The story it told[34] was one of the most interesting and frightening in the annals of magical practice, although the inquiry itself was investigating not magic, but violent death.

The affair had begun quietly enough a year earlier. A peasant named Gessner was working in his vineyard to protect his plants from the hard German winter when something attracted his attention. He picked it up, cleaned it off and discovered it was a coin. The inquiry did not record the exact nature of the coin, but it is reasonable to suppose it was old and probably silver. In any case, it was sufficiently valuable to persuade Gessner to abandon his work and hunt for more.

His efforts proved moderately successful and one or two more coins turned up. Gessner grew excited. He seems to have been an optimistic man, for he concluded these few coins were an indication of buried treasure, a hoard which would make him rich. He wondered where he could get a grimoire that would help him find it.

In our more rational age, this last point requires a word of explanation. Belief in magic was widespread throughout Europe in the early eighteenth century, and nowhere more so than in Germany where the nation's printing houses did a roaring trade in grimoires. (Gessner himself had actually owned one, a collection of conjurations entitled *Theosophia Pneumatica*.)

One reason for the popularity of these spell books was their concentration on the problem of buried treasure, an international obsession at the time. It was a common belief that spirits guarded such hoards, and the grimoires were full of advice on how to raise these entities and persuade them to part with the loot.

Doubtless the *Theosophia Pneumatica* contained similar advice, but that was no good to Gessner, who had lost his copy by the time he found the coins. Gessner discussed the problem with his friend, a tailor named Heichler, bemoaning the fact that he no longer had a grimoire which would enable him to find the rest of the treasure by magical means.

Heichler was sympathetic: he believed in magic too. Better still, he was able to introduce Gessner to a practising magician, a student named Weber. The latter was reputed to be the owner of various ritual implements and such rare grimoires as the *Clavicula Salomonis* and *The Key to Faust's Threefold Harrowing of Hell*.

The meeting took place in Weber's rooms, which he shared with a youth named Reche. Gessner asked for the magician's help, but Weber was hesitant. Conjurations are lengthy, tiresome operations, as we have already seen, and he had no intention of undertaking one unless he was sure it would be worth his while.

Faced with this reluctance, Gessner decided to massage the facts. He told Weber he had taken part in conjurations before (which may actually have been true). He claimed he had seen the treasure hoard in the vineyard – or at least seen its guardian spirit. As proof he produced the coins, which he pretended he had managed to steal despite the guardian's attempts to stop him.

Obviously not a man to do things by halves, Gessner went on to insist that he had seen other spirits in the area and described them in detail.

Weber was impressed. He agreed to lend his magical talents to the search and the two men worked out an arrangement by which Weber was to receive a portion of the treasure when it was found.

At this point, an individual named Zenner enters the story. He was, like Gessner, a peasant and seems to have bought his way into the conspiracy with the aid of a mandragore.

A mandragore is the specially prepared root of a mandrake plant. The tuber contains a toxic narcotic, which, if it fails to kill, will often produce vivid visions. Like other similar plants and fungi, the psychotropic action of the mandrake has led to a widespread belief in its magical properties. In the eighteenth century, it had a fearsome reputation among the superstitious, who believed it shrieked in agony when uprooted. So fearsome was this shriek that any living creature hearing it would die.

The prescribed method of harvesting mandrakes (safely) was to use a dog. The wretched animal was first half starved, then tethered to the growing mandrake. Food was left nearby as the dog's owner hurried out of earshot. The dog would naturally strain to reach the food and in doing so uproot the mandrake. The plant would scream, the animal would keel over, at which stage the owner would return to claim his mandrake and bury his dog.[35] Since the plant is inedible, mandrakes were harvested only for magical purposes. By an accident of nature, mandrake roots often take the shape – more or less – of a human figure: two arms, two legs and the abundant leafy growth taking the place of hair. Those creating a mandragore would heighten the effect by carving. The root, now looking like an ugly doll, could then be cured in vervain smoke to accompanying incantations.

All magical instructions for the creation of a mandragore unfortunately insisted that every stage of the operation had to be carried out at the astrologically appropriate phase of the moon. Consequently the entire operation became lengthy and burdensome. But the end result was ample justification: a mandragore was considered to be a talisman of enormous potency.

This then was the gift Zenner brought to the three treasure-hunters. It was not his own: he had stolen it from the husband of his mistress. He told Gessner, Weber and Heichler that it could open locks at a distance.

The four began their preparations. Working on the basis of Gessner's description, Weber concluded the guardian of the hoard was the spirit Nathael, an entity about whom I can find nothing in my own small collection of grimoires. Christmas Eve, only days away, was considered propitious for a spirit conjuration. All four conspirators wanted to be present, but Weber consulted his textbooks and discovered an odd number of participants was specified. Heichler, the tailor, was particularly busy during the pre-Christmas rush, and agreed to drop out.

The choice of a site for the operation proved rather more controversial. Heichler offered an empty room in his house. Zenner and Weber agreed, but Gessner objected. His esoteric studies had convinced him spirits were deceitful, and he was afraid they might try to fool his friends and himself by taking on the appearance of inhabitants of the house. It would be safer, he argued, to hold the conjuration in some remote spot.

After considerable discussion, their final choice fell on a little hut owned by Heichler. It was situated in the same vineyard where the treasure was buried.

The conspirators then fell to discussing luck pennies. These rare coins were supposed to reproduce themselves abundantly when the relevant ceremony was performed over them.[36] Was there, they wondered, a chance that the spirit might exchange luck pennies for ordinary pennies if they brought a few along? They decided it would be worth a try.

This was not as straightforward as it sounded – magic operations seldom are. According to the grimoires, each participant had to have a specific number of coins, carried in a bag of a particular material, purchased at a given price. Despite his other commitments, Heichler found he had to make the bags himself. In order to fulfil the remaining conditions, he gave them to his wife who, in turn, sold them at the specified price to this three colleagues.

Christmas Eve duly arrived. In the middle of the afternoon, Gessner and Weber called to collect Zenner. But Zenner had been having second thoughts. Now that the ordeal was close at hand, he was beginning to take fright. He urged his companions to change the venue to somewhere less isolated and suggested using an empty house of which he was the caretaker.

The three men went off to inspect the premises, but quickly discovered there were no shutters on the windows – an important consideration when one recalls the private nature of magical ritual and the severity of the Ecclesiastical Courts on matters of heresy. Besides, Zenner had mislaid his key.[37]

So, armed with lanterns and protective amulets, they set out for the vineyard hut that evening.

Before entering, Weber pencilled the word *Tetragrammaton* on the door. Tetragrammaton, which means 'the Name of four letters', is a substitute for the Hebraic JHVH, the most holy of all the names of God, which, according to rabbinical tradition should never be pronounced aloud. Magicians in Weber's day were nothing if not impressed by religion and often called on God and/or Christ for protection against the entities they evoked.

Thus fortified, the three men went inside to discover Heichler had left them some coals for their brazier and a tallow candle. The brazier itself was rather makeshift: they used a flower-pot and the fire gave off so many fumes that they were forced to open the door.

As we have seen from our examination of Lévi's evocation and the operation in the Colosseum, if a spirit is to be called up safely, various preparatory ceremonies have to be undertaken and a magic circle of protection drawn. In the case of Lévi, preparations took twenty-one days and this is by no means unusually long.[38] Weber, Zenner and Gessner had foregone such preparations altogether, apparently on the advice of Gessner who insisted he had called up spirits before without meditation, fasting or bathing.

They did, however, draw a magic circle. But Weber, the expert, drew it on the ceiling rather than the floor, an eccentricity which defies even magical explanation. He then began to read the conjuration from *The Key to Faust's Threefold Harrowing of Hell*.

It is probably true to suggest that most sensitive modern readers would find the content of medieval grimoires repulsive. The *Harrowing of Hell* is repulsive even for a medieval grimoire. One section conjures the demon Seloth 'by the tongue, liver and heart of the most holy Godhead, Jesus Christ'. Another throws out challenges to the Almighty in the manner of a nasty little boy attempting to manipulate his betters:

> In the name of Jesus Christ, if you are a living God, oh Jehovah, then conquer now the power of hell. Oh living God, if the blood of Jesus Christ is valid in your eyes as a hope and a boon to all men, then, O hellish spirit, must you be forced by that power to give what I desire. If, O most holy Trinity, you are almighty, then show your power here and now . . .

And so on, relentlessly: jeering, suggestive, whining and cajoling.

It is difficult to understand how this sort of nonsense could have produced any result whatsoever, but after a time Weber began to feel dizzy. He fought back the malaise and continued with the conjuration, but after a moment or two more blacked out, falling unconscious across the table. His last memory was of his two companions regarding him curiously.

The following day, Christmas, the tailor Heichler was attending church when something in the sermon must have pricked his conscience, for he slipped out and made his way to the hut to find out what the other three were doing. Two of them were doing nothing: Gessner and Zenner were both dead. Weber was alive, but apparently insane. He could not speak. When aroused from his torpor, the best he could produce was grunts and gibbering.

With enormous reluctance, Heichler called in the authorities, who stationed three watchmen at the hut to guard the corpses until they could be fully examined. The following morning, one of the watchmen was dead and the other two unconscious.

The judicial inquiry from which this account is drawn centred on the fate of Weber and his associates so that there is little information about the death of the watchman. But the record had a great deal to say about the would-be magicians. The body of the unconscious Weber was covered with marks and bruises. Zenner's corpse was in an even more appalling state: it was covered in huge weals and scratches. His tongue protruded horribly and there were many individual burns on his face and neck.

These were unexpected developments; and all the more so because no instrument was found in or near the hut that could have explained such injuries. The only source of fire was the flower-pot brazier, but this was undisturbed and the corpse nowhere near it.

How solid are the facts presented in the *True Account*? Dr E. M. Butler, formerly Schröder Professor of German at the University of Cambridge, certainly believed them. He went on record with the statement that:

> The circumstantial evidence is so realistic, even including a diagram of the scene; the account is so sober; the admissions of the one remaining witness ring so true; the judicial procedure was so meticulous; the strict adherence to known facts so close; that, together with the absence of torture, they positively command belief.

But if we believe the evidence, where does it point? How did Gessner and Zenner die? And what happened to poor mad Weber?

There is a limited number of rational explanations in this case. One is that the conspirators quarrelled and fought among themselves. Another is that they came under attack from an outside source. The official conclusion – that they succumbed to fumes from the brazier – does so little to explain the injuries sustained that it can, I think, be dismissed without further consideration.

It is likely enough that the three men may have quarrelled. We have already seen that they disagreed about a number of things. Nor is it beyond the bounds of possibility that their disagreements led to violence. But the injuries sustained could not have been inflicted without a weapon. The postulated battle royal left two men dead and the third unconscious. Who then hid the weapon?

An outside attack makes more sense, but not much. Doubtless there were criminals abroad in Germany in 1715, but one must ask what would attract them to a tiny hut in a remote vineyard. There was nothing of value for anyone to steal. In the depths of winter, there would not even have been grapes to eat.

Gessner and company seem so silly in many respects that it is easy to imagine they might have boasted about their treasure hunt, perhaps in a tavern, perhaps once too often. However difficult it is for modern minds to accept that spirits guard treasure, the belief was almost universal in their day. Thus they might have been followed to the hut by person or persons unknown, determined to steal the treasure for themselves. Yet if this was the case, why attack in the hut? Why not wait until the conspirators actually dug up their coins and move to take them then?

Again the question of a weapon arises. Nothing in the conventional armoury of the day would leave the sort of injuries the men sustained. Why was Zenner's face burned – and with what? If the attackers did not know about the little group's obsession with treasure, what was their motive in attacking at all? The victims were two peasants and a student, not wealthy merchants with fat purses worth stealing.

If the three were not attacked by robbers, is there any possibility they might have been attacked by an animal? There were wolves abroad in Germany at that time, but wolves, contrary to their unsavoury reputation, do not seek out humans to kill; and especially not in a smoke-filled little hut. Besides, the marks on Zenner were more like the claw marks of a giant cat than the canine bites of a wolf pack.

But the strongest objection to wolves, or animals of any sort, is the burn marks on Zenner's face. Only humanity carries fire. No known animal could have left those particular signs.

The more one thinks about it, the less convincing are the conventional explanations. Occultists, of course, would have no difficulty. Gessner, Weber and Zenner were amateurs dabbling in dangerous matters they did not fully understand. They called on spirits without proper preparation or safeguard (it is impossible to stand inside a circle drawn on the ceiling) and paid a heavy price for their stupidity. Something heard their evocation and crawled out of its alien dimension to do them harm.

This is almost impossible to swallow, even though it fits so many of the facts. One would rather assume the men were attacked by a maniac wielding a torch and some hitherto unknown weapon, both of which he carefully carried away with him. For, if we do not believe something like that, then we have to believe in the validity of magic in a very literal, objective sense.

CHAPTER

8

ENOCHIAN MAGIC

For a subject which has been a preoccupation of humanity since the Ice Age, it is surprisingly difficult to find unambiguous descriptions of magical operations and their outcomes.[39] There are a great number of anecdotes, like the story that Cornelius Agrippa once showed the Earl of Surrey his dead sweetheart in a magic mirror, or the marvellous post-mortem trial[40] of Pope Boniface VIII, who was reputed to have carried a spirit in his finger-ring and made the house shake when he retired to his room to consult with demons. But these are obviously romantic tales, exaggerated and distorted, with little use as evidence.

We might, however, add to the three case-studies already quoted an unusual account published by Meric Casaubon in 1659 and entitled *A True & faithful RELATION of what passed for many Yeers Between Dr JOHN DEE (A Mathematician of Great Fame in Q. Eliz. and King James their Reignes) and SOME SPIRITS*. The Dr John Dee of the title was Court Astrologer to Queen Elizabeth I and an Admiralty spy.[41]

Although best known in his day as an astrologer,[42] Dee was greatly interested in communicating with spirits and employed an Irish scoundrel named Edward Kelley[43] as a medium for the sum of £50 a year. The salary was not always paid, but the two stayed together all the same. Their experiments in crystal-gazing, using a shewstone now in the British Museum, began in 1582 and continued, despite various unconnected adventures, until 1587. Their flavour is caught quite neatly in the following extract:

> Suddenly there seemed to come out of my Oratory a *Spirituall creature*, like a pretty *girle* of 7 or 9 yeares of age, attired on her head with her hair rowled up before and hanging down very long behind, with a gown of Sey . . . and seemed to go in and out behind my books . . . and as she should ever go between them, the books seemed to give place sufficiently . . .
>
> DEE:[44]   I said . . . Whose maiden are you?
>
> SHE: Whose man are you?
>
> DEE: I am a servant of God both by my bound duty and also (I hope) by his Adoption.
>
> A VOYCE: You shall be beaten if you tell.
>
> SHE: Am not I a fine Maiden? Give me leave to play in your house, my Mother told me she would come and dwell here.
>
> DEE: She went up and down with most lively gestures of a young girle, playing by her selfe, and diverse times another spake to her from the corner of my study by a great Perspective-glasse, but none was seen beside her self.
>
> SHE: . . . Shall I? I will. (Now she seemed to answer one in the foresaid *Corner* of the Study.)
>
> . . . I pray you let me tarry a little (speaking to one in the foresaid *Corner*).
>
> DEE: Tell me who you are.
>
> SHE: . . . I pray you let me play with you a little and I will tell you who I am.
>
> DEE: In the name of Jesus then tell me.
>
> SHE: . . . I rejoyce in the name of Jesus and I am a poor little *Maiden*, Madini, I am the last but one of my Mother's children, I have little Baby-children at home.
>
> DEE: Where is your home?
>
> MA: I dare not tell you where I dwell. I shall be beaten.
>
> DEE: You shall not be beaten for telling the truth to them that love the truth, to the eternal truth all Creatures must be obedient.[45]

And so on. Although not entirely clear from the extract, Dee was communicating with Madini second hand. It was Kelley who spoke for the girl, or allowed the girl to speak through him. By June 1583, the experiments had taken a particularly weird turn. The two men believed themselves to be in contact with a number of entities including an impatient angel called Ave.

Ave dictated a series of Calls or evocations to the 'Watchtowers of the Universe', which were claimed to make up an entire system of magic known as Enochian. The curious method of dictation – letter by letter and backwards – was explained by the fact that the Calls were so powerful even writing them down in the normal way might stir up potent and unwanted magical currents.

The process of transcribing the Calls was bizarre. Dee and Kelley had somehow obtained, or created, more than a hundred large squares, or tablets, measuring 49 inches square on average, each wholly or partly filled by a grid pattern of letters. During the course of the experiments, Dee would place one or more of these tablets before him on a writing table, while Kelley would sit across the room staring into a crystal shewstone.

When contact was made, Kelley would report sight of the angel in the shewstone, along with the angel's own copies of the tablets. Using a wand, the angel would then point to certain letters on the tablets and Kelley would call out the rank and file of the letter indicated. Dee would then locate the letter in the same position in his tablet and write it down. Thus the Calls were gradually built up.

An example of the sort of message that came through is the following two lines:

Micma Goho Mad Zir Comselha Zien Biah Os Londoh
Norz Chis Othil Gigipah Vnd-L Chis ta Pu-Im Q Mospleh
Teloch . . .

This translates as, 'Behold, saith your God, I am a circle on Whose Hands stand Twelve Kingdoms. Six are the Seats of Living Breath. The rest are as Sharp Sickles or the Horns of Death . . .' which is only slightly less obscure than the original.

Perusing the *Faithful Relation* and various other accounts of his life, it is tempting to conclude that Dr Dee, an enormously naive man despite his learning and espionage training, was the victim of a confidence trick when it came to his dealings with spirits. The problem, of course, has always been Edward Kelley.

Before they met, Kelley had had his ears cropped for coining.[46] He is known to have lived on his wits and was involved – apparently more than once – in extracting money from the credulous on the pretence that he could make alchemical gold. He died in 1597 while trying to escape from jail. This is not the background of a reliable and honest man.

Nor can we suppose that Kelley's affection for Dee – which seems to have been genuine enough – was sufficiently strong to ensure the good doctor would be excluded from his con games. On one occasion he assured Dee that the spirits had told him they should 'hold their wives in common'.[47] Dee fell for it and an Elizabethan *ménage à quatre* ensued until the objections of the women forced him to abandon the arrangement.

In face of all this, it is easy to suppose that Kelley made up his talk of angels and spirits to keep his employer happy and ensure the continuation of his £50 a year, along with whatever other opportunities for profit might arise from his relationship with this well-connected man. Kelley was, after all, Dee's only link with the Otherworld: Dee could not see spirits for himself.

There are two difficulties with this. One is the claim that the Enochian Calls are not a code or cypher, but represent an actual language, internally consistent and with its own syntax. I am not qualified to evaluate this claim, but, if it is true, it certainly suggests there was more going on during the Dee/Kelley seances than a crude confidence trick.

It is not impossible that Kelley could have invented the Calls, for artificial languages have certainly been created: Esperanto is a modern example. But to do so would have required an enormous investment of time and effort, on top of which Kelley would then have been obliged to memorize the Calls – there are forty-eight of them in all, forming a substantial body of material – so perfectly that he was able to dictate them backwards. Given Kelley's dislike of honest toil, it would almost be easier to believe he really did talk with angels.

The second problem is that the Calls work. That is to say, they can be used to produce magical results. This fact is attested by the experience of, among others, the British poet Victor Neuburg.

In 1906, while Neuburg was an undergraduate at Cambridge, he fell under the influence of the magician Aleister Crowley. Crowley was an initiate of the hermetic Order of the Golden Dawn, an organization which trained many well-known people[48] in ritual and other magical arts. He had had a major mystical illumination two years earlier in Cairo and only a year after their first meeting was to establish his own magical Order, the *Argentinum Astrum*, or 'Silver Star'.

Neuburg was enormously attracted to Crowley; and not only because of his magical erudition.[49] By 1908, he was composing poems to his 'sweet wizard', which leave little doubt as to the depth of his feelings:

> Oh thou who hast sucked my soul,
> Lord of my nights and days,
> My body, pure and whole,
> Is merged within the ways
> That lead to thee, my queen.

And again:

> Let mè once more feel thy strong hand to be
> Making the magic signs upon me! Stand,
> Stand in the light, and let mine eyes drink in
> The glorious vision of the death of sin!

Three weeks before his finals, Neuburg travelled to London and took initiation into Crowley's *Argentinum Astrum*, vowing 'in the presence of this assembly to take a great and solemn obligation to keep inviolate the secrets and mysteries of this Order'. In the summer of 1909, he was at Crowley's house on the shores of Lough Ness, practising ritual magic and having his bottom flogged by Crowley with stinging nettles. In late autumn of the same year, the two unlikely lovers set sail for North Africa and docked at Algiers on 17 November. They took a tram to Arba, then walked south. By 21 November, they were in Aumale where Crowley bought Neuburg several notebooks. He was planning that Neuburg should use them to record the results of an operation in Enochian magic.

Crowley carried in his rucksack a copy of the Enochian Calls he had made from Dee's manuscripts in the British Museum. He had already experimented with two of the Calls and was now determined to find out what would happen if he used the rest. Over a period of days and nights they worked their way through the Calls until, by 6 December, they had reached what was technically known as the Tenth Aethyr, an area of magical reality inhabited, according to Kelley, by the 'mighty devil' Choronzon, Lord of the Powers of Chaos.

On a more mundane level, Crowley and Neuburg were stopping at Bou Saada. In the early afternoon they walked a considerable distance from the town to reach a valley of fine sand. There, in the desert, they traced a magic circle of protection, sealed with the words *Tetragrammaton*, *Ararita* and *Shadai el Chai*. The first of these we have already noted, the word pencilled by Weber on the door of the hut in the vineyard. *Ararita* is a magical formula,[50] while *Shadai el Chai*[51] is a Hebrew godname associated by magicians with the mudra chakra or subtle sexual centre of the human body.

In ritual magic, a circle is drawn for protection, its purpose being to keep malignant forces from gaining access to the operator. In certain types of ritual magic, notably evocation, a second geometrical figure is drawn outside the circle. This figure is an equilateral triangle, created for the manifestation of the entity evoked. Crowley and Neuburg traced the triangle too in the fine sand of the valley floor and fortified it with divine names. Crowley sacrificed three pigeons he had brought so that the released energy would give Choronzon something with which to manifest.

Neuburg moved into the circle. Crowley, acting on an impulse that experienced magicians must find as bizarre as Weber's drawing of the circle on the ceiling, entered the triangle.

(It is possible that Crowley, as eccentric in his

magical practice as he was in most other aspects of his
life, wanted to find out what it felt like to be possessed
by a demon. Jean Overton Fuller, who wrote the biography of Neuburg from which the account of this
magical operation has been drawn, considered Crowley
had 'ceased to be completely sane' by this stage, having
assumed the initiate grade of Master of the Temple,
following a homosexual act with Neuburg on an altar
set up on the summit of Dal'leh Addin mountain.)

Neuburg began the ceremony by chanting aloud the
following oath:

> I Omnia Vincam, a Probationer of the Argentinum
> Astrum, hereby solemnly promise upon my magical
> honour and swear by Adonai the angel that guardeth me,
> that I will defend this magic circle of Art with thoughts
> and words and deeds. I promise to threaten with the dagger
> and command back into the triangle the spirit incontinent
> if he should strive to escape from it; and to strike with the
> dagger anything that may seek to enter this Circle, were
> it in appearance the body of the Seer himself. And I will
> be exceedingly wary, armed against force and cunning;
> and I will preserve with my life the inviolability of this
> circle. Amen. And I summon mine Holy Guardian Angel
> to witness this mine oath, the which if I break, may I
> perish, forsaken of him. Amen and Amen.

This sworn, Neuburg then performed the Lesser
Banishing Ritual of the Pentagram. This ceremony,
which he presumably learned from Crowley, who in
turn had it from the Golden Dawn, remains the
standard method of preparing a place for a magical
working. It performs essentially the same function as
disinfecting an operating theatre prior to surgery.

First, Neuburg walked to the eastern quarter of the
circle, faced east and carried out a sub-ritual known as
the Qabalistic Cross. Raising his right hand, clasping
his magical dagger, to a point about three inches above

his head, he brought it down to touch his forehead and intoned the word *Ateh*. Then he brought the hand down to touch his breastbone and chanted *Malkuth*.

Still facing east, he touched his right shoulder while intoning *Ve-Geburah*, brought the hand across to touch his left shoulder while calling *Ve-Gedulah*, and finally clasped his hands together in the form of a cup at a level with his chest chanting *Le Olahim, Amen*.[52]

This done, he began the ceremony proper by tracing a pentagram with the dagger point in the air before him. He then stabbed the pentagram through its centre and intoned the name *JHVH*.

With his arm outstretched, Neuburg walked slowly clockwise to the south where he traced a second pentagram, stabbed it and vibrated *Adonai*. He continued to circle clockwise, stopping in the west to trace a third pentagram, stab it and changed *Ehehih*.

Arm still outstretched, he moved to the north and there traced a fourth and final pentagram. He stabbed it as before and called out the word *AGLA*.

Returning to the east, Neuburg completed the circle by bringing his outstretched fingers to the centre of where the first pentagram had been traced. For a moment he stood motionless, then stretched his arms out sideways in the form of a cross. In this position he solemnly intoned:

Before me Raphael.
Behind me Gabriel.
At my right hand Michael.
At my left hand Uriel.
Around me flame the pentagrams.
Above me shines the six-rayed star.

Finally, he repeated the Qabalistic Cross sub-ritual.

With the place prepared, Crowley, wearing a black

magician's robe, made the Enochian Call in his high-pitched, rather nasal voice:

> The thunders of judgment and wrath are numbered and
> are harboured in the North in the likeness of an oak whose
> branches are nests of lamentation and weeping, laid up for
> the Earth which burn night and day: and vomit out the
> heads of scorpions and live sulphur, mingled with poison.
> These be the thunders that 5678 Times (in ye 24th part)
> of a moment roar with an hundred mighty earthquakes
> and a thousand times as many surges which rest not
> neither know any echoing time herein. One rock bringeth
> forth a thousand even as the heart of man does his
> thoughts. Woe! Woe! Woe! Woe! Woe! Woe! Yea Woe! Be
> on the Earth, for her iniquity is, was And shall be great.
> Come away! But not your mighty sounds.[53]

It is difficult to see why such obscurities, even in the original tongue, would attract the attention of a demon, but something certainly happened. Neuburg heard Crowley's voice call out 'Zazas, Zazas, Nasatanda Zazas', followed by a string of blasphemies. Neuburg glanced towards the triangle and there discovered a beautiful woman, somewhat similar in appearance to a prostitute he had known in Paris. She began to call softly to him and make seductive gestures. Neuburg stolidly ignored her.

The woman then apologized for trying to seduce him and offered instead to lay her head beneath his feet as a token of her willingness to serve him. Neuburg ignored this too.

The demon – for so Neuburg considered the women to be – promptly changed into an old man, then a snake which, in Crowley's voice, asked for water. Unmoved, Neuburg demanded 'in the name of the Most High' that the demon reveal its true nature. The thing replied that it was Master of the Triangle and its name was

333.[54] A curious argument developed between Neuburg and the creature. Neuburg called on his own and Crowley's Holy Guardian Angels. The demon claimed it knew them both and had power over them. Neuburg firmly demanded that it reveal its nature and the demon finally admitted that its name was Dispersion and, as a consequence, it could not be bested in rational argument.

Equipped with the exercise book Crowley had given him, Neuburg was trying to write all this down when the demon cunningly swept sand over the boundary of the circle and leaped upon him in the form of a naked man.

An amazing scene ensued. The two, now locked together, rolled over and over on the sand, Neuburg trying desperately to stab the demon with his magic dagger. The creature in turn attempted to bite him in the back of the neck. Eventually Neuburg got the upper hand and drove the demon back to its triangle. He then retraced the part of the circle that had been obliterated with the sand.

After remarking that the tenth Aethyr was a 'world of adjectives' without substance, the demon asked permission to leave the triangle to get its clothes. Neuburg refused and threatened it with the dagger. After some further, rather childish, argument, the demon finally disappeared and the black-robed Crowley took its place. They lit a fire to purify the place, then obliterated both circle and triangle. The total ceremony had lasted two hours and exhausted both of them.

Since this account was extracted by Jean Overton Fuller from Neuburg's original notes, here at last we have a full, eye-witness description of what happens when a magical experiment is undertaken. But can we trust the witness? For all her fondness of Neuburg, Overton Fuller herself did not. She thought the common-sense explanation must be that Crowley had mouthed the words of the demon then thrown off his robe to leap naked onto Neuburg.[55]

It is difficult to disagree. Crowley had, of course, a propensity for leaping naked onto his lover and much of the nonsense spouted by the 'demon' sounds like the typical Crowlean mixture of schoolboy humour and Qabalistic learning. Neuburg insisted the demon kept imitating Crowley's voice. A dispassionate observer might have concluded it more likely that Crowley was imitating the demon.

There are, however, some aspects of the experience which do not quite fit the common-sense picture. Neuburg claims he saw a beautiful woman within the triangle. Was he taking poetic licence and referring to Crowley who, as we saw, he had already described as his 'queen'? Crowley had strong streaks of sexual masochism in his character and frequently took the passive role in his homosexual relationships. He would, within the cultural milieu of his day, have had no hesitation in pretending to be a woman in order to do so.

But what are we to make of Neuburg's claim that the 'woman' – whether demon or Crowley – subsequently transformed herself into an old man, then a snake? It is as well to realize that Neuburg himself thought he was speaking literally – a point made quite clear in his papers and subsequent conversations with friends. He believed he had wrestled with a demon. He believed he had seen a woman, an old man and a snake.

Here we begin to move closer to the heart of the matter. When a man sees things we believe he could not possibly have seen, we conclude he is hallucinating and look for the cause.

Had Neuburg taken hallucinogenic drugs? We know that Crowley experimented extensively with drugs, including the hallucinogen annalonium lewinii, and died a heroin addict. But there is no indication in the papers of either man that drugs formed part of the magic on this occasion.

Was Neuburg hypnotized? Hypnosis has been evoked quite frequently as an explanation of Crowley's supposed powers (as when he was reputed to have persuaded a London bookseller that all his shelves were empty). But as a hypnotist myself, I can see nothing at all in the reports of this Algerian working to suggest hypnosis was used.

Which leaves us with an interesting speculation. Is there something in the nature of magical ritual itself which triggers hallucinations?

CHAPTER

9

INNER WORKINGS

In one of the more readable historical studies of magic,[56] Francis King has this to say:

> Magic was defined by one initiate as 'the science and art of creating changes of consciousness' and to this phrase should, perhaps, be added the words 'and entering into contact with non-human intelligences'.

King's initiate was Mrs Violet Penry-Evans (née Violet Firth) better known by her pen-name Dion Fortune. Her definition of magic[57] has for many years been accepted as a baseline within the Western Esoteric Tradition.[58] In a footnote, King comments, 'Thus magic produces the same psychedelic effects as, for example, LSD, but without the harmful physical effects.'

This takes us another step towards the suspicion that magic may be a system designed – at least partially – to generate hallucinations; or, more kindly, to generate visionary experiences so vivid that they have often been confused with physical reality.

The picture of magic as a subjective system becomes even clearer when one considers the nature of magical training. After Aleister Crowley joined the Golden Dawn, he remarked disparagingly that the leaders of that organization had sworn him to secrecy by the

most terrible and fearsome oaths, then revealed to him
the signs of the Zodiac and the Hebrew alphabet. But
Crowley was exaggerating to make a point.[59] While the
work of the Neophyte did indeed include learning the
Zodiac signs and Hebrew alphabet – along with the
five Elements, the Sephiroth of the Qabalistic Tree of
Life, and the symbolism of his/her own initiation – the
most important aspect focussed on training the mind.

To this end, the practitioner was required to practise
rhythmic breathing followed by a specific meditation:

> Let the Neophyte consider a point as defined in mathe-
> matics – having position but no magnitude – and let him
> note the ideas to which this gives rise. Concentrating his
> faculties on this, as a focus, let him endeavour to realise
> the immanence of the Divine throughout Nature in all
> her aspects.[60]

The Golden Dawn did not, so far as I can discover,
require pre-initiation training of its members, but
many modern organizations in the same esoteric
tradition certainly do: the Fraternity of the Inner Light
and the Servants of the Light being two typical
examples. Such training can take anything up to five
years or more of daily meditations, combined with
specific exercises in visualization.

The practice of visualization was already very evident in the Golden Dawn, which, from the very start
of an initiate's career, required twice daily[61] use of the
Lesser Ritual of the Pentagram – that same short
ceremonial with which Victor Neuburg prepared the
place of working in the Algerian desert. But there was
more to the ritual than the external operation already
described in this book, for the working contained an
inner[62] aspect, which was considered far more
important than all the visible movements and gestures

put together.

When, for example, Neuburg was learning the Qabalistic Cross sub-ritual, he would have been taught the following visualizations which had to be synchronized with the relevant physical activities:

First, while standing upright, arms by his sides, body as relaxed as possible, he would have been told to visualize a glowing sphere of luminous white light (about the size of a child's football) floating a few inches above the crown of his head.

As he raised his hand to begin the ritual, he would have touched this imaginary sphere. Then, as he drew his hand downwards to touch his forehead, he would have been required to visualize a shaft of brilliant white light emerging from the sphere to pierce his body.

On touching his chest while intoning the word *Malkuth*, the shaft of light would be visualized as extending all the way through his body to end between his feet, so that he was now totally transfixed by a pillar of glowing white light.

In the Algerian desert, as Neuburg touched his right shoulder, he visualized a second, somewhat smaller sphere on a level with the shoulder, and partly interpenetrating it. He was taught to think of this sphere as a reservoir of energy.

Bringing his hand across his body, he next visualized a second shaft of brilliant white light from the right shoulder sphere crossing through his body to link up with a similar sphere at his left shoulder. The entire visualization to date left him transfixed by a massive (imaginary) cross of brilliant white light.

As he clasped his hands together, he would have visualized a small, steady blue flame between them.

The inner working did not, of course, end there. As

the Pentagram ritual proceeds, the visualizations associated with it become progressively more complicated.
The drawn pentagrams themselves are imagined as
being drawn in the blue flame which emerges from the
magician's fingertips or dagger-point. A circle of similar blue flame is drawn as the operator moves clockwise from east back round to east again.

When the archangelic names (Raphael, Gabriel,
Michael and Uriel) are called, each is visualized as a
vast, telesmatic figure guarding the particular quarter.
Raphael, for example, is seen as wearing shimmering
robes of shot silk in yellow and mauve, while the
magician strains to feel cool breezes emanating from
behind the figure.

So it goes until the ritual and the visualization are
complete. From the outside, the magician finishes the
ceremony much as he began it. Subjectively, however,
the operator sees himself as completely enclosed by a
floating circle of blue fire set with flaming pentagrams
at its cardinal points and guarded by gigantic figures,
each attributed to one of the four Elements, Earth, Air,
Fire and Water. Floating above the head of the
magician is the interlaced triangles of Solomon's Seal,
the ascending (point upward) triangle red, the descend-
ing triangle blue.

Magicians work very hard to ensure such visualizations are as vivid as possible. Regular practice is one
way of doing so, but often they will go to even greater
lengths to achieve the desired effect. In her *Ritual
Magic Workbook*, the very first lesson Dolores
Ashcroft-Nowicki offers to students is the building of
a temple workplace in their home. On the face of it,
this is an intensely practical chapter. Ashcroft-
Nowicki talks about electrical power-points, the
choice between wallpaper or paint, the dangers of

using a gas heater when one works in flammable robes, and similar mundane considerations. But only two paragraphs into the lesson, she has already indicated clearly that the mundane is not the important level:

> This is not something to take up as a hobby, you are laying the foundation stone of the 'Temple Not Made With Hands' that we all carry within us, this is and will always be the real temple.

What we have here is an extraordinarily interesting statement, the more so because it is so underplayed. Ashcroft-Nowicki is saying that the physical effort and financial investment that go into the building of a ritual temple are actually expended solely in order to help the mind to hold a similar temple in the imagination. Given the complexities embodied in temples of this sort,[63] it is a clear indication of the over-riding importance magicians attach to the use of the imagination.

The insight is swiftly confirmed in Ashcroft-Nowicki's own course in magic, embodied in *The Ritual Magic Workbook*. As early as the second month's training, she has this to say:

> By using your imagination to climb the staircase,[64] you are entering a new phase in your training, that of creative visualisation. You may already possess a good 'inner eye' but it will still need to be trained to create detail and to replicate sound, taste, touch and smell on the inner levels. If you do not have a fairly good imagination you will have to put in some hard work, for almost eighty per cent of magic depends upon this talent.

Exactly the same emphasis on training visualization abilities is found in virtually every major esoteric organization, sometimes as a central aspect – as in the practice of pathworking – sometimes as a side-effect of some other endeavour, such as astral projection[65] or manipulation of the chakras.[66] Nor is Ashcroft-Nowicki's estimate that almost 80 per cent of magical practice depends on visualization an exaggeration. Use of the imagination reaches far beyond the lodge rooms of the ritual magicians. The ceremonies of the Witch Cult all have their inner aspects. The notorious Voodoo doll of Haiti does no more than stand in place of the real image, which is a picture in the mind of the sorcerer. And, as we have already seen, the mystic journeys of shamanism all appear to take place in the realm of visual imagination.

For many years, details of esoteric training of the visual imagination were kept a closely guarded secret and, even today, very few people without personal experience of the occult realize quite how far the training goes. But W. E. Butler, a magician whose ideas have influenced the training of literally thousands of occultists world-wide, spelled it out clearly:

> . . . the training of the magician extends to all the senses . . . The technique . . . for visual work should be extended to cover all the other senses. In practice it will be found that the usual scale of success in these evokings will be headed by either visual or audible images, followed by taste, smell and touch in that order.[67]

This is moving towards a totality of inner experience far more vivid than that encountered by the average individual. And for the magician, every effort is made to push the process to its ultimate:

> A further stage, when proficiency has been attained in some measure at least, is to 'hear imaginatively' someone whose voice is familiar to you, giving a lecture. The lecture must first be formulated by you, but at some point you should cease to formulate and simply 'listen' men-

tally; the subconscious will carry on the lecture and you will simply listen to it.[68]

It was Butler who first announced to a general reading public that esoteric training of the imagination pushed into the magician's actual perception of the physical world. He gave this exercise as a cornerstone of magical ability:

... place the object [to be visualized] in a good light on a monochrome surface, either dark or light, and use a paper or cardboard tube some eight inches long and two and a half inches inside diameter, through which to gaze at it, using the left and right eyes alternately. Or the tube may be made rectangular, so that both eyes may be used at the same time. Then, as the object is being steadily held in the field of vision, the eyes should be thrown slightly out of focus as we sometimes do when we are 'day-dreaming' and the visual picture now apparently brought mentally within the head. This is a psychological 'trick' which is usually only acquired after a great deal of effort and failure ... Once the knack has been gained, it will be found increasingly easy to bring this visual image into mental apprehension. A further stage is reached when the student is able to see clearly inside his head, as it were, the picture of the object concerned, his eyes being closed in the meantime.

Once this has been accomplished, and practice has made it fairly easy, the complementary half should be essayed. The object chosen should be observed and the perception transferred in the usual way to the subjective mental screen. Meanwhile, a monochrome surface, such as a white disc on a black surround, or a black disc on a white surround, or a crystal or black concave mirror, should have been placed so that the student can use it as a screen upon which to project his mental picture.

He should not open his eyes sufficiently to see the disc or mirror (which should be in a dim light) while still holding the picture on the mental screen. Then by a quiet, calm effort of will, he should project the picture outwardly onto the screen.

> When the knack has been gained, it is possible to project such a mental image so clearly that it is to all intents and purposes as though one were perceiving it with the physical eyes.

'As though one were perceiving it with the physical eyes' . . . A great deal of Butler's impact on the world of Western magic can be accounted for by the fact that he was the first practising magician to write in simple, down-to-earth, non-technical, non-allegorical language what it was magicians actually did. There was seldom any need to interpret his words and no need at all to interpret them here. What Butler is describing, in the very fundamentals of magical training, is controlled hallucination, the practised ability to project the contents of the operator's imagination in such a way that it appears to be objective, physical reality.

CHAPTER
10

THE NATURE OF SPIRITS

Describing how the various mysteries and magical schools came into being, William G. Gray observed:

> In order to fulfil the essential condition of operating with one mind in one place at one time, occult practitioners agreed to construct an Inner Cosmos of their own in which their inner lives could be lived and related to the rest of existence . . .
>
> Some made Temples, some Groves, some Landscapes, some Castles, and in fact people of different types made whatever appealed to them most in the Innerworld. Their rituals were directed towards the maintenance and improvement of these realities, for reality is neither more nor less than anyone makes it.[69]

Thus, if we are to credit Gray, magicians are far more concerned with subjective reality than the objective world around them. The world of their adventures is the same world, somewhat differently constructed, as that of the Fantasy Role Play gamer who lives a portion of his life in a daydream scenario created according to the rules of *Dungeons & Dragons*. If this is the case and, as we have already seen, magicians also work hard to create visualizations so vivid that they are virtually indistinguishable from physical reality, then clearly we have gone some way towards explaining the experience of the shamanic journey and its modern equivalent, the pathworking.

But as we have also seen, journeys and pathworkings are by no means the totality of magic. Crowley and Neuburg, Dee and Kelley, Cellini and friends, Éliphas Lévi, Zenner, Gessner and the rest were all involved in the conjuration of spirits. Could spirits, considered since the Ice Age as entities and intelligences in their own right, actually be a part of this subjective reality? Francis King has no doubt about it:

> The fundamental theoretical postulates of Western Magic are few in number. First comes a belief in a system of correspondences between the universe as a whole (the macrocosm) and the individual human being (the microcosm). This correspondence must not, of course, be taken as crudely physical – rather it is an astro-mental relationship in which the soul of man is, to use the Golden Dawn phrase, a magical mirror of the universe. Thus any principle that exists in the cosmos also exists in man; the cosmic force that the ancients personified as Diana, for example, corresponds to the human reproductive instincts, while that same force in its evil and averse aspect, which the ancients personified as Hecate, corresponds to the human sicknesses of sterility and abortion.
>
> As a corollary of this theory, it is believed that the trained occultist can either 'call down' into himself a cosmic force which he desires to tap or, alternatively, 'call up' that same cosmic force from the depths of his own being. The first process is invocation and should never result in physical, as distinct from psychological, manifestation; the second is evocation in which the magician projects a 'spirit' (i.e. a factor in his own psychological make up) into his so-called Triangle of Art . . . [70]

Here then we have our first clear statement that spirits are not at all what they seem. King's explanation of them would not be out of step with modern psychiatric thought. But does this viewpoint represent the opinion of practising occultists?

The answer, surprisingly, seems to be a qualified yes. While there are undoubtedly magicians who believe, with their ancestors, that spirits are spirits, Israel Regardie, one of the most influential practitioners of the twentieth century, had this to say:

Analytical psychology and magic comprise in my estimation two halves or aspects of a single technical system. Just as the body and mind are not two separate units, but are simply the dual manifestations of an interior dynamic 'something' so psychology and magic comprise similarly a single system whose goal is the integration of the human personality . . .

It will be obvious, then, that by magic we are not considering a theatrical craft or jugglery – and certainly not that medieval superstition which was the child of ignorance begotten by fear and terror. These definitions should be expunged from our thinking . . .

Even today, the custodians of this [magical] knowledge . . . are still adamant in their traditional refusal to circulate a more accurate description of the nature of magic. Possibly even they have lost all understanding of its principles. No wonder is it that misconception exists. With the exception of a very few works which have attracted the attention of but a fractional part of the reading public, little has been written to act as a definitive exposition of what magic really is. Inasmuch as something of the nature of modern psychology is at least partially understood by a fair section of the educated world, were it said that magic is akin to and concerns itself with that same subjective realm of psychology, some notion of its character and objectives come within hailing distance.[71]

This is wordy, but clear enough. To Regardie, magic was a system of psychology, a means of manipulating subjective energies within the human psyche. He regarded the protective angels evoked in ritual as Jungian archetypes and thought spirits were 'semi-automatous complexes' – i.e. constellations of emotional energy which only appeared to be distinct from the individual involved.

Regardie was an initiate of both the original Golden Dawn and Crowley's *Stella Matutina* Orders so that his opinions were formed against the background of mainstream magical practice in modern times. Prior to his death in 1986, Regardie was acknowledged as one of the world's leading authorities on ceremonial magic, whose books were used in the training of generations of occultists.

It seems that at least one other great influence on the magical practice of the twentieth century would have agreed with him. Dion Fortune, whose definition of magic is quoted on the first page of Chapter 9, learned her magic, like Regardie, in the Golden Dawn, but subsequently went on to found her own Order. This Order, the Fraternity of the Inner Light, is widely regarded as having carried the torch of the magical tradition[72] when the Golden Dawn ceased to function in Britain. Certainly its doctrines had a profound influence on the founders of the Servants of the Light, one of the most important sources of magical training in Britain today. Thus it is safe to assume that the thinking of Dion Fortune permeates the wellsprings of contemporary magical practice.

But before Dion Fortune was a magician, she was a Freudian psychoanalyst and had no difficulty whatsoever in reconciling the two disciplines:

> I have had my full share of the adventures of the Path; have known men and women who could indubitably be ranked as adepts; seen phenomena such as no seance room has ever known, and borne my share in it; taken part in psychic feuds and stood my watch on the roster of the occult police force which, under the Masters of the Great White Lodge, keeps guard over the nations, each according to its race; kept the occult vigil when one dare not sleep

while the sun is below the horizon; and hung on desperately, matching my staying-power against the attack until the moon-tides changed and the force of the onslaught blew itself out.

And through all these experiences I was learning to interpret occultism in the light of psychology, and psychology in the light of occultism, the one counter-checking and explaining the other.[73]

But if occultists have not moved quite so far from orthodoxy than might have appeared the case, it nonetheless seems fairly obvious that the word 'complex' in Regardie's term *semi-automatous complex* is used in a special way. A complex, in psychiatry, is defined as a (wholly or partly unconscious) constellation of associated ideas which carry a high emotional charge. They are part of the way the mind works and while some – those which include feelings of inferiority, for example – can cause troublesome neuroses, it is difficult to see how such a constellation could manifest the personality characteristics and separate intelligence which are the hallmarks of a spirit.

But there are aspects of the psyche which, as psychiatrists have been swift to point out, sometimes act as spirits have historically been thought to act. When these manifest, the patient frequently concludes that spirits are actually involved.[74]

One such case was reported by Carl Jung[75] as part of an early family experience. While Jung was still a university student at Basle, his fifteen-year-old cousin, a shy, hesitant and poorly educated girl of pale, unhealthy appearance, became a prey to 'spirit voices'. She would cease to talk in her usual Swiss dialect and begin to use a smooth, assured, literary German. Spirits claimed to speak through her, including her grandfather and a long-dead North German noble.

The claims were taken seriously. The girl held regular Sunday evening seances during which she would bring through spirit messages. These seances continued until her early death, from tuberculosis, at the age of twenty-six. Jung concluded he was listening to aspects of the girl's own personality. One of these aspects manifested as a mature individual calling itself Ivenes. In sharp contrast to what Jung knew of his cousin, Ivenes presented herself as highly intelligent, confident and self-possessed. She also claimed to be the real cousin. Jung speculated that the girl somehow knew she was destined to die young and the Ivenes personality was an attempt to compensate for her lack of maturity.

Jung's cousin was not unique. The psychologist Pierre Janet cites the case of Leonie, a peasant woman who had been subject to attacks of somnambulism in childhood. Under hypnosis, a second personality emerged, more lively and vital than the first, which flatly denied being the same person as the waking Leonie. Leonie 2 actually considered Leonie 1 to be stupid.

As time went by, a third personality, Leonie 3, emerged. Leonie 3 was both different and superior to either of the others. She thought of Leonie 1 as good but essentially stupid and Leonie 2 as crazy.[76]

While Leonie showed three indwelling personalities, Doris Fischer produced five. They were studied by the Pittsburgh psychiatrist Walter F. Prince from 1910 onwards. Dr Prince noted that the various personalities were ranked in a sort of hierarchy which ranged from a very primitive entity at the bottom all the way up to a supposed spirit who claimed to have come in answer to the prayers of Doris' dead mother.[77]

A similar hierarchical structure was evident in the

psyche of Sybil Dorsett,[78] one of the most extreme cases of multiple personality on record, manifesting no fewer than sixteen separate personalities. Sybil developed her inner host in reaction to extreme ill-treatment by her mother, but the personalities themselves were among the most impressive ever studied. They included a builder, a carpenter, a writer, a musician and a painter. The separate, rounded nature of each personality was emphasized by the fact that the writer and the musician became firm friends, manifesting together in Sybil's body in order to hold conversations or attend plays and concerts. One other of the series, a mature woman who called herself Vicky, stood at or near the top of the hierarchy and often looked after the others. On one occasion she prevented Sybil committing suicide by throwing herself in the Hudson River.[79]

Even sixteen indwelling personalities does not exhaust the capacity of the human psyche. Truddi Chase, born in upper New York State, was inhabited by ninety-two of them, as the psychotherapist Robert A. Phillips Jr discovered when he went to treat her. The beings within included a giant, a poet and a child too young for speech.[80]

An analysis of cases like these soon shows the similarities between the secondary personalities of psychiatry and the spirits of magic. The indwelling personae appear as separate individuals, exhibiting personality traits and intelligence levels which may be at variance with those of the host. They can manifest as apparently objective voices or (hallucinatory) figures. They can take control of a patient in a process remarkably similar to possession, remain for a time, then withdraw. They have their own interests and areas of expertise. And besides behaving like spirits, many of them actually claim to be spirits.

But while it is easy to see why so many psychiatrists have concluded that the spirits of magic are simply misunderstood examples of personality fragmentation, there are differences between the two phenomena which are far less often analysed.

Perhaps the most obvious lies in the mental health of the host. With the exception of Jung's cousin, all the women mentioned in the foregoing case-studies were seriously ill; and even Jung's cousin did not appear particularly healthy. While multiple personality is rare, enough cases have now come to light to allow the emergence of a pattern. A common denominator in many studies is the experience of childhood abuse. Doris Fischer showed first signs of a dual personality at the age of three after her father threw her violently to the floor in a drunken rage. Truddi Chase was sexually abused by her stepfather between the ages of two and sixteen. And so on. Psychiatrists believe that the creation of alternate personalities is a defence against experiences too painful to be borne by the core persona, which hides behind and is protected by the others. Truddi Chase's ninety-two indwellers refer to themselves as 'the troops' in a clear indication of their protective role.

Practitioners of magical evocation may be thought eccentric, perhaps even foolish, but there is no suggestion that they are insane.[81] Unlike those with personality fragmentation,[82] magicians seem perfectly able to function effectively in the real world; and some, like W. B. Yeats, Algernon Blackwood, Florence Farr and Sax Rohmer, have pursued unusually successful, even distinguished, careers.

Then there is the question of who is in charge. Despite Neuburg's unfortunate experience, magically evoked spirits do not normally break free from the triangle of art or enter the circle of protection. Nor, unless something has gone badly wrong, do they take possession of the magician's body. Spirits of magical evocation are controllable. The whole point of magical method is that they should be. Evocation calls up a spirit at a particular time, and banishes it at the magician's will. This is in stark contrast with the studies in the psychiatric casebooks, where the unfortunate patient is forced to accept every upsurge of the secondary personalities with no measure of control at all – at least until a cure is effected.

For these reasons if no other, it does seem that, despite the immediate similarities, it would be unwise to assume that the spirits of magic are necessarily the secondary personalities of the operator who evoked them.

But if not secondary personalities, what are they?

11

CREATING A GHOST

An odd thing happened to the novelist Margaret O'Donnell while she was working on her fictional reconstruction of history, *The Goddess*. As a writer, she was accustomed to designing her books carefully, researching, outlining and conscientiously constructing plotlines with a diligence which would have done credit to an army general planning a campaign. This had worked well until a stage of the novel where her protagonists were caught up in the violent upheaval of Alexandria at the time of Hypatia and the burning of the Library.

O'Donnell knew where her characters were going, of course. She had already decided that, with the Library burning, they would leave the building, make their way to the coast and there take a ship to Rome. It was to be a straightforward section of the book with no plot twists or unexpected turns.

Her characters left the burning Library on schedule. But only minutes later, their astounded author found herself describing how they had turned round and come back. They had, they said, been unable to get through the crowd!

The fact that fictional characters take on a life of their own is a cliché of creative literature. But few outside the writing profession can appreciate how literal a phenomenon this is. It is not *as if* fictional characters take on a life of their own. Taking on a life of their own is what *actually* happens. When a novel gathers momentum in an author's mind, the characters themselves will often decide where they want to go and there is little or nothing the novelist can do to stop them, short of abandoning the work completely.

This sounds ludicrous when stated so baldly, yet remains a fact of many, if not most, author's lives. Seamus Cullen, whose convoluted fantasies[83] are characterized by extraordinary intricacies of plot, once remarked that he had never actually written a book in his life – they had all written themselves through him. Typically, he would get an idea for an environment or theme, the characters would take over and the whole story would unfold itself, as much to the author's surprise and delight as the reader's.

How seriously one must take the separate 'life' of fictional characters is underlined by the fact that at one stage of his career, Cullen decided for financial reasons to create a novel in a category that was enjoying a marketing vogue at the time. He quickly found he could not do so. The characters in his head would not permit it.

I have had personal experience of the phenomenon in the writing of my own novels. When commissioned to produce my first work of fiction[84] in the late 1970s, I was required to create a detailed synopsis for the US publisher Doubleday, who had strong ideas about both setting and content. This I did without too much difficulty and the result seemed sufficiently promising to warrant the issue of a contract. But when I began to write the book, I quickly discovered that the characters simply would not stick to the outline. The work went its own merry way and, when complete, bore little resemblance to the book that had been commissioned. Fortunately Doubleday, a long-established and experienced literary house, realized books do not always lie within the author's control and liked the end product sufficiently well to publish it anyway.

Since that time, I have learned to relax with my characters, let them develop their adventures and trust the result will be of interest to the reader. So far this approach has worked, but that is little more than a fortuitous accident. In point of fact, I now know it is the only way I can write fiction.

Watching a novel unfold in this way is a fascinating experience. It is like looking through a window into a different dimension and reporting on the activities of the individuals one finds there. Time and again, I have been amused by my characters' wit, surprised by their actions, concerned at their fate ... all because 'my' characters were not my characters at all, but creatures capable of doing their own thing. They are like spirits I have called up and set loose on the page, not puppets whose strings I control.

This similarity of fiction characters to spirits has not gone unnoticed. In his classic collection of science fantasy tales, *The Martian Chronicles*, the American author Ray Bradbury tells how the first visitors to the planet Mars discover it is haunted, not by ghosts of the Martian dead, but by Mr Pickwick, Rip Van Winkle and a host of other famous characters from literature. Bradbury speculated that the affection and interest of generations of readers gave them a reality of their own. But as a novelist he must have known no readers are required. The process begins at the moment of creation, in the mind of the author.

Bradbury's *Chronicles* were written with a light, deft touch and sold as fiction not philosophy. How seriously then should we take his suggestion – and my own – that created characters may have something in common with spirits?

Travellers to Tibet have brought back reports of a curious practice which may have a bearing on this question. Prior to the Chinese invasion of 1950, this remote and isolated country had a monastic tradition so strong that one man in four throughout the entire population was a monk. Although the focus of monastic work was religious, the religion concerned was a unique blend of shamanism and Buddhism which greatly encouraged the practice of meditation and the personal examination of psychic contents. As a result, Tibetan lamaseries became, over the centuries, rich repositories of information about the nature and structure of the human mind – a fact now quite widely appreciated by Western psychologists, despite the differences in terminology.[85]

Out of this repository comes details of a creative process involving a mythic creature called a Yidam, one of Lamaist Tibet's tutelary deities.

Pupils of Tibetan gurus were often instructed to meditate on the Yidam and study pictures of it in the sacred scriptures. This revealed the creature to have a fearful, almost demonic aspect: something not uncommon in Tibetan deities. When the student was thoroughly saturated in Yidam lore, he – students were almost always male – would be advised to find a remote cave and there draw a magic circle (known as a kylkhor) using powdered chalk. The purpose of the circle was to aid the visible appearance of the Yidam.

In order to achieve this, the pupil was instructed strongly to visualize the Yidam within the circle. Over a period of weeks, or even months, the pupil would be encouraged to continue with the exercise until a full-scale hallucination resulted and the Yidam appeared. The similarities between this process and W. E. Butler's description of the training of Western magicians are too obvious to require much comment except to point out one important cultural difference. In the West, magicians accept that the outward projection of visionary contents is no more than that. In Tibet, however, the bed-rock assumption would have been that correct meditations would tend to call up a given deity, thus the ceremony of the Yidam would be viewed as an evocation, rather than a visualization.

At the point when the Yidam appeared, the pupil would be told he had been remarkably successful in his endeavours and was obviously favoured by the god. For his next step, he would have to persuade it to leave the circle.

Here, of course, we move beyond Butler's basic exercise altogether. The visualization, involving movement, is substantially more complicated and difficult. It might have taken several more weeks or months, but eventually the pupil would report that the god had indeed stepped out of the kylkhor. He would be congratulated, then told to see if he could manage to get the Yidam to speak to him and accompany him wherever he went.

At this point, despite the bizarre nature of the exercise, it is possible to recognize that the pupil is really being asked to engage in the creation of a fictional character, albeit one firmly based on scriptural authority. For while the appearance of the Yidam is a matter of simple visualization, any conversations held must require precisely the same creative input as an author writing dialogue.

There is no doubt at all that the Lamas who

developed the exercise recognized this as well, for the whole experience was actually a test of the pupil. If he succeeded in creating a Yidam that would walk and talk with him, his teacher would tell him his studies were ended since he now had the wisest and most powerful teacher possible. The pupil who accepted this was deemed a failure – and sent off to spend the rest of his life in a comfortable hallucination. The pupil who expressed doubts had learned the lesson that even the most powerful deities were no more than creations of the human mind.

If Tibet seems a long way to go to establish a link between spirits and fictional characters, it may be as well to point out that a wholly scientific experiment somewhat closer to home makes the same point. I described the experiment fairly fully in my book *Mindreach*[86] and can do little better than quote the relevant passage here:

A group of investigators from the Toronto Society for Psychical Research, under the leadership of Dr George and Mrs Iris Owen, decided to attempt one of the most remarkable experiments in the entire history of their speciality. They set out to make a ghost . . .

First, in the manner of a fiction writer, they created a character, then invented a background and life to go with him.

The group's character, Philip, would have done full justice to any historical thriller. It was decided he had lived in the time of Cromwell, in a house called Diddington Manor. As part of the overall life story, Philip fell in love with a beautiful Gypsy woman named Margo and subsequently had an affair with her.

Dorothea, Philip's wife, found out about the relationship and took her revenge by accusing Margo of witchcraft. Margo was tried, convicted and burned at the stake. Philip, mad with grief, committed suicide by throwing himself off the battlements of his home.

It must be stressed that all of this was fiction, with one sole exception: there actually was a Diddington Manor, pictures of which had been obtained by the group. But no one named Philip had ever lived there, nor did Margo or the jealous Dorothea ever exist.

Having formulated this tale, the group then tried to bring Philip to life (so to speak) by means of a series of seances. Photographs of the manor were placed around the seance room and the group met regularly to concentrate on the fictional Philip and his dramatic life story.

For several months nothing happened. It seemed as if the experiment was to be a failure. Then the group decided on a different approach. The intensive concentration was abandoned in favour of a much more informal atmosphere. The group chatted about Philip and their experiment. At one point they even sang a few songs.

Surprisingly, this latter approach proved productive. At one seance, a rap was heard. The group promptly set up a code and communication was established ... sure enough, the 'spirit' was Philip, claiming the life history they had invented for him.

This was an extraordinary development, given the circumstances of the experiment. As the seances continued, the fictional Philip continued to behave exactly as seance room spirits have always behaved. It caused raps and table movements and brought through such a richly detailed description of the Cromwellian period that the experimenters actually felt compelled to double check that they had not based Philip on a real life character. In the event, they confirmed that they had not. He was fiction through and through, but like Bradbury's Martians, no less capable of haunting for all that.

The Toronto experiment has been successfully duplicated by other groups, one of whom dispelled any lingering doubts about the fictional nature of the spirit by communicating with an ethereal talking dolphin named Silk. The work to date has all been within the pseudo-Spiritualist seance room framework. No one, so far as I am aware, has attempted to create a fictional character for conjuration within a magician's circle. Or at least, not consciously, for the Toronto experiment must surely suggest that creating fictional characters is what magicians have been doing all along.

'All of literature is a footnote to Faust,' comedian Woody Allen once remarked in the hope of producing an impressive quotation. From what we have learned so far, he may well have been right.

And yet . . .

12

SPIRITS VISIBLE

The Hermetic Order of the Golden Dawn, that archetypal training organization for the Western Esoteric
Tradition, was structured in a series of levels, degrees
or grades. The first step of the hierarchy was the grade
of Neophyte. Above this came Zelator, then Theoricus,
Practicus, Philosophus and so on up to the rank of
Ipsissimus, described by John Symonds[87] as 'that lofty
height occupied by the one God and a host of lunatics'.

Movement through the levels was not automatic.
The entire Order operated something like a school,
where progress from one class to the next depended on
how well one did one's homework and performed in
end-of-term exams.

The examinations typically consisted of written
papers, prepared both under time constraints at the
Lodge and at home in the manner of a thesis, and of
practical demonstrations. These might involve the
construction of a talisman or showing familiarity with
various magical rituals, like that of the ubiquitous
Pentagram. It was a rule of the Order that any
ceremonies performed by the candidate must 'show
effect' as well as verbal accuracy. Depending on the
grade, one or more examiners might be involved in
the test.

When a candidate at the level of Zelator wished to

pass on to the grade of Theoricus Adeptus Minor, he or she was required, among other things, to perform a ceremony based on formulae contained in Order Ritual number Z-2 and witnessed by an examiner. The ceremony had to meet with the examiner's approval as to method, execution and effect. The instructions given for the ritual include the following passage:

> He [the operator] is then to take back the Sigil to between the Pillars, and repeat the former processes, when assuredly that Spirit will begin to manifest, but in a misty and ill-defined form . . . Now as soon as the Magician *shall see the visible manifestation* of that Spirit's presence, he shall quit the station of the Hierophant and consecrate afresh with Water and with Fire, the Sigil of the evoked spirit . . .
>
> The Magician, standing in the place of the Hierophant, but turning towards the place of the Spirit and fixing his attention thereon, now reads a potent Invocation of the Spirit unto visible appearance, having previously placed the sigil on the ground, within the circle, at the quarter where the Spirit appears. This Invocation should be of some length; and should rehearse and reiterate the divine and other Names consonant with the working. That Spirit should now become *fully and clearly visible*, and should be able to speak with a direct voice, if consonant with his nature.[88]

So Ritual Z-2 was a spirit evocation to visible appearance. The candidate was deemed to have failed unless the spirit appeared to have a consistency at least equivalent to steam.

This is a remarkable requirement by any criterion. If we have defined magic as a collection of techniques designed to stimulate visionary experience, and spirits as fictional creations little different to Prospero or Pickwick, are we now to suppose that such subjective visions can actually be shared?

In common with most practising magicians, W. E. Butler would have insisted that the answer must be yes.

> A further stage in this mental projection [of visualized images] is one which is not often met with outside the occult lodges. It is possible, if the magician has the materialising type of body, or can employ a materialising medium, to cause such mental images to be clothed with ectoplasmic substance and become visible to the physical senses of all present.
>
> Another way in which an apparent objectivity can be given to the projected images is by a process of 'telepathic radiation'. Here the projected image, localised in one point of space, becomes what the psychic researchers term a 'phantasmogenetic centre' and the simultaneous telepathic radiation by the magician induces what is known as a 'collective hallucination' in those around. Again, this is not usually experienced outside the lodges, except apparently accidentally.
>
> The technique of this latter method depends upon certain training which allows the conscious mind to be more closely linked with its subconscious levels. The magical feat known as the 'Operation of Invisibility' is based on this technique, though, in some cases, something more enters into it, for the ectoplasmic substance can produce some very unusual effects. The present writer once took a photo of a high grade occultist. On developing the film, there was no trace of the figure of the person concerned, though all the chair in which he was sitting at the time showed quite clearly. It was just as though a photo had been taken of an empty chair.[89]

Is this sort of thing really possible? Coincidentally, I heard a similar story, without the magical overtones, several years ago from a woman who was not an occultist, but a trained scientist. Following the break-up of her marriage and serious financial difficulties, she had gone through a period of severe depression during which her evaluation of her own worth sank to such a low ebb that she became prey to the feeling she did not exist at all. During the worst of her depression, she was encouraged by friends to pose for an outdoor photograph. When the film was developed, there was no sign of the woman, while the tree against which she had been standing was clearly visible.

Perhaps both cameras were faulty – although the appearance of the 'hidden' objects (chair and tree) in each case is curious. But whatever about the projection of negative subjective states, the very structure of the Golden Dawn would seem to predicate that positive mental images can be shared. Furthermore, it would appear that the sharing can involve more than two people. Francis King writes:

> On May 13th, 1896, for example, she[90] with the assistance of Alan Bennett, Charles Rosher and Frederick Leigh Gardner, evoked the mercurial spirit Taphtharthareth to visible appearance – or so the four of them believed.[91]

In certain circumstances, orthodox psychologists would have less difficulty with this sort of thing than one might imagine – and without any need to evoke exotica like ectoplasmic substance or telepathic radiation. Experiments in peer pressure suggest that if, for example, a subject is required to decide which is the shorter of two fairly similar lines, he will have little difficulty in doing so, unless peer pressure is exerted. But if enough of his colleagues seriously insist that the longer line is actually shorter, then the subject will eventually conclude they are correct. He will begin to see the lines not as they really are, but as his peers insist them to be.

Such experiments clearly indicate that our perceptions of reality are, at least to some extent, conditioned. Predictably, individual response to peer pressure varies and a few stubborn individuals will insist they are right about the damn lines no matter how many people claim otherwise. But there are more than enough subjects whose perceptions can be influenced in this way to make peer pressure a definite factor in what most people think they see.

Another, perhaps even more important factor, is expectation. Psychologists have noted again and again that what we expect to see profoundly influences our interpretation of what we actually do see. Closely associated with this factor is setting. It is a matter of common experience that we will often pass by a familiar tradesperson in the street without recognizing him. He is no longer in his familiar setting, thus our expectations of meeting him have been diminished. Equally, positive expectations condition our perceptions of objects of uncertain interpretation. Every motorist has had the experience of imagining a shadow on the road to be a body, particularly when tired.

How far such influences can go was brought home to me several years ago in conversation with the entertainer Peter Silverman.[92] At the time, Silverman pursued a career as a stage hypnotist while claiming, however, that he did not use hypnosis at all or, alternatively, that his 'powers' went beyond hypnosis. In a sense the latter was quite true, since he often used little more than psychological manipulation to persuade his subjects to behave in an amusing manner on stage. Over a period of years, he had achieved a substantial international reputation in those countries which still permitted public demonstrations of this type.

Silverman was fascinated by what he referred to as the 'witch-doctor syndrome' – the fact that the more profoundly his audiences believed in his abilities, the easier it was to convince them of the truth of a particular illusion. As an illustration of this effect, he quoted his own promise to levitate during the final performance of a particular stage run.

This promise was made primarily to ensure a full house for his last night, but he repeated it with every appearance of conviction at the end of several shows during the run, urging members of the audience to book at once so that they should not miss such a spectacular feat. When the time came to make good his word, he did not attempt to use mechanical trickery. Instead, with lights dramatically lowered, he lay down on a specially constructed platform in the middle of the stage, warned the audience to remain absolutely quiet, then pretended to pass into trance.

For a time he simply lay there while the expectation built. Then, when he judged the tension to be at its peak, he sat up abruptly, clutched his chest and collapsed. The curtains swung closed and a loudspeaker appeal was made for any doctor who might be in the house. A statement was subsequently issued to the effect that Silverman had had a heart attack, brought on by the intense strain of his attempted levitation.

The 'heart attack' was as non-existent as Silverman's ability to levitate, a point he admitted to me freely. But the interesting aspect of the anecdote concerned what happened after the abortive levitation attempt. On chatting much later with members of the audience on the night in question, Silverman found a substantial number prepared to swear they actually had seen him levitate somewhere between a foot and eighteen inches from the platform. He was, they insisted, floating before he clutched his chest.

Any policeman will confirm that good witnesses are

rare. Within hours, or even minutes, the average individual has a distorted memory of what took place. But when expectation and peer pressure are simultaneously brought to bear – as they were in Silverman's demonstration – the situation becomes much worse: there are always some who can be persuaded to believe they have seen something that did not happen at all.

Is this then what occurred in the Golden Dawn? Did members, expecting to see a spirit evoked in the highly charged emotional environment of the Lodge room, persuade each other and themselves that a spirit was there when none really appeared? This would certainly seem to be a possibility in the 13 May operation of Florence Farr and her three colleagues. But it is a little more difficult to accept in the altogether cooler atmosphere of an examination – even an examination in the magical arts. The test was applied again and again, by different examiners in different Golden Dawn temples, as more and more members successfully passed into the particular grade. Can it have been purely a matter of self-deception and shared illusion every time?

The question is complicated by that final phrase in the passage we have already quoted: 'That Spirit should now become fully and clearly visible, and should be able to speak with a direct voice, if consonant with his nature.'

This goes beyond Butler's instructions for projecting an imaginary image of a static object. It goes beyond Silverman's feat of persuading members of his audience that he was levitating. In evocations of the type described, we are not dealing with the fleeting appearance of a spectral figure, but rather the production of an entity which can talk with sufficient clarity to answer questions. In the vineyard at Jena, one could imagine its being asked the location of the treasure hoard, with three pairs of eager ears straining for the answer. It is more difficult to decide what the elaborately robed members of the Golden Dawn would ask, but doubtless they found some topic of interest to discuss with the manifest entity. And since there are no records of any disagreements arising out of what has been said by spirits during evocations, we must conclude they all heard essentially the same thing.

The conclusion is not, of course, based on the Golden Dawn experience alone. Spirit evocation has been a major aspect of magical practice since the Ice Age and there have been broad sweeps of history during which it was a public occupation. In classical times, spirits were called to give oracular pronouncements. While the meaning of such announcements has, historically, often been obscure, there are few disagreements on exactly what was said.

In the face of spirits manifesting visibly and talking audibly, is it still possible to hold to our earlier conclusion that these entities are constructs of the human mind? However confident I may be about my skills as a novelist, I would find it difficult to conceive the possibility of creating a fictional character of such power that it could be seen and heard.

Yet even here, it seems, there is some evidence for just such a thing happening, although once again we have to turn eastward, to Tibet, to find an explanation of the mechanics of Western magic.

The Tibetan term *sprulpa*, more usually rendered *tulpa*, is defined as an illusory creation of magic, a phantom generated sometimes as the result of a lengthy ceremony, sometimes almost instantaneously, by an adept. Occasionally, the process of creation is unconscious, as Madame Alexandra

David-Neel reported:

> A Tibetan painter, a fervent worshipper of the wrathful deities, who took a peculiar delight in drawing their terrible forms, came one afternoon to pay me a visit.
>
> I noticed behind him the somewhat nebulous shape of one of the fantastic beings which often appeared in his paintings. I made a startled gesture and the astonished artist took a few steps towards me, asking what was the matter.
>
> I noticed that the phantom did not follow him and, quickly thrusting my visitor aside, I walked to the apparition with one arm stretched in front of me. My hand reached the foggy form. I felt as if touching a soft object whose substance gave way under the slight push, and the vision vanished.[93]

Although it transpired that the painter had been performing a rite of evocation over the previous few weeks, David-Neel concluded the real effect of the ceremony had been to create a particular state of mind. He had further been working on a painting of the deity. 'In fact,' remarked David-Neel, 'the Tibetan's thoughts were entirely concentrated on the deity . . .' It was this, she was quite certain, that had caused the phantom to appear.

The conscious creation of a tulpa was regarded as highly dangerous for anyone who was not fully aware of the psychic processes at work . . . and who had not reached a state of high spiritual enlightenment. Experts believed that the tulpa would instinctively free itself from its maker's control once it had obtained sufficient vitality to do so. There were stories of magicians battling for mastery of rebellious tulpas and being killed in the attempt.

> Tibetan magicians also relate cases in which the tulpa is sent to fulfil a mission, but does not come back and

pursues its peregrinations as a half-conscious, dangerously mischievous puppet. The same thing, it is said, may happen when the maker of the tulpa dies before having dissolved it. Yet, as a rule, the phantom either disappears suddenly at the death of the magician or gradually vanishes like a body that perishes for want of food. On the other hand, some tulpas are expressly intended to survive their creator and are specially formed for that purpose.[94]

Fantastic though they seemed, David-Neel considered that the reports of tulpa creation emanated from people she had found trustworthy. She was sufficiently impressed to embark, despite all warnings of the dangers, on her own experiment.

In order to avoid being influenced by the forms of the Lamaist deities, which I saw daily around me in paintings and images, I chose for my experiment a most insignificant character: a monk, short and fat, of an innocent and jolly type.

I shut myself in tsams and proceeded to perform the prescribed concentration of thought and other rites. After a few months the phantom monk was formed. His form grew gradually fixed and life-like looking. He became a kind of guest, living in my apartment. I then broke my seclusion and started for a tour, with my servants and tents.

The monk included himself in the party. Though I lived in the open, riding on horseback for miles each day, the illusion persisted. I saw the fat trapa, now and then it was not necessary for me to think of him to make him appear. The phantom performed various actions of the kind that are natural to travellers and that I had not commanded. For instance he walked, stopped, looked around him. The illusion was mostly visual, but sometimes I felt as if a robe was lightly rubbing against me and once a hand seemed to touch my shoulder.[95]

It transpired, however, that there was something to the warnings of danger after all. After a time, David-Neel found the process of separation beginning.

> The features which I had imagined when building my
> phantom, gradually underwent a change. The fat, chubby-
> cheeked fellow grew leaner, his face assumed a vaguely
> mocking, sly, malignant look. He became more trouble-
> some and bold. In brief, he escaped my control.[96]

The tulpa had, by this time, achieved sufficient
objectivity to be seen quite clearly by others. One of
them, a herdsman, mistook it for a visiting lama. It
also proved remarkably difficult to disperse. David-
Neel says she succeeded, 'but only after six months of
hard struggle'.

One of David-Neel's publishers described her as 'the
original travelling sceptic'. She was a Knight of the
Legion of Honour in her native France and recipient of
a gold medal from the Geographical Society of Paris.
She became the first European woman ever accorded
the rank of Lama and has long been acknowledged in
the West as a scholarly authority on Tibetan esoteric
doctrines. Against this background, it is impossible to
dismiss her report of a personal experience as trivial.

This leaves both rationalists and true believers in an
uncomfortable position. So far, it is evident that the
magical techniques of 'spirit evocation' do produce
results which, at face value, would seem to confirm
some of the claims made by magicians through
the centuries.

But closer examination suggests that spirits may not
be what they seem. Their evocation may involve
mechanisms perfectly familiar to orthodox psychology, and their nature appears to be an extension of a
creative process practised by artists and, particularly,
by writers.[97] The case is not yet proven, but the
evidence is mounting.

CHAPTER

13

SPIRIT KNOWLEDGE

One of the most frequently quoted examples of magical evocation appears in the Old Testament First Book of Samuel describing a time when the Philistines were ranged against Israel. The relevant passage, beginning at Chapter 28, verse 3, reads:

> Now Samuel was dead, and all Israel had lamented him, and buried him in Ramah, even in his own city. And Saul had put away those that had familiar spirits, and the wizards, out of the land.
>
> And the Philistines gathered themselves together, and came and pitched in Shunem: and Saul gathered all Israel together, and they pitched in Gilboa.
>
> And when Saul saw the host of the Philistines, he was afraid, and his heart greatly trembled.
>
> And when Saul enquired of the Lord, the Lord answered him not, neither by dreams, nor by Urim, nor by prophets.
>
> Then said Saul unto his servants, Seek me a woman that hath a familiar spirit, that I may go to her, and enquire of her. And his servants said to him, Behold, there is a woman that hath a familiar spirit at En-dor.
>
> And Saul disguised himself, and put on other raiment, and he went, and two men with him, and they came to the woman by night: and he said, I pray thee, divine unto me by the familiar spirit, and bring me him up, whom I shall name unto thee.
>
> And the woman said unto him, Behold, though knowest what Saul hath done, how he hath cut off those that have familiar spirits, and the wizards, out of the land: where-

fore then layest thou a snare for my life, to cause me to die?

And Saul sware to her by the Lord, saying, As the Lord liveth, there shall no punishment happen to thee for this thing.

Then said the woman, Whom shall I bring up unto thee? And he said, Bring me up Samuel.

And when the woman saw Samuel, she cried with a loud voice: and the woman spoke to Saul, saying, Why hast thou deceived me? For thou art Saul.

And the king said unto her, Be not afraid: for what sawest thou? And the woman said unto Saul, I saw gods ascending out of the earth.

And he said unto her, What form is he of? And she said, An old man cometh up; and he is covered with a mantle. And Saul perceived that it was Samuel, and he stooped with his face to the ground, and bowed himself.

And Samuel said to Saul, Why hast thou disquieted me, to bring me up? And Saul answered, I am sore distressed; for the Philistines make war against me, and God is departed from me, and answereth me no more, neither by prophets, nor by dreams: therefore I have called thee, that thou mayest make known unto me what I shall do.

Then said Samuel, Wherefore then dost thou ask of me, seeing the Lord is departed from thee, and is become thine enemy?

And the Lord hath done to him, as he spake by me: for the Lord hath rent the kingdom out of thine hand, and given it to thy neighbour, even to David:

Because thou obeyedst not the voice of the Lord, nor executedst his fierce wrath upon Amalek, therefore hath the Lord done this thing unto thee this day.

Moreover the Lord will also deliver Israel with thee into the hand of the Philistines: and tomorrow shalt thou and thy sons be with me: the Lord also shall deliver the host of Israel into the hand of the Philistines.

Then Saul fell straightway all along on the earth, and was sore afraid, because of the words of Samuel: and there was no strength in him; for he had eaten no bread all the day, nor all the night.[98]

I have quoted the passage in full because commentators have more often associated it with witchcraft and/or mediumship than magical evocation. The
use of the term 'familiar spirit' and the sex of the
magician is generally considered sufficient to warrant
a link with witchcraft, while the fact that the woman
obviously saw the spirit before Saul did, is taken to
indicate mediumship.

The key point, however, would seem to be Saul's
instruction to 'bring me him up, whom I shall name
unto thee' and the woman's skill in so doing.
Spiritualist mediums are virtually unanimous in their
insistence that they do not command spirits, merely
give free spirits an opportunity to communicate with
the living.

> . . . spirit people cannot be called back against their will
> to communicate with those on earth. They come only if
> they wish to do so. There can be no question of 'raising
> the dead' as so many people erroneously assert.[99]

Nor is the type of evocation described typical of
witchcraft, ancient or modern. It is, in fact, an act of
necromancy and as such is firmly the province of the
magician. It is accepted, for example, that Dr Dee and
Edward Kelley attemped a necromantic evocation in a
lonely cemetery prior to their departure from England
for Europe. An early engraving shows the two of them,
armed with torch, wand and book, crowded in a
cramped circle protected by the mystic names
Raphael, *Rael*, *Miraton*, *Tarmiel* and *Rex*. A shrouded
spirit stands at attention before them.

But the point at issue is not really whether this was
a magical, mediumistic or Craft evocation. The point
is the reason why the evocation took place: and here
there is no disagreement at all – the spirit of Samuel

was called because King Saul needed information.

This is, in fact, the most commonplace reason for evoking spirits. The unfortunate conspirators at Jena wanted information about buried treasure. Dee and Kelley wanted information about Enochian magic. Saul's request (I have called thee, that thou mayest make known unto me what I shall do) lays down a pattern for a multitude of evocations since biblical times. In each case the spirit is asked for advice; often advice that would involve foreknowledge.

This is certainly what happened with King Saul. He wantd to know what would happen in the looming Israeli–Philistine confrontation and the spirit Samuel told him:

> . . . the Lord will also deliver Israel with thee into the hand
> of the Philistines: and tomorrow shalt thou and thy sons
> be with me: the Lord also shall deliver the host of Israel
> into the hand of the Philistines.

Stripped of its religious overtones, the spirit predicted that Saul and his sons would be killed the following day and the Philistines would win the battle against the Israelites . . . which was, as it transpired, exactly what happened.

> Now the Philistines fought against Israel: and the men of
> Israel fled from before the Philistines, and fell down slain
> in mount Gilboa.
>
> And the Philistines followed hard upon Saul and upon
> his sons; and the Philistines slew Jonathan, and Abinadab,
> and Melchishua, Saul's sons.
>
> And the battle went sore against Saul, and the archers
> hit him; and he was sore wounded of the archers.
>
> Then said Saul unto his armourbearer, Draw thy sword,
> and thrust me through therewith; lest these uncircum-
> cised come and thrust me through, and abuse me. But his
> armourbearer would not; for he was sore afraid. Therefore

Saul took a sword, and fell upon it.

And when his armourbearer saw that Saul was dead, he fell likewise upon his sword, and died with him.

So Saul died, and his three sons, and his armourbearer, and all his men, that same day together.

And when the men of Israel that were on the other side of the valley, and they that were on the other side Jordan, saw that the men of Israel fled, and that Saul and his sons were dead, they forsook the cities, and fled; and the Philistines came and dwelt in them.

Whether one accepts the story as literally true is unimportant. What is important is that it remains typical of the sort of encounters magicians are supposed to have had with spirits over the centuries. If we suspect the spirit of Samuel was a creation of the mind of the woman Saul consulted (or, just possibly, of Saul himself) then we must ask if it is possible for a fictional character to exhibit knowledge that its creator did not know. This may sound unlikely, but it is, in fact, simply another way of asking whether an individual may obtain information he or she does not already know without going through the usual channels. There seems no doubt whatsoever that the answer to this must be yes, although the process itself can be analysed out under three quite different categories.

The first of these is information not consciously known, but stored nonetheless in the individual's unconscious. In one of my earlier books, I quoted a personal experience of this which occurred while writing a novel:

The central character of the novel was an Egyptian Pharaoh whom I called Nectanebo. The character grew in my head for several months before I actually began to write, with the result that the creation was extremely detailed. I knew, for example, the era in which Nectanebo lived, the outline of his career, some details of his death and the fact that he had a fearsome reputation as a sorcerer.

With the fictional character firmly in mind, I began research into the history of Ancient Egypt in order to provide authentic background for the book. I was stunned to discover Nectanebo had actually lived – and that his life had followed essentially the pattern I had created for him.

At the time, the discovery came as a shock. It was only later that I realised I had already read the same source-books I was using to research Egyptian history. That had been some years previously and I had forgotten much of the content – certainly I had no conscious memory of Nectanebo whatsoever – but the relevant information had obviously been filed away in my unconscious.[100]

There was an even more dramatic instance of this process in what appeared to be an evidential case-study in reincarnation. The late Arnall Bloxham, a Welsh hypnotherapist with substantial experience in regression techniques,[101] was approached in 1969 by a client called Jane Evans[102] who was suffering from rheumatism and whom he quickly persuaded to take part in a reincarnation research experiment.

On the face of it, the experiment was strikingly successful. A deep trance subject, Jane Evans regressed to six 'previous lives' including one as Livonia, the wife of a tutor to the children of a Roman legate named Constantius around the turn of the third and fourth centuries AD. She had lived, she recalled, in Eboracum, the Roman name for York.

This far memory was particularly rich in detail. The entranced Jane Evans named the wife of the legate as Helena, his son as Constantine, her own husband as Titus, the legate's deputies as Caius Flaverius and Curio; and so on. She was consistent in referring to

British cities by their Roman names – Bath became Aquae Sulis, for example. The impressive nature of the experiment can be gauged by the following brief extract from many hours of tape recordings.

> LIVONIA: A messenger has come from Rome for Constantius. He has called Titus and me and the *domina*[103] already knows the news that a man called Allectus has come with a message for Constantius. He has been summoned back to Rome. Rome now has two emperors – two emperors.
>
> BLOXHAM: Who are they?
>
> LIVONIA: The Emperor Diocletian and the Emperor Maximianus. There are now two emperors of Rome.
>
> BLOXHAM: How will this effect you?
>
> LIVONIA: Not at all, except that the legate has to go to Rome to Maximianus who is now in charge of Britain, who now governs Britain. The empire has been split in two – Diocletian has one half and Maximianus the half which includes Britain.

The material certainly impressed Jeffrey Iverson, a BBC television producer who made a documentary and subsequently wrote a book on the subject.[104] Iverson's historical research led him to conclude that Livonia was talking about Aurelius Valerius Constantius, who rose from the ranks of the legions to become Caesar. Iverson consulted the Roman expert Brian Hartley, who admitted cautiously that the material was on the whole 'fairly convincing' and checked, so far as it was possible to do so, against known historical facts.

Despite all of this, however, the experiment subsequently proved to be indicative not of past life recall, but of the phenomenon of cryptomnesia, or 'hidden memory', exactly like my own experience of Nectanebo. The researcher Melvin Harris subsequently discovered a novel by Louis de Wohl entitled *The Living Wood* which told essentially the same

Roman story as Jane Evans, naming the same names and showing the same quirks (like the unusual abbreviation of Verulamium to 'Verulam'). The novel was published in 1947.[105]

No one makes the slightest suggestion that Bloxham or his subject, Jane Evans, were anything other than scrupulously honest about their experiment. It is accepted that Jane Evans had no conscious recollection of having read de Wohl's book, yet the conclusion seems inescapable that its content lay buried somewhere in her unconscious mind.

The second method by which the human mind may gain access to information while circumventing normal channels is embodied in the hypothesis formulated by a scientific group led by Professor William MacBain at the University of Hawaii:

> If one individual has access to information not available to another, then under certain circumstances and with known sensory channels rigidly controlled, the second individual can demonstrate knowledge of this information at a higher level than that compatible with the alternative explanation of chance guessing.[106]

This is the sort of statement that gives science – or perhaps just scientists – a bad name among those who like to understand what they read. What is actually being described is telepathy, the ability of one mind to tap directly into another and extract information from it. Professor MacBain's team established their hypothesis through tests on twenty-two psychology students divided into eleven pairs.

In the experimental series, twenty-three concepts were chosen as the target communications, selected both for the wide range of emotional responses they were likely to invoke and for the fact that they could be represented by simple line drawings.

'Senders' and 'receivers' of each team sat before identical rows of display panels. A symbol would illuminate on the sender's panel for a period of twenty-five seconds, during which the sender would concentrate. Then the light would go out, the sender would relax for five seconds, and the receiver would press a button indicating which symbol he thought was being sent.

Although senders and receivers were in separate rooms more than thirty feet apart, the experiments showed results 'significantly different from random distribution', indicating that a factor other than chance was involved in their production. Interestingly, analysis of the students' personality profiles indicated certain psychological factors associated with success as a sender or a receiver.

The MacBain experiments are, of course, only a small part of the mass of statistical evidence on telepathy dating back more than a century to the early 1880s when two academics, Malcolm Guthrie and James Birchall, carried out a series of 246 experiments in the telepathic transmission of drawings to specially gifted subjects.

The third category by which the human mind may obtain information via extra-sensory channels is the most peculiar of all – a sort of direct perception that has so far defied rational analysis. There have been a number of mathematical prodigies who exhibited the talent to a marked degree. George Parker Bidder, born in 1802, the son of an Exeter stonemason, was a case in point. A few days prior to his death in 1878 he was asked to calculate the number of lightwaves needed in one second to produce the visual effect of red on the human retina. His answer, 444,433,651,200,000, was computed mentally.

There have been individuals with a mathematical talent that is explicable by the normal processes of calculation. The Derbyshire man Jedidiah Buxton, for example, was able mentally to calculate the 39-figure result of doubling a farthing 139 times, then correctly squared the total in his head. Impressive though this was, he calculated as anyone else might have done, the sole difference being that an exceptional memory allowed him to hold the totals and sub-totals in his mind. But Bidder was different. He did not calculate at all, but rather arrived at the (correct) answer by a process of intuition, often instantaneously.

Individuals of this type are rare, but not all that rare. Quite a number have been examined over the past two hundred years and their powers well attested, without, however, the implications being fully grasped. For the implications are surely that some human minds are capable of achieving a direct perception of data without any intervening steps. The data, in Bidder's case, was mathematical, but once the principle is established, it seems reasonable to suggest other data types might be perceived as well.

In fact, the reality of this perception does not rest on inference. In the early 1930s, the father of modern parapsychology, Dr J. B. Rhine, set up a series of telepathy tests using card guessing techniques, the results of which were then compared with chance expectation. It quickly transpired that some sort of mind-to-mind transference of data was actually occurring since several receivers scored significantly higher than chance. But then Rhine tested subjects without the aid of a sender. In these instances, the 'receiver' was asked to guess the order of cards in a shuffled pack. Once again, several subjects scored well above chance expectation, ably demonstrating the capacity of the mind to extract information directly from its environment. Later on, both Rhine and other scientists using Rhine's methodology tested for the reality of precognition – essentially the ability to see into the future – and found that too had a statistically valid basis.

All this, of course, clearly points to the fact that the human mind retains a mass of information of which it is not consciously aware; and appears to have some very mysterious means of absorbing even more. If this sort of information is available to the mind, it is perfectly logical to suppose it may also be available to a creation of the mind. Thus the fact that 'spirits' have often been reputed to furnish information (consciously) unknown to the magician who evoked them does not, after all, destroy the thesis that the spirits might themselves be fictional creations.

But if we accept the possibility that such fictional creations may sometimes behave like a spirit (Philip), may sometimes be seen by others (Madame David-Neel's tulpa), may sometimes act as conduits for information not known consciously by their creators, is it not stretching credulity to its limits to suggest they may be capable of acting directly on the physical world, as spirts have long been reputed to do?

Stretching credulity it may be, yet it is in precisely this area that the evidence for our thesis is at its strongest.

14

SPIRIT ACTION

In November 1967, the lighting system in the Rosenheim office of a German lawyer, Sigmund Adam, began to go wrong. Strip lights kept failing so consistently that he ordered a special meter installed. The device showed sudden – inexplicable – surges of current.

Rosenheim is a small town south-west of Munich. The local electrical company, the Stadtwerke, were called in to investigate and came to the conclusion that there was something wrong with the power lines. They tried installing a direct cable, but still the lights malfunctioned.

An exasperated Sigmund Adam had his own generator put in and changed every strip light for an ordinary bulb. It made no difference at all. He was still wondering what to do when his phone bill arrived, showing a massive increase over his usual level of calls. With a growing feeling of paranoia, Adam insisted on an investigation by the phone company. Technicians installed a monitor which showed someone was dialling the speaking clock for hours on end, four, five and even six times a minute. This, however, a physical impossibility: tests showed it took a minimum of seven seconds to make the connection.

A local reporter heard about the story and turned up

to investigate. When a light bulb fell out of its socket as he was leaving, he decided a spirit was involved and wrote up a report on the Rosenheim spook. The story was taken over by the national press and attracted the attention of one of Europe's leading parapsychologists, Professor Hans Bender of the Institute of Paranormal Research at Freiburg.

Bender mounted a full-scale investigation and it soon became very apparent that the Königstrasse office was the focus of a full-scale haunting. Lights would swing for no apparent reason, pictures turned on the wall and a heavy filing cabinet was moved by unseen hands. But the spirit was not a spirit. All the phenomena – and more – were associated with a teenage girl, Anne-Marie Schaberl, who had joined the company two years previously. When she walked along the corridor, the overhead lights would begin to swing back and forth and the mysterious surges of current occurred only when she was in the building.

With equipment still going wrong all around her, Adam fired the girl. She took a job in another office where similar phenomena broke out. When she went ten-pin bowling with her fiancé, the electronic equipment ceased to function properly. She took a mill job, but left when a machinery malfunction led to the death of a co-worker.

This was not a case of a haunted human in any traditional sense of the phrase. When first tested by Bender, the girl showed no indication of paranormal abilities, but once her emotions were aroused – by questioning her about a painful illness – she showed extraordinary ESP abilities, including a high degree of telepathic awareness. There seems no doubt at all that Schaberl, a tense, unhappy, suspicious and aggressive individual, created the 'spirit' at an unconscious level and flung it outwards to do its mischief.

In this she was by no means unique. Colin Wilson[107] estimates there are probably more than a thousand recorded cases of poltergeist hauntings. Many, if not most, of these involve a 'carrier' like Schaberl. In a few, the effects seem to be consciously produced. A classic example was the notorious 'Phantom Drummer of Tidworth'.

The first published account of the Phantom Drummer was written by the Reverend Joseph Glanvil in 1666. He described how he went to a house in Wiltshire[108] and there found 'two modest little girls in bed between seven and eleven years old'. There was a mysterious scratching sound coming from behind the bolster. Glanvil was certain the noise could not have been made by the girls – their hands were in view. He searched the room without discovering any cause, but later did find a linen bag with something moving about inside it, like a rat or a mouse. He drew the bag inside out. It was empty.

This was not the beginning of the case. It all started on a March day in 1661 when a magistrate named John Mompesson visited the village of Ludgershall in east Wiltshire. While trying the day's cases, Mompesson's deliberations were disturbed by the sound of drumming outside. He asked the local constable to investigate.

The constable was soon able to tell him that the cause of the noise was a tinker named William Drury, who had arrived in the village a few days earlier. He added that Drury had requested public assistance on the strength of various papers signed by eminent magistrates. So far the request had been refused. It was suspected the papers were forgeries.

Irritated by the drumming, Mompesson ordered that

this tinker should be brought before him. He examined the papers and pronounced them forged, then committed Drury to jail until the next sitting of the assizes and confiscated his drum. The loss of the drum upset Drury more than the prospect of jail and he pleaded for its return, but the magistrate refused. The case was closed and Mompesson went on his way. Drury went to jail.

But not for long. Within a day or two, the tinker escaped, without, however, managing to get his drum back. For want of anything better to do with it, the court bailiff sent it off to the magistrate Mompesson. It arrived at Mompesson's home in Tidworth while he was away in London. Mompesson came home to a haunting. Terrified servants told him there had been knocks and raps in the house for three nights running. The magistrate suspected villainy and went to bed with a loaded pistol.

What happened next was pure farce. The sounds started up and Mompesson leaped out of bed brandishing his pistol. He rushed into the room where the noises came from, only to find they had moved to another room. The magistrate followed. The noises moved again. He followed and they moved again. Soon he was chasing them all over the house. Eventually they moved outside. Mompesson gave up and went back to bed. As he lay there, the noises continued. Among them he could clearly hear the sound of drumming. The noises returned the next night and the next. Often they went on for hours on end. But still nobody could find where they were coming from.

Suddenly they stopped. For three weeks there was peace, then they started up again, worse than ever. They took to following the Mompesson children around. Small articles began to move of their own accord. Invisible hands tugged a breadboard away from a manservant. When a minister arrived to pray, the noises grew louder than ever, accompanied by the small of burning sulphur.

This was a poltergeist haunting with a vengeance. The Mompesson house was filled with knocks, raps, bangs, slamming doors and mysterious lights. One morning the magistrate's horse was found on its back with a hind hoof jammed in its mouth. A visitor had his sword snatched away. Another found the coins in his pocket had turned black. The local blacksmith was attacked with pincers. The spirit developed a voice. Witnesses claimed it shouted 'A witch! A witch!' at least a hundred times. The contents of ash-cans and chamber-pots were emptied into the children's beds.

Two years after the trouble started, the tinker William Drury stole a pig at Gloucester and was jailed for his pains. When a friend came to visit him, Drury asked for news of Tidworth. They began to discuss the haunting (which was common knowledge by this time) and Drury smugly claimed he had been the cause of the trouble. He had, he said, plagued Mompesson and would continue to do so until the magistrate made amends for taking away his drum.

It was a stupid claim to make, for the friend inevitably talked. Drury was charged with witchcraft and deported. As soon as he left the country, the haunting stopped.

There is, of course, no way of determining whether Drury was engaged in idle boasting to make himself appear important, but his claim is interesting nonetheless; and all the more so in the light of an extraordinary case in which I was personally involved.

In 1972, following the break-up of my marriage, I lived with a journalist named Julie Johnson,[109] who was, at the time, suffering from a disfiguring skin complaint. Julie was understandably embarrassed by the condition and sought the help of a number of specialists without, however, finding anyone who could alleviate the problem. In desperation, she took to discussing her predicament with anyone who would listen. One of those she spoke to was Thomas Brooke-Jones.

Brooke-Jones was a student of poltergeist phenomena and a practising occultist – he referred to himself as a 'witch', although he was not a member of the modern Craft movement and seemed to use the term in its old sense of someone interested in practical magic. He listened sympathetically to Julie's dilemma and promised to see what he could do to help.

Within a week, Julie's skin condition started to improve; but then one afternoon I arrived home to find her in a state bordering on hysteria. There was, she claimed, an invisible presence in the house. She had gone upstairs to take a bath, and as she climbed into the tub had felt something furry brush against her, like a small animal. She told herself she was imagining things, but while she was in the bath, the creature – whatever it was – had burned her on the arm and bitten her on the thigh. When she left the bathroom, it had pushed her so that she fell downstairs, fortunately without injuring herself beyond some bruising.

She showed me the bitemark and the burn. The former was a smallish wound on the inner thigh like the bite of a cat or similarly sized animal. The latter was circular, as if someone had stubbed out a lighted cigarette on her arm.

Although the injuries could certainly have been self-inflicted and no one actually witnessed her fall downstairs,[110] I could see no reason (then or now) why

Julie should have decided to fabricate such a preposterous story. I also suspected I knew what had happened. Later that same afternoon I went calling on Brooke-Jones and, without mentioning Julie's experience, asked him what methods he had used in his attempt to cure her skin complaint.

It was a favourite theory of Brooke-Jones that the 'elemental servants' of magic and historical witchcraft were, in fact, controlled poltergeists, called up from the unconscious of the practitioner or, alternatively, called up by the practitioner from the unconscious mind of the person who was the focus of the particular 'spell'. On this occasion, he had decided to test his theory by attempting to call up a poltergeist to cure the skin complaint. He had done so the previous Saturday through an act of concentration and imagination, then forgotten the whole thing.

I told him he seemed to have succeeded all too well and suggested he might like to recall his troublesome creation. He promised, with embarrassed apologies, to do so. Julie Johnson suffered no further phenomena, but the improvement in her skin condition reversed itself and it was some months before she achieved a cure with the help of a more orthodox medical practitioner.

The conscious 'sending' of a poltergeist in this way is accepted as commonplace in South America. Colin Wilson quotes Hernani Andrade, founder of the Brazilian Institute for Psycho-Biophysical Research, as saying:

Any Brazilian is well aware that this country is full of backyard terreiros of quimbanda [black magic centres] where people use spirit forces for evil purposes ... To produce a succesful poltergeist, all you need is a group of bad spirits to do your work for you, for a suitable reward,

and a susceptible victim who is insufficiently developed
spiritually to be able to resist.[111]

It is evident from this that Andrade accepts
poltergeists as spirits in the traditional sense of the
word, but closer to home there is substantial evidence
that these noisy and destructive 'ghosts' can be
manufactured just as easily as the more subdued Philip
in Toronto. The first indication that this might be
possible came in an article in the *Journal of the Society
for Psychical Research* dated September 1966. It was
drily titled 'Report on a Case of Table Levitation and
Associated Phenomena' and was written by the
psychologist Kenneth J. Batcheldor.

Batcheldor was interested in the generation of
psychokinetic (PK) phenomena and had approached it
via the largely neglected Victorian Spiritualist practice
of table-turning. Within a group context, Batcheldor
quickly discovered that by starting out with little or
no rigid controls and permitting 'artifacts' – impressive,
but essentially non-psychic phenomena brought about
by involuntary muscle movements etc. – he could
create an atmosphere conducive to genuine PK
manifestations.[112] How spectacular these manifestations became is indicated by the following extract:

> When the power had built up, various experiments were
> tried . . . Sometimes we took our hands off and watched
> the table moving without contact . . . In most sittings,
> attempts were made to communicate with any directing
> intelligence, occasionally with considerable response, but
> more often than not with no response . . . Other spon-
> taneous phenomena which could occur in a sitting were:
> breezes, intense cold, lights, touchings, pulling back of
> sitters' chairs, movement of objects (rattle, trumpet),
> 'gluing' of the table to the floor so that it could not be
> budged and 'apports'.[113]

The similarity between the phenomena described and 'spirit' – especially poltergeist – manifestations is too obvious to require further comment. Even more violent 'poltergeist' activity arose in a student group at the University of Aston in Birmingham, so that the sitters were forced to abandon their experiments altogether.

Despite the similarities, Batcheldor was never happy with the hypothesis that spirits were involved, although for some time he did consider the possibility that one of his sitters was a natural medium. Later he concluded that the important factor did not rest with any individual, but with the group as a whole and was, in fact, a question primarily of mindset.

> Relevant to this theme is the fact that when sitters trained themselves to inhibit discursive thinking, the levitated table or tube remained suspended in the air for a much longer period, whereas any intrusive thought caused it to come crashing down.[114]

From all this, it is quite clear that anything credited to spirits can be duplicated quite effectively by creations of the human mind. Does this mean that we should consider all evoked spirits as tulpas called from the depths of the Jungian unconscious by techniques imperfectly understood? Several modern investigators, among them Colin Wilson and Guy Playfair, consider that there is still a place in our philosophy for traditional ideas about spirits. Even Jung himself, despite a public stance which insisted paranormal phenomena could be explained in terms of psychology, had serious private reservations:

> I once discussed the proof of identity for a long time with a friend of William James, Professor [James] Hyslop, in New York. He admitted that, all things considered, all

these metaphysic phenomena could be explained better by the hypothesis of spirits than by the qualities and peculiarities of the unconscious. And here, on the basis of my own experience, I am bound to concede he is right. In each individual case I must necessarily be sceptical, but in the long run I have to admit that the spirit hypothesis yields better results in practice than any other.[115]

If Jung was correct – and there are few individuals in the twentieth century who knew more about the human mind than he did – then our investigation of magic is already leading us into complex and difficult speculations, with both natural and artificial spirits clamouring for attention in the magician's triangle. But before diving any deeper into that particular controversy, it is as well to remember that the practice of magic is not confined to spirit evocation.

15

OCCULT ANATOMY

Sometime between the first century BC, and the second century AD, there developed a body of mystical, philosophical and religious literature, the precepts of which were to have a profound influence on occult thought. Collectively referred to as the *Corpus Hermeticum* or, more simply, the *Hermetica*, the literature was studied by virtually every major magical practitioner of antiquity, including Paracelsus, Agrippa and Fludd. A fundamental maxim of the *Hermetica* was:

> Upon that which is below is imprinted the objective reflection of that which is above and the Perfect Archetypal Lord, although subjective and dwelling above, is also, paradoxically, indwelling in all that is below . . .[116]

This maxim, more concisely stated 'As Above, So Below', suggests that the microcosm – the body, mind and spirit of the individual human being – is a model in miniature of the macrocosm, or cosmos as a whole. Such thinking pervades traditional astrology[117] and underpins the notion that planetary positions can somehow influence human lives. It is also found in Qabalah, with its doctrine of the *Adam Kadmon*, or 'Heavenly Man', a picture of the universe as the body of a great being, constructed on similar lines to the smaller beings inhabiting planet Earth. The Qabalistic

Tree of Life, central glyph of the entire Qabalistic system, is presented as a map of both the cosmos and the human soul.

The third-century theologian Origen voiced the same idea in his statement, 'Know that you are another world in miniature and that in you there is a sun, a moon and stars too.' Modern esoteric thought does not take the theory quite so literally, but it remains a fundamental just the same, as does its corollary that a sort of 'resonance' exists between macrocosm and microcosm, allowing one to influence the other. Such influence is not all astrological – the universe acting on the individual. Magicians believe the effect can travel the other way, outwards from the individual to the cosmos . . . or at least that portion of the cosmos which concerns the magician.

Consequently, almost all magical training begins with exercises designed to stimulate certain inner aspects of the individual. This, it is believed, will enable him or her to manipulate not only personal wellbeing, but also the course of events in the external world. Israel Regardie began one of his shortest, most influential works with the words:

> Within every man and woman is a force which directs and controls the entire course of life. Properly used, it can heal every affliction and ailment to which mankind is heir. Every single religion affirms this fact. All forms of mental or spiritual healing, no matter under what name they travel, promise the same thing.[118]

But it is not only healing for which the mysterious 'force' is used, as Regardie makes clear towards the end of his book:

> The preliminary stimulation of the psycho-spiritual centres within, and then formulating clearly and vividly

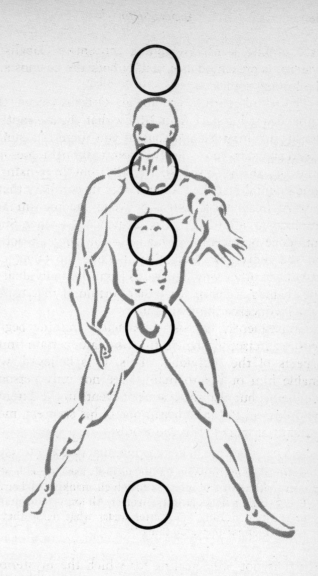

Astro-mental centres.

one's demands upon the universe is capable of attracting almost anything required, so long, naturally, as it exists within the bounds of reason and possibility.[119]

Like so much else in magical practice, this is difficult to accept at face value, but may reward closer investigation. Once again, it seems useful to begin with an examination of what it is magicians actually do in training.

Magical training is based on the theory that the universe is filled with a vast sea of energy, vital to all life. It is further believed that immediately surrounding the human body is an individual energy field – called the aura – in the shape of a gigantic egg. This field contains a series of control centres for the forces that circulate within the aura. Certain of the centres act as contact points and 'transformers' for the universal energy through which we move. A schematic representation of the more important centres is shown on page 149.

The 'universal energy' of the Western Esoteric Tradition seems identical to the prana of Hindu yoga or the 'Heavenly Ch'i' of traditional acupuncture which the Chinese believe is manufactured in the sun. No modern scientist would argue against the proposition that our solar system – and indeed the entire cosmos – is a sea of radiation. It is also agreed that certain wavelengths – broadly those perceived as light and heat – are necessary for the continuation of life; and it is known that specific aspects of the spectrum influence our wellbeing, as when ultra-violet light reacts on the human skin to trigger the production of vitamin D.

The concept of an aura is a little more controversial. The idea of an energy field surrounding the human body[120] is very old indeed. Representations of religious figures – the Buddha, the gods of Hinduism, Christ or the Christian saints – frequently show a luminous nimbus, particularly around the head where, in Christian iconography especially, it is sometimes stylized as a ring halo. Such figures are believed to be so highly evolved that they develop an exceptionally pure and powerful aura.

Despite the artistic convention, auras are normally only visible to rare individuals with specific psychical talents. The medium Eileen Garrett, for example, claimed[121] she saw every plant, animal and person 'encircled by a misty surround'. In 1911, however, a London doctor named Walter R. Kilner developed a series of screens based on a dicyanin dye which he claimed could be used to train the eye to see auras.

Kilner distinguished several layers in the aura and, like the industrial chemist Baron Karl von Reichenbach half a century before him, insisted his screens showed auras emanating from magnets.

A particularly interesting aspect of his work was his conviction that changes in the appearance of the aura could be used as a diagnostic tool – a belief shared by many psychics. Fatigue, diseases or even mood swings could alter the perceived size and colour, as could hypnosis and the application of electricity.

Despite his empirical approach, Kilner's findings remained a little too subjective for the scientific community. (Subjects using his screens might, for example, be reacting to suggestion and only imagining they could see the human atmosphere.) But a more technical approach to the aura was on the horizon.

When the electrical engineer Semyon Kirlian, visited Russia's Krasnodar Hospital in 1939 to collect some technical equipment for repair, he chanced to see a patient receiving treatment from a new high-frequency generator. As the electrodes were brought close to the patient's skin, there was a small flash of light. Kirlian recognized this as the type of flash that occurs as a gas is being charged by an electric spark and wondered what was being charged here, since no gas was present.

The problem intrigued him sufficiently to prompt an experiment. He and his wife Valentina set up two metal plates to act as electrodes and placed a photographic film on one of them. Then he put his hand between the plates and switched on a high frequency current. He received a severe burn,[122] but when the film was developed, it showed Kirlian's hand surrounded by a luminescent halo.

It was the start of something very interesting indeed. The Kirlians refined their techniques and eventually created the technology to develop a whole new branch of photography.

> Basically, photography with high frequency electrical fields involves a specially constructed high frequency spark generator or oscillator that generates 75,000 to 200,000 electrical oscillations per second. The generator can be connected to various clamps, plates, optical instruments, microscopes or electron microscopes. The object to be investigated (finger, leaf etc.) is inserted between the clamps along with photo paper. The generator is switched on and a high frequency field is created between the clamps which apparently causes the object to radiate some sort of bioluminescence onto the photo paper. A camera isn't necessary for the photography process.[123]

The Kirlians used the new technology to make a great many pictures. Those which involved living tissue – even plant tissue like a leaf – showed sparks and flares of energy in patterns as dramatic as they were beautiful. A dead leaf showed nothing of these patterns. When a portion of a leaf was torn or cut away, a ghostly image of the missing piece clearly showed.

Research projects using Kirlian photographs of human volunteers confirmed some of Kilner's findings by showing that the aura effect varied in relation to a subject's mood and was influenced by personality interactions: the Kirlian auras of young men brightened when a pretty woman entered the room. One of the most dramatic results of the experiments was the discovery that subjects lit up like a Christmas tree moments after drinking a shot of vodka.

In the Neuropsychiatric Institute at the University of California at Los Angeles, the scientific team of Thelma Moss and Ken Johnson constructed Kirlian apparatus which showed energy flares emitted by the fingertips of faith healers as they exercised their art. There was also a discovered linkage with Chinese acupuncture in that many traditional acupuncture points show as small flares in a Kirlian photograph.

Since many occultists have seized on Kirlian photography as proof positive of psychics' claims to see the aura, it may be as well to point out that what the Kirlian equipment photographs is not a field generated by the human body, but rather interference patterns on a field generated by the equipment itself. Thus Kirlian photography shows the aura only by inference, and not directly.

If orthodox science has gone some way towards establishing the reality of human 'atmosphere', the same cannot (yet) be said for the esoteric postulate of specific centres within it. These do not appear on Kirlian plates and are amenable only to psychical investigation ... and rather specialized psychical investigation at that.

Many occultists refer loosely to the centres of the

Western Esoteric Tradition as the chakras, a Sanskrit term translated as lotuses or wheels and derived from Oriental yoga systems. But while some of the Western centres coincide with the Oriental chakras, others do not. Even the limited number of centres shown on page 149 is enough to highlight the differences. While the throat and genital centres conform with Eastern chakra doctrine, the uppermost centre is a little too high to coincide exactly with the crown chakra of the East; two major chakras on the trunk of the body have been absorbed into a single centre, which coincides with neither; and the lowest centre, between the feet, has no counterpart in the Oriental system at all.

When Western scientists first investigated Eastern notions of the chakras, they noted the coincidence between chakras placement and certain nerve plexi and glandular centres in the physical body. This led to the theory that the chakras were really no more than the plexi and glands themselves. Yoga practitioners have vigorously denied this, insisting that, while certainly linked, the chakras are an energy system which, so to speak, 'stands behind' the endocrine and nervous systems of the physical body. Careful study of the astro-mental centres of Western magic suggests they represent a system one further step removed, which stands behind the chakras, as the chakras stand behind the glands.

Except that while we must make do with the chakras we are born with, just as we must make do with a routine set of glands, magical training actually allows the establishment of new astro-mental centres which did not, presumably, form part of the individual's birthright. This is most clearly seen in Qabalistic training. Central to Qabalistic thought is the glyph of the Tree of Life shown opposite.

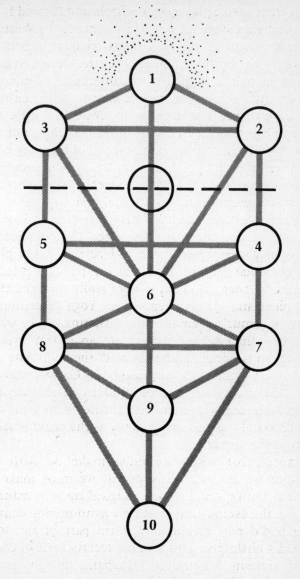

Tree of Life.

One of the earliest tasks set for the trainee Qabalist is 'the establishment of the Tree within the aura'[124] *see opposite*. The wording is significant, for if the centres shown on the Tree were already there, they would not require to be established, merely stimulated or strengthened. My own experience suggests that while some centres[125] may be pre-existent, the remainder most certainly are not. I have yet to find a psychic who claims to have detected any outer (as opposed to central) sphere in the auras of those who have not undergone Qabalistic training.

The method by which the Tree is placed in the aura is visualization. Trainees are required, on a daily basis, to visualize the Sephiroth (spheres) of the Tree as glowing energy centres within their own auras. They are also taught techniques believed to control the flow of energy between the spheres, particularly those of the 'Middle Pillar' which coincides with the spinal column and centre of the body. These techniques too are almost exclusively based on visualization.[126]

The question naturally arises, do they work? On a purely personal level, the answer seems to be yes, although not everyone is likely to accept the evidence for such a conclusion.

Simply visualizing the astro-mental centres – particularly those on the central axis – is supposed to increase physical energy levels and one's resistance to disease. These are difficult claims to substantiate . . . or, indeed, to refute. Energy levels are so intimately related to mindset that one can never be certain whether the boost (which certainly seems to follow esoteric training in most cases) is an automatic process occasioned by the centres or simply a useful example of self-suggestion. Resistance to disease is relative.

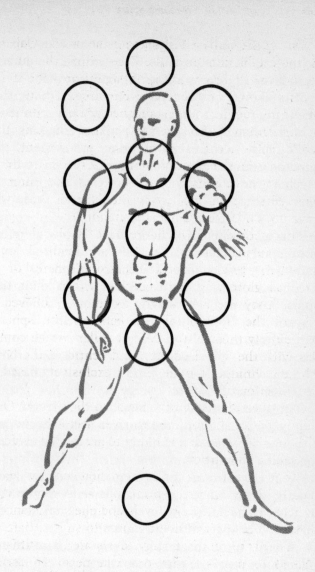

Tree of Life within the aura.

Even if one falls ill despite establishment of the centres, it is still possible to argue one would have been more ill, or more often ill, without them.

If, however, one accepts clairvoyant investigation, the intriguing fact remains that many psychics report a brightening of the aura and chakra centres in those who engage in the exercises. Some psychics will even report seeing the astro-mental centres themselves.

I have, however, my own reasons for accepting that the visualization techniques are effective. While it is true to say that for most trainees, the immediate results of manipulating the centres are low key, there are certain personality (or possibly physical body) types in which they can be very spectacular indeed.

On one occasion, for example, I was called upon to assist a woman who, while engaged in an esoteric experiment, had become prey to irresistible trembling which mounted into violent shaking and eventually convulsions. For reasons which need not concern us here, it seemed likely that she was suffering from a gross imbalance of energy within her chakras, possibly associated with a 'blockage' in one or more of the channels. I attempted to treat this directly using acupuncture-related techniques, but succeeded only in obtaining partial symptom relief. By working to balance the astro-mental centres, however, total relief was obtained. Since the woman herself was not aware of what I was doing on the second occasion, the usual objection of suggestion does not arise.

A rather more spectacular example of how effective manipulation of the astro-mental centres can be arose out of a hypnotic trance experiment in which the subject's centres were first 'awakened', then the energy circulated through them. The technique will normally do little more than increase energy and bring a sense of wellbeing. Occasionally a slight 'buzz' is felt. In this case, however, the woman experienced pressure and pain in the head which built to a point where she was convinced she had begun to bleed from the ears. In fact she had not, but she was certainly in considerable pain. The symptoms continued to build for close on fifteen minutes until they became so acute that I was forced to apply an emergency acupuncture technique at the crown of the head. This resulted in the subjective sensation of, in the woman's own words, 'blood spurting in a fountain out of the top of my head'. Here again, no actual bleeding was involved, but relief of both pain and pressure was almost immediate.

The fountain sensation lasted several minutes, then died down and eventually stopped altogether. Following the totality of this rather frightening experience, the woman involved discovered she had developed 'second sight' and was able, for the first time, to 'see' auras, sense her surroundings while blindfold, and 'see' energy fields such as those associated with electrical wires and magnets.

CHAPTER

16

MAGICAL INFLUENCE

It is accepted that there is a linkage between mind and body. Worry can cause ulcers, hypnotic suggestion is enough to create blisters on the skin, and there is at least some evidence to suggest a positive attitude combined with visualization can slow, possibly even reverse, the spread of cancer.[127] In view of this, it is perhaps not surprising that manipulation of the astro-mental centres should produce personal results. But magicians go further. They claim that such manipulation can actually influence external reality, attracting wealth, generating good luck or blighting crops, for example.

The way this is supposed to come about is interesting, for it involves the use of mental associations – chains of linked ideas reaching out towards the thing or situation desired. These associations are not absolutes, but are built into the mind of the operator via protracted meditation and practice. Although various schools have standardized their own systems and these have, over the years, become hallowed by tradition, it would appear that the associations may be quite arbitrary and still work. The important thing is that they are consistent and firmly established in the mind of the individual magician.

Those trained in Qabalah tend to use chains

of associations so extensive that Aleister Crowley literally filled a book with them.[128] They can, however, be considerably simplified without, apparently, losing their effect. Israel Regardie, for example, created a workable mini-system based on seven planetary associations. The planet Mercury was associated with:

> Business matters, writing, contracts, judgment and short travels. Buying, selling, bargaining. Neighbours, giving and obtaining information. Literary capabilities and intellectual friends. Books, papers. Positive colour, yellow; negative colour orange.[129]

Also built into the chain was the Hebrew Godname *Elohim Tzavoös*.

Regardie explained the use of the system as follows:

> Suppose I am engaged in certain studies requiring books that are not easily obtainable from booksellers ... The result is that for the time my studies are held up. This delay reaches the point when it is excessive and irritating and I decide to use my own technical methods for ending it. At certain prescribed intervals, preferably upon awakening in the morning and before retiring to sleep at night, I practise the rhythmic breath and the Middle Pillar.[130] By these methods I have made available enormous quantities of spiritual power and transformed the Unconscious into a powerful storage battery, ready to project or attract power to fulfil my need. This I circulate through the auric system.
>
> My next step consists of visualizing the negative or passive colour of Mercury, orange, so that meditating upon it changes the surrounding auric colour to that hue. Orange is used because books, which I need, are attributed to Mercury; and I employ the negative colour because it tends to make the sphere of sensation open, passive and receptive. Then I proceed to charge and vitalize the sphere by vibrating the appropriate divine name again and again until it seems to my perceptions

that all the mercurial forces of the universe react to the magnetic attraction of that sphere. All the forces of the universe are imagined to converge upon my sphere, attracting to me just those books, documents, critics, friends and so on, needed to further my work. Inevitably, after persistent and concentrated work, I hear from friends or booksellers quite by chance, so it would seem, that these books are available. Introductions are procured to the right people and taken by and large my work is assisted. The results occur, however, in a perfectly natural way.[131]

Regardie had no patent on magical systems of this type. Crowley operated in essentially the same way. In the first volume of his *Magic in Theory and Practice*, he insisted that the magician

... may attract to himself any force of the Universe by making himself a fit receptacle for it, establishing a connection with it, and arranging conditions so that its nature compels it to flow toward him.[132]

In typical Crowleyan fashion, he illustrated the precept by informing the reader that if he wanted to drink water, he would dig a well and allow the laws of hydrostatics to fill it. But later in the book he leaves no doubt about the actual nature of 'connecting with the universe'.

It may be that our process resembles creation – or rather imagination – more nearly than it does calling-forth. The aura of a man is called the 'magical mirror of the universe'; and, so far as anyone can tell, nothing exists outside of this mirror. It is at least convenient to represent the whole as if it were subjective. It leads to less confusion. And, as a man is a perfect microcosm, it is perfectly easy to re-model one's conception at any moment.

Now there is a traditional correspondence, which

modern experiment has shown to be fairly reliable. There is a certain natural connexion between certain letters, words, numbers, gestures, shapes, perfumes and so on, so that any idea ... may be composed or called forth by the use of those things which are harmonious with it and express particular parts of its nature ... Let it be said yet again! not only is his [the magician's] aura a magical mirror of the universe, but the universe is a magical mirror of his aura.[133]

Crowley accepted the maxim 'As Above, So Below' and the use of the visual imagination to generate objective effects, as did Dion Fortune and the magicians of the Golden Dawn. Today's generation of magicians are trained to the same approach. There are variations in detail, but the fundamentals remain the same. In the instructions on sex magic given to members of America's Great Brotherhood of God, for example, the following passage appears:

Every endeavour of man takes time ... Three minutes would accomplish very little. It takes much more than that to build up the magickal visualization of the desired object and the inspiration necessary for its accomplishment ... A general rule is not under twenty minutes and usually it would take an hour or more for the best accomplishments.[134]

The contemporary magician Marian Green follows the Tradition in laying stress on visualization as an essential of successful magic. She writes:

Creative visualization ... is a method of directing what you see and of creating from fragments already in your memory, a new place or condition. It is the most important key to practical magical work and allows you to direct your will effectively, through the images you create ...

Magic has always relied upon symbols and upon the use

of items of equipment which may seem archaic or clumsy at the end of the twentieth century, but these are very powerful in the world of inner reality. In really elaborate rituals there are long lists of instruments, regalia, banners, altars, signs and symbols and to use all of them could mean a considerable outlay of cash. Many of these items can be seen in the mind's eye, or represented by some more ordinary objects, which, for the duration of the ceremony, appear to be the magical equivalent.[135]

Even outside of the Western Esoteric Tradition, the same 'magical' technology appears time and again under differing guises. Dr Joseph Murphy writes:

> You are like a captain navigating a ship. He must give the right orders and likewise you must give the right orders (thoughts and images) to your subconscious mind which governs all your experiences ... Change your thoughts and you change your destiny.[136]

In an introduction to this system of psychogenesis, Jack Ensign Addington has this to say:

> The world and all that it contains is made up of ideas made manifest. The manifest or physical universe is really only the afterglow, the lingering evidence of that which has already taken place in Mind. That which the world calls real had to have started with psychogenesis. It had to have a beginning in the invisible world of Mind.[137]

And his first step in the practical application of his system is defined as:

> Set up for yourself the ideal mental image.[138]

Dr Herbert Benson echoes the same thought in his advice on maximizing the power of your mind. After eliciting what he calls the 'relaxation response' he suggests:

You may well find that, given your particular interests,
you should go to other sources to find relevant thoughts
and words to focus upon. Or, you may simply want to
visualize the desired skill or the perfect game.[139]

So it goes for system after system with a consistent
central thesis that thoughts – and particularly visualizations – can influence external reality. Is there any
reason to suppose such an outlandish thesis might be
true? As a first step towards finding the answer, it may
be useful to ask an even more fundamental question:
can the mind, under any circumstances, directly
influence matter to however small a degree?

The key word here is directly. The Russian PK
(psychokenetic) medium, Nina Kulagina, showed herself capable of moving matchsticks, compass needles,
fountain pens and other small objects simply by
concentrating on them. She survived intensive tests in
both Soviet and American laboratories and on one
occasion caused a journalist's half-eaten sandwich to
crawl across the table during an interview. Madame
Kulagina's abilities looked very like mind over matter,
but Kirlian photography showed she had actually
learned the trick of pulsing and concentrating her
personal energy field to such a degree that it could act
on physical objects. She found the process exhausting,
often lost as much as two pounds in weight during a
single session, and on one occasion drove herself to the
point of collapse with heart trouble.

With the more gross forms of PK, there is always the
suspicion that some factor other than mind may have
become the causal factor, as was the case with Madame
Kulagina. But during the latter part of the 1960s, a
series of experiments carried out by the distinguished
British neurophysiologist, Dr W. Grey Walter, showed

conclusively that mind can influence matter; and do so directly.

Grey Walter announced the results of his experiments during his 1969 Eddington Memorial Lecture. His procedure was based on the fact that the human brain generates minute but measurable electrical signals. Electrodes were attached to his subjects' scalps over the area of the frontal cortex. These transmitted any brain electrical activity via an amplifier to a specially constructed machine. Set before the subject was a button which, when pressed, caused what Grey Walter described as an 'interesting scene' to appear on a TV screen.

When you or I decide to take a particular physical action, such as pressing a button, a 20-microvolt electrical surge occurs across a large area of our brain cortex. This is known technically as a readiness wave, and both its presence and effect have been familiar to neuro-specialists for several years. What Grey Walter did was amplify this readiness wave to such a degree that it could directly trigger the TV picture a fraction of a second before the button was actually pressed. He called the process 'auto-start'.

Subjects usually figured out what was happening fairly quickly and trained themselves to 'will' the pictures onto the screen without touching the button at all. The subjective mental state was all important. For the trick to work, the subject had to duplicate his/her mindset in pressing the button. If attention wandered or the mind locked itself in on focussing on the necessity of concentration, the brain wave potential failed to rise and no picture was delivered. But once the knack was developed, subjects could combine auto-start with auto-stop, will pictures onto the screen directly, then dismiss them with the relevant thought when finished.

The triggering of screen pictures was not, of course, an example of mind acting directly on matter since the switch was triggered by a perfectly ordinary electrical surge originating in the subject's brain. But once subjects learned they could produce the pictures without pressing the button and began to do so by an act of will, their minds were directly influencing matter – the physical matter of their own brains. A decision of the mind, applied in a particular way, was all it took to change the electrical potential of the frontal cortex. There was no physical aspect to the cause: as the subjects got into their stride, the button was neither pressed nor attempted to be pressed. The totality of cause lay in the mind.

Although a 20-microvolt surge is a small thing, its implications in this case are enormous. It is enough, for example, to settle once and for all the bitter controversy about the independent reality of the mind.

Broadly speaking, there have been two schools of thought about the human mind throughout most of the twentieth century. One suggests the mind is a thing in itself, intimately connected with the body and operating the brain as a driver might operate a car. The other, supported by the Behaviourists among others, claimed that 'mind' was no more than a convenient collective term for a host of subjective impressions generated by the electrical activity of the brain – that mind was, in effect, 'given off' by the brain as a kettle gives off steam.

Grey Walter's experiment now shows the Behaviourists to have been wrong. It is the mind that controls the brain and not the other way about.

Another implication, of substantially more importance to our present examination of magic, is the establishment of a principle. If the mind can directly influence the physical matter of the brain, as these experiments show it does, it then becomes reasonable to inquire whether the mind can have a direct influence on any form of matter other than the brain. To move outside the skull in this respect is an enormous step which would require substantial proof, but once the principle has been established, there is nothing intrinsically ridiculous in attempting to take it.

CHAPTER

17

SYNCHRONICITY

Although there is no theoretical limit to the reach of coincidence, very few people hear of Monsieur Deschamps and the plum-pudding without concluding something very odd is going on. The story was first told by the astronomer Camille Flammarion in his book *The Unknown* and extensively quoted by a variety of authors since the turn of the century.

Deschamps, as a boy in Orléans, was introduced to the delights of plum-pudding by a Monsieur de Fortgibu, who gave him the first piece of it he had ever tasted. The pudding is more widely known in Britain than it is in France and it was a decade later before Deschamps had an opportunity to sample it again. He spotted it on the menu of a restaurant he was visiting and, with fond memories of M. de Fortgibu, ordered a helping.

An apologetic waiter returned moments later with the news that there was only one piece of plum-pudding left and it had, unfortunately, already been ordered by another patron of the restaurant ... Monsieur de Fortgibu.

Many years later, while attending a dinner party, Deschamps was invited by his hosts to sample a gastronomic rarity, a piece of plum-pudding. Deschamps readily agreed and explained this would be only the

second time in his life he had eaten plum-pudding.
He told the story of his experience in the restaurant
and remarked as he was served the pudding that the
only thing lacking to make the occasion complete was
de Fortgibu.

As this point, the door burst open and an old, old
man entered, obviously hopelessly disoriented. It was
Monsieur de Fortgibu, who had mistaken the address
and burst in on the party by accident.

Paul Kammerer, the heretic scientist who spent
much of his career attempting to demonstrate the
Lamarckian theory that acquired characteristics may
be inherited, was fascinated by coincidence and spent
twenty years collecting examples of the phenomenon,
many of which matched the remarkable plum-pudding
story. But Kammerer collected every coincidence he
could, simple or complex.

In the former category was the story of his own wife
who, while reading a magazine in a doctor's waiting
room, was impressed by some reproductions of
pictures by a painter named Schwalbach. She made a
mental note of the name in the hope that she might
one day see the originals. At that point, the doctor's
receptionist opened the door and called, 'Is Frau
Schwalbach here? She is wanted on the telephone?'

One of the more complicated examples in
Kammerer's collection also concerned his wife. It
began with her reading about the character Mrs Rohan
in Hermann Bang's novel *Michael*, while travelling in
a tram. As she was reading, she saw a man who
reminded her irresistibly of her friend Prince Josef
Rohan. Frau Kammerer then overheard the man who
looked like Rohan being asked whether he knew the
village of Weissenbach on Lake Attersee. When she left
the tram she called into a delicatessen where the

assistant promptly asked her if she knew Weissenbach on Lake Attersee. That same evening, Prince Rohan called to see the Kammerers unexpectedly.[140]

This sort of thing, Kammerer found, extended into all aspects of life. In November 1910, for example, he discovered that his brother-in-law had gone to a concert where he had seat No. 9 and cloakroom ticket No. 9. The following evening, at another concert, he had seat No. 21 and was issued with cloakroom ticket No. 21.

Kammerer was so fascinated by coincidence that he spent hours in public parks, making careful note of the people who went by and classifying them by age, dress, sex and such things as whether they carried umbrellas or parcels. He did the same thing on long journeys by tram or train. After adjusting for common-sense factors like weather or rush-hour, he was forced to conclude:

> We have found that the recurrence of identical or similar data in contiguous areas of space or time is a simple empirical fact which has to be accepted and which cannot be explained by coincidence – or rather, which makes coincidence rule to such an extent that the concept of coincidence itself is negated.[141]

In other words, his studies showed so many and so consistent examples of 'coincidence' that he was no longer prepared to accept coincidence as an explanation. He finally decided that alongside the familiar sequence of cause-and-effect, there was an acausal principle active in the universe which tended towards unity. This 'force', he believed, had a selective action tending to bring similar configurations together in space and time. Einstein read Kammerer's book on the subject and found it 'original and by no means absurd'.

Another intellectual with an interest in collecting coincidences was Carl Jung. On 1 April 1949, he recorded:

Today is Friday. We have fish for lunch. Somebody happens to mention the custom of making an 'April fish'[142] of someone. The same morning I made a note of an inscription which read: 'Est homo totus medius piscis ab imo.' In the afternoon, a former patient of mine, whom I had not seen in months, showed me some extremely impressive pictures of fish which she had painted in the meantime. In the evening I was shown a piece of embroidery with fish-like sea monsters in it. On the morning of April 2, another patient, whom I had not seen for many years, told me a dream in which she stood on the shore of a lake and saw a large fish that swam straight towards her and landed at her feet. I was at this time engaged on a study of the fish symbol in history. Only one of the persons mentioned here knew anything about it.[143]

Jung wrote these lines while sitting beside a lake. Just as he had finished the sentence, he walked towards the lake and there lay a dead fish, which had not been there the previous evening.

The same sort of thing happened in the lives of his patients. In a frequently quoted incident . . .

A young woman I was treating had, at a critical moment, a dream in which she was given a golden scarab. While she was telling me this dream I sat with my back to a closed window. Suddenly I heard a noise behind me, like a gentle tapping. I turned round and saw a flying insect knocking against the window pane from outside. I opened the window and caught the creature in the air as it flew in. It was the nearest analogy to a golden scarab that one finds in our latitudes, a scarabaeid beetle, the common rose-chafer *(Cetonia aurata)* which, contrary to its usual habits had evidently felt an urge to get into a dark room at this particular moment.[144]

The experience proved to be a turning point in the treatment of the patient. In another, rather more sinister study, Jung reported:

> The wife of one of my patients, a man in his fifties, once told me in conversation that, at the deaths of her mother and her grandmother, a number of birds gathered outside the windows of the death-chamber. I had heard similar stories from other people. When her husband's treatment was nearing its end, his neurosis having been removed, he developed some apparently quite innocuous symptoms which seemed to me, however, to be those of heart-disease. I sent him along to a specialist, who after examining him told me in writing that he could find no cause for anxiety. On the way back from this consultation (with the medical report in his pocket) my patient collapsed in the street. As he was brought home dying, his wife was already in a great state of anxiety because, soon after her husband had gone to the doctor, a whole flock of birds alighted on their house. She naturally remembered the similar incidents that had happened at the death of her own relatives, and feared the worst.[145]

Cases like these led Jung to the same conclusion as Kammerer: that an acausal connecting principle was present in nature. He named it *synchronicity* and collaborated with the physicist Wolfgang Pauli in an essay to describe it. The result, in Arthur Koestler's words, was 'sadly disappointing'.[146] Jung seemed to have considerable trouble in coming to terms with what he wanted to say and much of the essay was vague and somewhat rambling.

Interestingly, Jung elected to illustrate the principle of synchronicity with reference to astrology. It would be difficult to find a competent modern astrophysicist willing to entertain the notion that the planets might have a causal influence on terrestrial events,[147] but the sheer persistence of astrological practice – it began in ancient Chaldea – has been enough to encourage statistical evaluation of its claims. To the forefront of this work has been Dr Michel Gauquelin, who as a traditionally trained astrologer had every motivation to substantiate its validity, yet reached a diametrically opposed conclusion:

> In France we have been involved for several years in a systematic verification of astrological propositions . . . Our first task was to evaluate the statistical methods employed by the astrologers themselves. Their techniques were found to be severely limited: the laws of chance are ignored and conclusions are reached without support . . . the statistical laws of chance in every case superseded the purported laws of astrology.
>
> Another step in our research was to calculate the horoscopes of more than fifty thousand people whose lives indicated some exceptional characteristic – a special aptitude, or gift, or stroke of luck – and also those whose lives were marred by exceptionally adverse conditions. For all these people we noted not only the day but also the hour of birth.
>
> In no case did we find a statistically significant difference favouring the traditional laws of astrology . . .
>
> Modern astrology, as a predictive method, relies on the survival of a hopelessly outdated view of the world and of life. It ignores the progress of astronomy and of human biology, as well as all the variables that affect behaviour through a lifetime. Every effort made by astrologers to defend their basic postulate . . . has failed.[148]

For all this, traditional astrology works, as anyone who has put it to the test must recognize. That is to say, a competent astrologer is capable of making reasonably consistent and accurate character analyses and predictions based on the 'hopelessly outdated view of the world and life'. Since Gauquelin's research shows this cannot be because traditional planetary positions really do influence human life, there is a continuing mystery about how astrologers get their results.[149]

Gauquelin's findings in any case came too late for Jung who made his own examination of 483 horoscopes for the classical Sun/Moon conjunction indicative of marriage. Sure enough, he found the conjunctions present in the horoscopes of marriage subjects to an unlikely degree. Three batches of horoscopes yielded results which had a chance expectation of 1:1,000; 1:10,000; and 1:50 respectively. Jung's base was too small for the findings to represent anything remotely resembling a proof of astrology – and besides which, his investigations were strictly limited to the 'marriage' conjunction – but he did feel they were a clear example of synchronicity.

> The statistical material shows that a practically as well as theoretically improbable chance combination occurred which coincides in the most remarkable way with traditional astrological expectations. That such a coincidence should occur at all is so improbable and so incredible that nobody could have dared to predict anything like it. It really does look as if the statistical material had been manipulated and arranged so as to give the appearance of a positive result. The necessary emotional and archetypal conditions for a synchronistic phenomenon were already given, since it is obvious that both my co-worker and myself had a lively interest in the outcome of the experiment.[150]

Both Jung and Kammerer concluded that an investigation of coincidence pointed towards an acausal connecting principle because they could find no indication of the more familiar causal link. But the cause of the phenomena may have been, if not exactly under their noses, at least under their hats.

A common denominator of the cases under investigation is *meaning* – Jung actually defines synchronicity as *meaningful* coincidence. But meaning is a function of the human mind: without an observer to observe, no sequence of events, however bizarre, could carry any meaning whatsoever. So we know that in Jung's synchronicity and Kammerer's seriality, the mind is involved. As scientists, Jung and Kammerer found it impossible to take the final step towards the idea that the mind might actually be the *cause*. Magicians have no such problem: their entire technology is based on the assumption that mind can influence events.

Once the step is taken – once, that is, we decide that the sorts of events studied may have been caused by something in the minds of their participants – we soon discover that the magical analysis of synchronicity fits the facts rather well.

Most magicians agree that the three essential elements of their art are concentration, visualization and emotion. Concentration directs the particular effort towards the desired result. Visualization creates the actual mechanism by which the result is achieved. Emotion fuels the boiler and provides the driving force. Although Crowley advised his followers to 'inflame themselves with prayer', the actual balance between these three aspects varies greatly depending on the operation to be undertaken and the results expected. For some magic, the emotion experienced by the magician is no more inflamed than a feeling of confidence. If the directive element of concentration is lacking or weak, it will not necessarily prevent the achievement of results, but they will tend to pop up unexpectedly, all over the place.

With all this in mind, it is well worth examining our synchronistic case-studies.

The young Deschamps was first fed plum-pudding

by the ubiquitous de Fortgibu when the former was a child. Food is important to children – many characters in the most popular comics seem to be obsessed by it – and unusual or exotic food has an emotional impact far stronger than it would have on an adult. The plumpudding, a rare treat in France, became clearly associated in the boy's mind with de Fortgibu.

There is no doubt that Deschamps was very taken by his treat. It had sufficient impact for him to notice it at once on the restaurant menu ten years later and to call for a piece without hesitation. As he did so, we are safe in assuming he thought – and possibly visualized – the associated de Fortgibu. The excitement and anticipation of the moment, the visualization, the concentration on certain linked ideas, combined to create a synchronistic situation. A trained magician, required to 'call' de Fortgibu, would have done it no differently.[151]

In the third leg of the coincidence, the magical elements appear even more clearly. Deschamps was consciously thinking of de Fortgibu, visualizing the earlier incident as he told the story and even expressing the wish that de Fortgibu should appear . . . as, indeed, he did.

It is noteworthy that Kammerer's wife, in the doctor's waiting room was concentrating on the *name* Schwalbach and it was the name, rather than the person, which subsequently 'manifested' in the receptionist's question. In the second quoted incident, however, Frau Kammerer was actually involved in visualizing a person, albeit a fictitious person, as she enjoyed Hermann Bang's novel. Possibly she found herself emotionally involved with the Mrs Rohan character. Thus two out of the three magical elements appeared in the incident, enough to set the wheels of synchronicity in motion. Without concentration – for Frau Kammerer obviously imposed no direction on the situation – events simply fizzled and sparkled like random fireworks until that evening.

Jung's 'fish' series has all the hallmarks of a magical operation. The essential factor here is that he was 'engaged in the study of the fish symbol in history'. Jung had a highly visual mind – his autobiography is largely a record of visions and hypnopompic experiences. The fish symbol, like any other symbol, is a visual thing and Jung, we know, was fascinated and excited by symbolism. Once again, all the magical elements are present. Driven by the power of a massive intellect, the magical results were forthcoming, but this time in specific direction: fish symbols – and a fish itself – began to appear all over the place.

There is no way of telling, of course, but I suspect the golden scarab was 'called' to the window by Jung rather than by his patient. He was a conscientious and caring physician, strongly attracted to women and with the quirky turn of mind that is drawn to the unusual and bizarre. It may have been that while he listened to his patient's description of her dream, he engaged in a little fantasy himself, imagining a 'miracle' which would aid her recovery. If I am right, then the appearance of the beetle followed the laws of magical reality, even if it remained inexplicable by the laws of science.

What we are looking at here is, of course, the apparent ability to apply magical methods quite unwittingly, to engage in a practice of magic without the realization of what one is actually doing. The question naturally arises as to why, if it is as easy as all that, we are not surrounded by unconsciously produced magical phenomena every day of the week?

But it is not as easy as all that. Magic is as much an art as a science and great magicians are as rare as great pianists or painters. But just as there are 'naturals' who can pick out a tune on the keyboard with no formal training, so there are 'natural magicians' who manage to influence events in accordance with traditional magical techniques, but without realizing what they are doing. It is my thesis that Jung was one such natural magician. Kammerer may well have been another – his wife certainly was.

The theory of the 'natural' or 'unconscious' magician goes at least some way towards explaining the mystery of astrology. Rationally, physically and statistically, traditional astrology cannot work. Yet, in practice, for certain people, it manifestly *does* work. I would argue that astrology works when it does work because it is a truly magical art – one of the oldest practised by humanity. Its most successful exponents are unconscious magicians, highly motivated, emotionally involved, trained to accept without question the system they use and accustomed to opening their minds to the vast (visual) vistas of the solar system and interstellar space. When their calculations 'predict' a certain sequence of events for themselves or for a client, it is the astrologer's mind which ensures they come about. Such results will no more show up in mass statistics than Leonardo da Vinci's painting of the *Mona Lisa* would show up in statistics on the sale of paint, but they are no less real for that.

Jung himself may have suspected something of this sort was going on. 'Synchronicity,' he said, 'is a phenomenon that seems to be primarily connected with psychic conditions, that is to say, with processes in the unconscious.'[152] He was criticized for the insight by, among others, Arthur Koestler, who felt he could not break the habit of thinking causally about an acausal phenomenon. But if the phenomenon was not acausal after all, Jung may have moved closer to the truth than his critics suspected.

In one of my earlier books,[153] I made the suggestion that magic was a sort of controlled synchronicity.[154] I now believe the exact reverse to be true: that the phenomena labelled synchronistic are frequently, if not always, examples of uncontrolled magic. But worse is to come. I think there is substantial evidence to suggest a large body of people in modern society may use magic in a controlled, targeted and highly effective way . . . without realizing for an instant what it is they are actually doing.

CHAPTER

18

ALCHEMY

Several years ago, a colleague of mine found himself caught up in a police raid. The officers were searching for illegal drugs and since my colleague was carrying several packets of small, white tablets, he was arrested. Despite his protestations that the tablets were for medical use, they were temporarily confiscated and samples sent for analysis. When the results came back, he was promptly released.

As he was leaving the station, a puzzled detective drew him to one side. 'You're free now and clear of all charges,' he said, 'so you don't have to pretend the pills are medicine. But tell me: what on earth do you *really* do with them?' The lab analysis had confirmed they contained no active ingredients whatsoever.

The analysis was accurate. The sugar base of the little tablets was unadulterated by any chemical, drug or even vitamin. But the detective was wrong to suggest this meant they could not be used medicinally. They were, in fact, homoeopathic prescriptions for migraine and nervous tension.

Homoeopathy is an alternative therapy now so widely accepted that it has become part of Establishment medicine.[155] It reverses traditional theory in claiming like should be used to cure like. The system was developed by the German doctor Samuel Hahnemann

(1755–1843), who came to believe that drugs which caused certain symptoms could be used in tiny doses to cure diseases showing those same symptoms.

This sounds similar to the principles of vaccination, but actually is not. Hahnemann experimented with such deadly toxins as aconite and strychnine, using a technique known as 'potentizing' to create dosages so minute that not a single molecule of the original substance could be chemically detected in the medicine. When his system worked, he concluded he was actually stimulating the body to call on its own reserves of healing. Anyone less desperate for a theory might have stopped to wonder how an undetectable substance could stimulate the body to do anything.

Modern homoeopathic practitioners still talk confidently about 'potentizing' and 'like curing like', but the plain fact is nobody really has the least idea why homoeopathy works – only that it does. If ever there was a magical medicine, it is not to be found in the witch-doctor's hut, but rather in those tiny lumps of sugar potentized to cure disease in a way that nobody quite understands. The bizarre nature of homoeopathy becomes clear when we examine it one step removed from its medical origins.

In the early months of 1924, the Silesian nobleman Count Keyserlingk held an agricultural conference on his estates at Koberwitz. His objective was to promote the (then quite revolutionary) idea that the earth and nature should not be the objects of short-sighted financial exploitation. A pioneering method of conservationist farming was introduced, as was a radically new type of pest control.

Pest control was a problem close to Count Keyserlingk's heart: his estates were almost overrun by rabbits. At one time, like most nobles, he had limited their numbers by organized hunting, but during World War One, the shortage of manpower led to loss of control. As a result the rabbit population had multiplied alarmingly on all farmland in the area.

By the time the war ended, Keyserlingk had adopted the green ethic and declined to return to the old ways of shooting wildlife. Worse still, he refused to permit the use of poison on his estates. He was, he said, searching for some alternative method of pest control. Six years later, at his agricultural conference, he announced he had found it.

The man who was to deliver the miracle was the Austrian philosopher, scientist, artist and occultist Rudolf Steiner. Steiner was the originator of the esoteric system anthroposophy, which asserts that humans possess a faculty of spiritual cognition functioning independently of the senses. He was also noted for the development of a special system of education, for a new artform called eurhythmy, and for a whole new branch of medicine which combined the principles of homoeopathy and herbalism. Now, it appeared, he had become an expert on the humane elimination of rabbits.

Steiner, an accomplished public speaker, delivered a series of lectures at the conference, probably on biodynamic farming, a discovery of his own that uses moon phase in order to promote plant growth. To demonstrate his new method of pest control, he first ordered the shooting of a male rabbit from the estate. This done, he set up a temporary laboratory where he removed spleen, testicles and a portion of skin from the unfortunate beast. These he burned to ashes.

The ashes were then mixed with milk sugar and potentized in the traditional homoeopathic manner. The resultant mixture, in liquid form, was carried in buckets by Steiner and his helpers to the four corners of the estate and widely sprayed by dipping brushes and flicking them in all directions.

For two days nothing happened. Steiner assured conference delegates that this sort of thing took time – he estimated a minimum of three days for results. At dawn the following day, thousands of rabbits were clustered around an old ashtree in the paddock, with more running to join them. The animals seemed nervous and agitated.

The cluster round the tree was not unique. Within hours reports were coming in of similar clusters in different parts of the estate. By late afternoon, the individual clusters had joined in a single, seething mass on the outskirts of the lands. Shortly before dusk, the entire warren swarmed away north-east. It was years before there was any sign of a rabbit on the Keyserlingk estate again.

This sort of thing is frankly weird and an examination of Steiner's reasoning does little to explain it. Steiner concluded, for reasons he did not disclose, that spleen, testes and skin were the physical basis of a rabbit's survival instinct. By burning, then homoeopathically potentizing them, he created a mixture which would, theoretically, induce contra-survival behaviour in the species. Rather than remain in the safety of their burrows, the rabbits would, he predicted, congregate in the open and eventually take off in a suicide migration like lemmings. The requisite homoeopathic doses were dispersed widely throughout the rabbits' habitat by the men with brushes. The rabbits subsequently *breathed* them in. This all sounds naive to the point of silliness, but the fact remains that it worked.

Was it possible that the secret of Steiner's remarkable experiment in pest control lay, like the secret of all homoeopathic action, in the potentizing? Dr Ernst Lehrs, an expert in the field, describes the process:

> The method of diluting or 'potentising' is as follows: A given volume of the material to be diluted is dissolved in nine times its volume of distilled water. The degree of dilution thus arrived at is 1:10, usually symbolised 1X. A tenth part of this solution is again mixed with nine times its bulk in water. The degree of dilution is now 1:100, or 2X. This process is continued as far as it is necessary for a given purpose. Insoluble substances can be dealt with in the same manner by first grinding them together with corresponding quantities of a neutral powder, generally sugar of milk. After a certain number of stages, the powder can be dissolved in water; the solution may then be diluted further in the manner already described.
>
> We can carry the dilutions as far as we please without destroying the capacity of the substance to produce physiological reactions. On the contrary, as soon as its original capacity is reduced to a minimum by dilution, further dilution gives it the power to cause even stronger reactions, of a different and usually opposite kind. The second capacity rises through stages to a variable maximum as dilution proceeds.
>
> A simple calculation shows that not a single molecule of the original substance will remain in solution after a certain degree of dilution is reached. Yet the biological and other reactions continue long after this, and are even enhanced.

It is very difficult to understand why this procedure should achieve anything at all, let alone become the foundation of a potent system of medicine. Dr Lehrs is of little further help here. He states:

> What this potentising process shows is that, by repeated expansion in space, a substance can be carried beyond the ponderable conditions of matter into the realm of pure functional effect.

Which only means, I suspect, that the good doctor does not know why it works either. In fact, the system of homoeopathic potentizing resembles nothing so much as certain techniques of ancient alchemy.

Alchemy is one of the most difficult of all academic studies. Carl Jung commented:

> In my opinion it is quite hopeless to try to establish any kind of order in the infinite chaos of substances and procedures. Seldom do we get even an approximate idea of how the work was done, what materials were used, and what results were achieved. The reader usually finds himself in the most impenetrable darkness when it comes to the names of the substances – they could mean almost anything ... Moreover, one must not imagine for a moment that the alchemists always understood one another. They themselves complain about the obscurity of the texts and occasionally betray their inability to understand even their own symbols and symbolic figures.[156]

Nonetheless, it was not quite the impractical mishmash modern scholars sometimes represent it to be. The works of Jabir ibn-Hayyan, a practising Spanish alchemist of the fourteenth century, became the textbooks of medieval alchemy and contained not only mystical theory but also important practical recipes. Arnold of Villanova described distillation; Roger Bacon gave a recipe for gunpowder and directions for constructing a telescope.

In time, alchemists turned from attempting to make gold towards preparing medicinals. A leader in this movement was Philippus Aureolus Paracelsus, who was the first European to mention zinc and use the word alcohol to refer to the spirit of wine. The *bain marie*, still used to keep food hot without spoiling, is named for its inventor, a medieval alchemist called

Mary the Jewess.

But behind the practical results – and there were enough of these to establish the foundations of modern chemistry – lay some very odd practices. Processes like distillation, reduction, heating and cooling could be repeated over and over, quite literally for years. Alchemists considered prayer and meditation were necessary in order to achieve results.

The theory of alchemy – in so far as there was any unifying theory at all – was based on the *Corpus Hermeticum*, the body of esoteric literature referred to in Chapter 15. At first, for Western alchemists at least, the contact was second-hand, via Arabic works. In the second half of the fifteenth century, however, Marsilio Ficino made accessible, in Latin, some of the original thought by translating a Greek manuscript which had reached Italy from Macedonia.

With such roots, it is not altogether surprising to find that one of the most important aspects of alchemy was the *imaginatio*, or use of the visual imagination to influence the work at hand, as Jung was quick to point out:

> A somewhat different aspect of the psyche's relation to the chemical work is apparent in the following quotation from the text of an anonymous author: 'I pray you, look with the eyes of the mind at this little tree of the grain of wheat, regarding all its circumstances, that you may also be able to plant the tree of the philosophers.' This seems to point to active imagination as the thing that sets the process really going.[157]

Jung believed this to be an indication of projection, a well-known phenomenon by which psychological contents are mistakenly considered to be aspects of the external world. But he recognized that the alchemists themselves did not share his belief:

> Ruland says, 'Imagination is the star in man, the celestial
> or supercelestial body.' This astounding definition throws
> a quite special light on the fantasy connected with the
> *opus*. We have to conceive of these processes not as the
> immaterial phantoms we readily take fantasy-pictures to
> be, but as something corporeal, a 'subtle body' semi-
> spiritual in nature . . . It was a hybrid phenomenon, as it
> were, half spiritual, half physical: a concretization such as
> we frequently encounter in the psychology of
> primitives.[158]

The nature of imagination as a phenomenon is something we will have to return to at a later stage. For the
moment, the only point is that visual imagination
played a critical part in alchemy, establishing the now-
familiar mind/matter interaction which confirms that
alchemy was a magical art. We may ask, as we have
already asked in relation to other magical arts, did
it work?

A central preoccupation of alchemy was the transformation of base metal into gold.[159] This was usually
achieved by melting the original metal in a crucible
and adding a mysterious powder known as the Philosopher's Stone. The real trick, of course, was making
the Stone.

Historically, there have been many claims for the
successful manufacture of alchemical gold, usually
explained by modern scholars as mistaken or fraudulent. There is no doubt that fraudulent practice was
commonplace. John Dee's medium, Edward Kelley,
was jailed for it and, as late as 1782, James Price
committed suicide rather than repeat an apparently
successful alchemical experiment under test
conditions.[160] But even the most cynical historians
stop short of suggesting fraud was universal.

Many modern chemists tend to the view that
alchemists were sufficiently naive to believe any

yellow metal must be gold – yellow brass, made from calamine and copper, is a quoted example. The manufacture of pseudo-silver was even easier. Arsenic compounds, known to have been used by alchemists, create silver-coloured alloys in reaction with copper. But however naive the alchemists may have been, there was nothing naive about the professional gold- and silver-smiths who tested the alchemical products and found them genuine.

Those who insist there must have been *something* genuine in alchemy (which, after all, preoccupied some of the world's finest minds for centuries) are still faced with the fact that the ability to manufacture gold seldom made practitioners rich. In 1541, Paracelsus, accepted as one of the greatest alchemists of his age, signed a will which showed his most valuable possession was a four-ounce ornamental silver chalice. The remainder of his estate was made up of books and routine personal property.

This has led Hans Biedermann to suggest an intriguing alternative explanation of considerable relevance to our present thesis:

> It is possible – though certainly not proven – that the long and intense concentration of an alchemist on his materials and operations, and the physically exhausting toil of the work, might induce an unusual condition of mind in which the alchemist was able to cause abnormal chemical reactions in his materials. These might be termed 'parachemical' reactions, possibly accounting for the alchemist's success.
>
> If this were so, we would expect it to occur only very rarely and for very short periods of time – which would explain the inability of successful adepts to grow rich by making large quantities of gold.
>
> On this hypothesis, the 'grace of God' for which alchemists devoutly prayed and without which, they said, the work could not succeed, would be interpreted as the

rare and fleeting psychic ability to cause parachemical change in the alchemist's materials – an ability which in a pious age seemed to be something coming from outside the alchemist himself, as a gift from God. The reading and rereading of mysterious books, rich in symbolism, might create a suitable mental atmosphere, a condition of mental exhaustion and 'headiness', a kind of drunkenness of the imagination. And the same mental condition might also be contributed to by the exhaustion produced by long concentration on the chemical operations themselves, performed over and over again.[161]

One wonders whether there might be a parachemical explanation for homoeopathy, which so resembles alchemy in its central process. But before considering that, we need to know whether this sort of thing is really possible, not as a historical inference, but as a matter of modern day experience.

19

IMPOSSIBLE OBJECTS

While we were enduring the ministrations of a television studio make-up department, Dr Lyall Watson told me of a fascinating incident he had experienced during his last trip abroad. He had met up with a psychokinetic child who, while playing with a tennis ball, had suddenly concentrated. There was an abrupt *plop* when the child tossed the ball. Watson caught it to find it had mysteriously been turned inside out. The ball itself was undamaged, but now the smooth inside rubber was on the surface and the fabric pile (presumably) inside.

If I had not been so excited at the prospect of appearing on television, I might have thought to ask if he had kept the ball, for it would surely have provided valuable support for several paranormal theories. But even if the inside-out ball has not survived, at least two other impossible objects certainly have; and both are now under serious consideration as evidence for the theory that mind can directly influence matter.

One of these objects, the subject of speculation and controversy for centuries, is the Shroud of Turin.

The Turin Shroud is a length of linen 14 feet 3 inches long by 3 feet 7 inches wide. Apart from a three-and-a-half inch strip running along one side, it is a single piece. Faintly imprinted on this linen is a pale sepia monochrome double image of the back and the front of a tall, naked, powerfully built man, laid out as if in preparation for entombment. According to Ian Wilson:

> The face on the frontal image has a masklike quality about it with owl-like 'eyes'. It seems detached from the rest of the body because of the apparent absence of shoulders. While the crossing of the hands across the pelvis is quite well defined, the legs fade away below the knees, the feet being just a blur.
>
> The image of the back is more consistent but similarly indefinite throughout. In everyday terms, both images most resemble the faint scorch marks typical of a well-used linen ironing-board cover.[162]

The marks coalesce to show a man who was scourged and crucified. Since its first known public exposition in 1357, people have believed the Shroud to be the actual burial cloth of Christ, miraculously imprinted with the holy image. Radiocarbon dating carried out in 1989 finally confirmed it could be nothing of the sort: the cloth is medieval.[163]

With the announcement of the scientists' results, there has been widespread media and public assumption that the mystery of the Shroud has somehow been solved. In fact, if anything, it has deepened. Unpalatable though it might be to rationalists, a miraculous origin for the Shroud would at least explain how the image got on the cloth. To date, nothing else has.

The most obvious inference has always been that what appears on the cloth is the remnants of a painting, an example of religious art. But there are immediate problems with this theory. The first is that careful analysis has shown the figure depicted suffered scourging, wrist and feet wounds like those experienced in crucifixion and head lacerations consistent with a crown of thorns. While these are precisely the features which led to the belief that the Shroud was the winding cloth of Christ, they are also genuine features of a first-century Roman crucifixion; and, more importantly, they are technically correct.

It is this technical correctness that poses the first problem. Conventional religious art shows the nail wounds in the palms of Christ's hands. In reality, nails placed in this position will not support a victim on a cross: the Romans took a firmer fixing through the bones of the wrist – which is where the nail marks are shown on the Turin Shroud. So if there was a painting, it was certainly not a conventional religious painting. Experts are equally unhappy about the depiction of the blood flows from the wounds. Here again, forensic examination shows them to be technically correct. The question is asked, how did anyone in medieval times obtain such exact and detailed information about first-century crucifixion? And having somehow obtained it, where did any medieval artist find the skill to depict it so precisely?

This latter question is itself further complicated by an early development in the examination of the Shroud. In 1898, a special exposition was arranged as part of the fiftieth anniversary celebrations of the Italian Constitution. A request was made that the Shroud should be photographed and its owner, King Umberto I of the House of Savoy, eventually agreed that this should be done. The man chosen for the job was Secondo Pia, a middle-aged lawyer who had won several awards as an amateur photographer.

These were the early days of photography and the job to be done proved far from easy. A platform had to be built to raise the camera to the necessary height. The floodlights Pia was using cracked due to overheating and without them exposures of between fourteen

and twenty minutes were necessary. When Pia developed the glass plate, his first emotion was one of relief
when a negative image started to emerge.

His next emotion was awe, for the negative image
was not negative at all, but something more akin to a
photographic print. The picture on the Shroud had lost
its grotesque, mask-like appearance and become an
impressive portrait of a well-proportioned man with
long hair and a full beard. The blood flows from his
wounds could be clearly seen. This meant only one
thing – the image on the Shroud was itself similar to
a photographic negative.

This does not absolutely rule out painting, but it
does make it even more unlikely. The argument that
no medieval artist had the skill to portray such an
anatomically correct representation may be weak – a
forgotten genius is always a possibility – but it is
reasonable to ask why any artist would have created a
negative image even if he could. If a representation was
wanted, surely it would have been painted in the usual
way? In medieval times there were no cameras to
reverse the image.

The negative image discovery led to the theory that
the imprint on the cloth might have been just that –
an imprint. A German writer was the first to suggest
that a life-size statue, or even a corpse, was coated with
pigment and the cloth pressed upon it to offset the
image. The bloodstains could then have been painted
on afterwards.

Reasonable though this sounds, it is not the answer
either. Experts, including a French professor, have
attempted to duplicate such a procedure experimen-
tally. The results have been abysmal.

The mystery deepened in 1976 when the physicist
Dr John Jackson and the image-enhancement expert

Bill Mottern subjected a photograph of the Shroud to an Interpretation Systems VP-8 Image Analyser. To their astonishment, the machine showed the photograph contained sufficient data to produce a perfect three-dimensional relief. An ordinary photograph will not give this result. Indeed nothing known to science was capable of giving it before the development of holography. The discovery of so much encoded data in the Shroud absolutely precludes the possibility that it was painted; and virtually precludes imprinting.

How then did the image get there? Colour-scan technology applied in 1973 indicated that all features of the figure had an identical spectroscopic analysis to the burn marks produced when the Shroud was slightly damaged by fire during one of its historical expositions. This was confirmed by the Shroud of Turin Research Project who reported in 1984 that the image is made up of yellowed surface fibrils 'in a more advanced stage of degradation than the non-image linen. The chromophore is a conjugated carbonyl.' This means, in effect, that the closest known thing to the Shroud image is a scorch mark.

Commenting on the similarity between the scorched image and shadow imprints left on buildings in Hiroshima following the dropping of the atomic bomb, Ian Wilson has this to say:

> The concept of a force is implicit from the manner in which the image seems to have been created with a marked upward/downward directionality, without any diffusion, and leaving no imprint of the sides of the body or the top of the head. Also the image-forming process seems to have shown no discrimination between registering the body surface, the hair, the blood and even inanimate objects ... All would seem to have been imprinted on the cloth with the same even intensity, and

with only the most minor colour variation in the case of the blood.

The idea, then of some form of thermo-nuclear flash being the force in question is obviously more than idle speculation.[164]

Wilson was writing before the definitive carbon dating of the Shroud and thus tended towards the conclusion that the artifact might be the genuine grave-wrapping of Jesus. Against such a background, the inference was that the body of Christ miraculously disappeared in a flash of light, leaving its imprint as it did so. Since this postulate is no longer tenable, the mystery remains.

In 1990, however, César Tort published what he called an 'incredible yet tantalising hypothesis on the genesis of the sindonic image'. He believes it to be an example of retrocognitive thoughtography.

Retrocognition is the ability to obtain information about the past by paranormal means – the exact reverse of precognition, in fact. Thoughtography is an unwieldy term describing the apparent ability of certain individuals (or groups) to impress imagined images on photographic plates and other surfaces. The best known proponent of the art is Ted Serios, an American who frequently demonstrated under test conditions his ability to conjure pictures onto Polaroid film.

Serios' abilities came to light when Dr Jule Eisenbud of the University of Colorado Medical School received a press cutting which claimed Serios could produce photographs merely by staring into the camera lens with deep concentration. The report further insisted that Serios had been tested by scientists and photographers, who were unable to discover fraud or a rational explanation. Eisenbud arranged for a demonstration.

This was carried out in a Chicago hotel where, after several attempts, Serios produced two blurred but recognizable photographs of city buildings.

Eisenbud brought Serios to Denver, where a series of more stringent scientific tests took place. Before a committee of distinguished scholars, Serios managed to produce, among other things, a picture of the Westminster Abbey clock tower, which he had seen in a magazine photograph the day before.

Serios was not a particularly sympathetic test subject. He had a drink problem, limited intelligence and a self-centred personality. During one demonstration he became drunk and incoherent. He failed to turn up for another. Despite these difficulties, he was eventually persuaded to produce more than a hundred mental photographs under test conditions. They varied in content from people to rockets and some were in colour.

One important point which emerged from the tests was that the cameras used were largely a matter of convenience: Serios could produce pictures whether or not there was a lens. This and other examples indicate that conventional photographic techniques form no part of the process, nor is sensitized film a necessity for success. In the circumstances, the suggestion that thoughtography might be involved in the production of the Shroud image certainly does not run contrary to the little we know of the process.

Tort considers so much data on first-century crucifixion was embodied in the Shroud that only retrocognition can explain it. The image itself, he believes, may have been the result of a mass-PK (psychokinetic) effect occurring at Lirey in France, shortly after the Battle of Poitiers in 1356. He postulates that a devout audience, living in the aftermath of the Black Death, identifying strongly with the suffering Jesus, and faced with the ecclesiastical display of a plain unfigured cloth supposed to be the grave-shroud of Christ, were sufficiently hysterical and energized to 'project' a collective image onto it paranormally. However far-fetched this hypothesis might seem, Tort claims – with some justification – that it is the only one so far advanced that actually accounts for all available data on the Shroud.[165]

Is thoughtography really possible? Ted Serios developed a reputation as a 'difficult' test subject, but long before he came to prominence in the world of paranormal research, one investigator was engaged in experimentation which, while less well known, is a convincing indication that the human mind can influence a photographic plate.

In 1910, T. Fukurai, a Professor of Psychology at the Tokyo Imperial University, became interested in psychical research after running some tests on a clairvoyant. He began to investigate a second medium and discovered that, in attempting to guess the picture content of undeveloped film, she seemed to be affecting the film itself. It soon transpired that she could imprint mental pictures on a photographic plate, which did not need to be in a camera at the time.

The promising series of experiments stopped abruptly when the medium died. Fukurai found his career in jeopardy when the press discovered what he had been doing and denounced him with such vehemence that he was forced to resign his university chair. But it did not stop his interest in paranormal research. In 1928, be travelled to England to begin a whole new series of thoughtography experiments with a psychic named William Hope. Two years later, he published

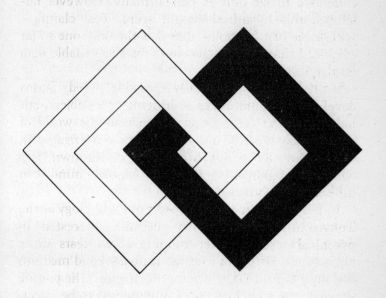

Meyer's 'Impossible Object'.

his results, which included evidence that his medium could select the particular photographic plate he wished to influence, could split his thoughtform between two different plates, and target in on a specfic area of a roll of film.

While none of this proves Tort's theory that the Turin Shroud might be the result of thoughtography, it does at least show the possibility exists. Even the fact that the Shroud linen is not a light-sensitive plate does not create a barrier. Freak photographic effects have occurred using a variety of (apparently) non-sensitive materials.[166]

The second 'impossible object' is substantially more recent in origin than the Shroud. It was created by the paranormally gifted Silvio Meyer while under investigation by a research team from Berne, in Switzerland.

Meyer had been the subject of a study since 1974 and shown himself unusually consistent in the production of phenomena, both spontaneously and under test conditions. In December 1987, while filling in time at work, he cut two square frames from, respectively, the aluminium foil in which his sandwiches had been wrapped and a piece of paper from a notebook.

Next, Meyer slit the side of the paper frame and inserted the uncut aluminium frame so that one was looped into the other. He then held the cut portion of the paper frame between thumb and forefinger, concentrating, for ten minutes. As a result, the paper 'fused', became once again continuous and the two frames were intertwined as seen on the previous page.

Although researchers had only Meyer's word for what happened, they had every opportunity to study the impossible object itself. In doing so, they allowed two possibilities, based on the assumption that the object was *not* made by paranormal means. One was that the frames were somehow constructed around one another. The second was that while constructed separately, one of the frames was then cut, the two joined and the frame glued or welded back together.

On analyzing the first postulate, the possibility of manufacturing the aluminium frame around the paper was dismissed. The melting point of aluminium is 660°C, more than 200°C higher than the temperature at which paper catches fire. Thus the process of constructing one frame would simultaneously destroy the other. A further problem is the fact that kitchen foil is the result of pressing and rolling using specialized industrial machinery (to which Meyer did not have access). Duplication of its characteristics by casting would certainly be extremely difficult: the experts tended to think it actually impossible.

Manufacturing a paper frame around the aluminium would certainly have been a great deal easier – well within the capabilities of any competent home handy-man, in fact. But the problem in this case turned out to be the nature of the paper. It had not the coarse, fibrous quality of hand-made paper, but rather displayed the smooth texture and grain of notebook paper. Analysis showed it was optically brightened with a bluish fluorescence such as one would expect to find in paper created by mass production methods in a mill – which is, of course, exactly what Meyer claimed it to be.

Having dismissed the first option, the researchers turned to the second which, on the face of it, seemed far more promising. A substantial battery of tests was applied to the object itself, including microscopic inspection, laser-beam surface reflection analysis and radiation analysis. There is no indication of a join in the paper, no sign of any glue, no thickening, no cuts or shifts in the microscopic grain. The aluminium frame showed none of the characteristic overlap thickening of cold welding – which in any case requires machine pressures in excess of ten tonnes – and no hint of the oxidation which occurs in heat welding.

The end result of the testing was that the experts were unable to find any rational means by which the object could have been created. Investigations continue at the time of writing, but in the interim, the object remains 'impossible'.

Unless, of course, one accepts Meyer's own explanation and allows the possibility that mind can manipulate matter directly. Such an admission reinforces the possibility of parachemical reactions in alchemy, which in turn supports the notion that homoeopathic practitioners may themselves be unwitting alchemists in the preparation of their nostrums.

If so, they are not the only doctors practising magical medicine.

CHAPTER

20

WITCH-DOCTORS

Warts are small growths on the skin, usually measuring from 2 to 10 millimetres (0.08 to 0.4 inches) across. They occur chiefly on exposed areas of the body such as the hands, fingers, face, scalp and soles of the feet, and are caused by viruses. Most pharmacists carry a range of proprietary preparations designed to banish them and in desperate situations they can be surgically removed. But any doctor worth his salt will refer his troubled patients to a wart-charmer.

Wart-charmers are individuals with the ability to cure warts by magic. Sometimes the talent is inherited from a parent, sometimes 'passed on' in the form of a spell, procedure or talisman, by another practitioner. The techniques used vary widely, ranging from prayer to burying a piece of string that has first been looped around the wart. They really have only one thing in common: they work.

I became a wart-charmer by an odd route. While I still practised as a hypnotherapist, a friend asked me if I was prepared to treat a work colleague who was severely depressed. The colleague, Jean Manchester,[167] was a woman in her early twenties. The cause of her depression was a disfiguring outbreak of warts on her face.

When Jean called to see me, it was immediately

obvious she was in a very bad psychological state. She sat head bowed, her long hair pulled forward to cover her face, and only with extreme reluctance allowed me to inspect the warts. There were forty-eight of them. They had appeared, over a matter of days, about eight months before. She had tried various preparations, but in vain. Because of their location and number, her doctor had firmly advised against surgical removal.

It was very obvious that Jean's depression was reactive. The way to cure it was to cure the warts. I felt there was a possibility I could do so. Recent research had shown that, despite their viral nature, warts reacted to hypnotic suggestion, often very quickly. I placed Jean in trance – she was a reasonably good subject – and told her firmly that her warts would disappear overnight: she would wake in the morning with a clear skin.

The experiment was a failure. Jean woke the following morning with no difference in her condition. The warts were still there the next day and the day after. I tried hypnotic reinforcement, again without result.

Three weeks went by during which I decided that if hypnosis had ever cured warts, it was certainly not going to cure them in this case. Then I had an urgent call from Jean. She wanted to see me right away, but refused to say why. She walked into the room with her hair drawn back and head high. Her skin was clear: every wart was gone. They never returned.

Jean gave me credit for the cure, but I was less certain. It is in the nature of warts that they will sometimes disappear of their own accord. As much out of curiosity as anything else, I began to experiment with the effect of suggestion on warts. I quickly discovered hypnosis was not necessary to achieve a result. Almost any technique would do, so long as the patient believed in its validity. This included a variety of the old wart-charming rituals.

But then came the crunch. I began to experiment with individuals who had no faith whatsoever in the techniques I was using. (I made a point of applying the most outrageously folksy practices to the warts of my most sophisticated and scientifically minded subjects.) They still worked.[168]

Since it seemed to me unlikely that I had been born with some mysterious – and highly specific – power to destroy warts, this outcome left me puzzled. It is widely accepted that faith often heals, which is another way of saying that when a patient believes something will do him or her good, the mind will often ensure the body reacts accordingly. But this factor was not present in the case of disbelievers. What, then, cured the warts?

Suggestion, like faith, is a well-documented healer. It was case-studies of hypnotic suggestion applied to warts that set me on my wart-charming career in the first place. Nor does suggestion have to be explicit, as in hypnosis. It may be implicit, as in the application of a folk ritual known to be a wart cure. The problem was, as I quickly discovered, I was unable to achieve comparable results using suggestion in any condition other than warts.

It did, however, occur to me that there was one common denominator in all my wart cures – my own belief that I could do it.

The conviction was firmly founded. Its starting-point was the (strictly scientific) research which insisted warts responded to hypnotic suggestion. I knew from long experience that I was a competent hypnotist, thus I accepted without question that I should be able to cure warts by hypnosis. When my first experiment eventually succeeded, this reinforced the belief and laid the foundation for the next step, the idea that suggestion alone, apart from hypnosis, should achieve results. In retrospect, it may have been that I was curing warts by methods other than those I believed I was using at the time, but this does not matter. What matters is that my self-confidence was being reinforced with every case I took.

The end result was the development of a total, unquestioned assumption that I could cure warts using virtually any method I chose. Did the cures actually *depend* on this assumption? In other words, could the state of mind of a healer – wart-charmer or doctor – influence the outcome of a cure?

One man who thought so was the essayist, lawyer, statesman and philosopher, Francis Bacon, who gave this advice in 1626 on how to cure a sick gentleman:

> First pick out one of his servants who is naturally very credulous; while the gentleman is asleep, hand the servant some harmless concoction and tell him that it will cure his master in a certain space of time. The [energies] of the servant, made receptive by his complete faith in your medical powers, will be powerfully stamped with the image of this future cure; they will flow out and similarly stamp the [energies] of his master, also in a state of receptivity because he is asleep.[169]

This is an extraordinary insight, even for a man who has earned his place in history. It reinforces Biedermann's parachemical theory of alchemy, provides a possible explanation for homoeopathic potentizing, and anticipates recent experiments in Kirlian photography which indicate that energy 'imprinting' of certain materials – among them vials of water or oil – is possible. More to the point, it is directly in line with modern research into one of the most fascinating of all medical phenomena, the placebo effect.

According to E. A. Green:

> A placebo is an inert substance made to appear indistinguishable from an authentic drug. Its most common use is in the testing of new drugs to provide an evaluation by comparison. Also, a placebo may be prescribed when there is no apparent organic basis for an illness. The 'placebo effect' is attributed to psychological factors. In conditions involving the central nervous system, such as pain or anxiety, placebo effects often mimic the effects of an active drug.[170]

But Green makes one important mistake in this definition. Placebos may be successfully prescribed even where there is a very evident organic basis for an illness. One of the most dramatic examples of this was reported by B. Klopfer in the *Journal of Projective Techniques* in 1957. His paper was entitled 'Psychological Variables in Human Cancer' and told the story of a patient he called Mr Wright.

Wright had contracted lymphosarcoma, cancer of the lymphatic system, one of the most insidious and virulent known forms of the disease. He had tumours in his neck, groin, chest, abdomen and armpits along with serious enlargement of liver and spleen. Fluid had to be drained regularly from his lungs and, while the clinic where he was being treated had managed to keep him alive using oxygen, his physician, Dr Philip West, considered he was unlikely to survive more than two weeks.

At the time, however, newspaper reports began to appear about a new cancer treatment using a drug called Krebiozen. The drug was still in its test phase but, coincidentally, one of the facilities chosen for testing by the American Medical Association was the very clinic where Mr Wright was dying. Wright read the reports and asked Dr West if he could have the drug. West was reluctant. There is a specific procedure for the testing of drugs and terminally ill patients seldom feature in it, but eventually he decided to allow Wright to have Krebiozen on compassionate grounds.

The injection was administered at a weekend. When West reported for work two days later, he was delighted to find Wright dramatically improved. His tumours were only half their original size and he felt fitter than he had done since developing the disease. After a further ten days on Krebiozen, he was discharged from hospital with his cancer in full remission. At this stage he felt so well he even took up his old hobby of flying. His breathing was so free he found he could manage without oxygen at heights where it was normally used.

Perhaps the most interesting aspect of this miracle cure was that Wright was the only Krebiozen patient who showed a positive response. The remainder either continued to deteriorate or held their own. This experience was repeated in other clinics within the test programme, a fact duly reported in the press. Wright read the reports and promptly relapsed. He was readmitted into the clinic and went back under the care of Dr West.

West realized his patient must be an unusually good placebo reactor and decided to experiment. He told Wright the newspaper reports about Krebiozen had not been strictly accurate. The drug, he said, lost potency very quickly and the negative results had arisen out of the use of exhausted stock. This problem had now been solved and the clinic was awaiting supplies of highly refined, double-strength product.

Wright was injected with what he believed to be the new double-potency Krebiozen the next day. In fact, the injection was nothing more potent than water. All the same, Wright promptly recovered and went back to his flying. He was symptom free for two months, approximately the time it took for the American Medical Association to complete its trials of Krebiozen. These showed conclusively the drug was useless against cancer.

When the findings were announced, Wright had his second relapse and died within days.

Wright's case demonstrates that a placebo can be highly effective against organic illness, even in its terminal phase.[171] It is, however, a demonstration within the classic placebo mould. What healed, in this case, was Wright's faith (assisted to some degree by West's suggestions). As soon as his faith waivered, his illness returned. But there are many recorded instances in which the faith of the patient is, as Bacon suggested, less important than the faith of those who administer the nostrum.

In the late nineteenth century, for example, the French physician Dr Hippolyte Bernheim conducted an experiment in which he told the mothers of his youngest patients that a bottle of plain water was a potent treatment for whatever happened to ail their children. Out of twenty-six cases (some resistant to orthodox treatment) involving patients whose ages ranged from thirty-three months down to nineteen days, Bernheim's magic bottle failed only once. He had nineteen complete cures and six improvements.

It is evident that the patients' faith played little or no part in their recovery. Nor, of course, did that of Bernheim, who knew the bottle contained plain water. What seems to have worked is the faith of the mothers, which acted exactly as Bacon predicted.

The curious action of placebos is well documented

in medical research which, however, has tended to raise more questions than it answers. In a study carried out by F. Evans, for example, various placebos were respectively found to be 54 per cent as effective as morphine, Davron and asprin . . . despite the fact that each of these drugs has a different potency. What this research means is that the degree of pain control achieved by a placebo is a standard percentage of the relief which would be expected from the drug for which it has been substituted. The question arising, as J. Finlay Hurley put it succinctly,[172] is how does a placebo know which drug is which?

The answer, of course, is that a placebo does not. Nor, usually, does the patient. But the administering physician does. Once again, we have evidence that mindset can directly influence the technical action of an inert substance.

This sort of finding falls well within the definition of magic that we have been developing throughout the present book. And the magical aspect of placebo action is further reinforced by the discovery that, whatever the faith of patient or doctor, not all placebos have precisely the same degree of effect. To get the best from a placebo pill, you should ensure it tastes bitter and is either small and red or yellow or large and brown or purple. Two (inert!) pills will always work better than one, an injection will typically work better than a pill, and a new placebo will generate better results than one which has been around for a while.[173]

Doctors are understandably reluctant to see themselves as magicians, however many placebos they administer. (And as little as a century ago the bulk of Western medicine depended almost entirely on the placebo effect since modern analysis has shown that virtually every remedy in common use was either neutral or downright harmful in action.) The orthodox stance remains that placebos work through suggestion – either self-suggestion in cases where the patient is aware of the expected action, or some sort of communicated suggestion via the physician.

There is no doubt at all that where a patient believes a certain result will follow the introduction of a particular substance into his body, then suggestion will go a long way towards bringing that result about. In his paper on 'Cardiovascular Reactions to Symbolic Stimuli',[174] S. Wolf noted that 85 per cent of those who die from snakebite each year do not have enough venom in their blood to kill them.

Nor is there any controversy about the possibility of broad influence by the physician on the patient: we have already seen how Dr West's confident nonsense about new 'highly refined, double-strength' Krebiozen caused a full remission of cancer in his patient, Mr Wright. Even where no overt claims are made for the placebo by the physician, experts insist that attitude, body posture and vocal intonation can all provide subtle clues to the expected reaction – the reason why tests of new drugs against placebos are now almost always of the 'double-blind' variety where neither the subjects nor the administering physicians are aware of which is the real drug and which the purple pill.

All the same, it is difficult to see how attitude, posture or vocal intonation could convey such precise information about drug effect that a patient is able (by producing the predictable result) to differentiate between placebo aspirin and placebo morphine.

One other possibility remains: the notion of *telepathic* suggestion. Telepathy has been a fact of scientific life since the 1930s when Dr J. B. Rhine set up his famous Zener card experiments to establish a statistical validity for ESP phenomena.[175] Telepathic suggestion is a little more controversial, but there is ample evidence of its existence in certain circumstances.

I made my own small experiments with the technique after studying Russian reports of telepathically induced hypnotic trance. These involved an unusually responsive subject named Léonie, whom I first placed in trance – and subsequently awoke – telepathically on a summer's afternoon while we were sunbathing together.

The second experiment occurred after some colleagues protested that, given the circumstances of a warm, drowsy day, Léonie might have passed spontaneously into trance on the first occasion. This was a perfectly valid objection, so that the second experiment was carried out at a party while Léonie was anything but relaxed. She passed into trance while chatting to a friend who watched bemused until she awoke. She was unaware of what had happened and rationalized that she must have inexplicably dozed off.[176]

A much more striking example of telepathic hypnotic induction coincidentally also involved a subject named Léonie. It occurred in 1886 following a dinner party attended by six prominent academics including Professor Pierre Janet, Dr M. Gilbert, Frederick Myers and Julius Ochorovicz – all noted for their interest in psychical research.

The discussion centred on whether Gilbert could hypnotize Léonie by telepathy and call her to him. While Gilbert retired to his study to begin the experiment, the remaining five hurried to surround Léonie's home, almost a mile away.

As the experimenters watched from the shadows, Léonie emerged from the house, eyes shut, walked as far as the gate then, inexplicably, turned around and went back. It was later discovered that Gilbert, at this point, had allowed his concentration to waver and dozed off.[177]

After a few moments, Janet emerged from hiding to find out what was going on and was almost knocked down by Léonie who suddenly emerged from her cottage, walking extremely quickly. Despite the fact that her eyes were shut, she negotiated lamp posts and traffic for ten minutes while the scholars trailed behind, then suddenly stopped and looked around her in confusion. Gilbert, it later transpired, had decided the experiment was a failure and had begun to play billiards. After a short time, however, he resolved to give it another try. Léonie obligingly fell back into trance and continued on her way.

She reached Gilbert's home in time to collide with him in the doorway, knocking him down. Unaware of who he was, she climbed over the recumbent body and ran through the house shouting, 'Where is he?' Gilbert picked himself up and called her mentally. Léonie 'heard' and answered, bringing the experiment to a successful conclusion.

Dr Edward Naumov, the Soviet parapsychologist, recorded an experiment in which a test volunteer was successfully commanded to fall ten times out of ten using telepathy. Eight times out of the ten he fell in the specific direction commanded.

The founder of modern hypnotic practice, the Marquis de Puységur, repeatedly demonstrated 'mental suggestion', particularly with a subject named Madeline. Not only was de Puységar able to direct her movements, but he also seemed able to pass this ability on to others, who could direct her mentally to walk, sit and pick up specific objects.

In the light of these findings, it seems likely, perhaps even inevitable, that telepathic suggestion plays a part in certain placebo effects. But it is equally obvious it cannot explain them all: Bernheim's bottle is a case in point. When all else is stripped away, we are left – at least in some instances – with a picture that is uncomfortably close to that painted by Bacon. Certain effects and potencies can, apparently, be 'imprinted' on suitable carriers by an action of human will. The carriers will then trigger the relevant effect when applied, divorced from any mind-to-mind influence, verbal suggestion or personal faith.

This is, of course, a description of magic in action: the manufacture of an amulet, charm or talisman under a different name.

CHAPTER

21

ASTRAL PLANE

Magic is a collection of techniques, used by humanity for a minimum of 40,000 years and based on the conviction that what happens within the human mind has a direct influence on the physical world. Apart from the testimony of those who have experimented with the techniques, eyewitness accounts tend to confirm that magic works. There has been no direct scientific study of magical methods, but evidence drawn from the fields of parapsychology, psychical research, academic study and medicine at least shows the claims of the magicians are not impossible. There is a further suggestion that some of the beings known for centuries as 'spirits' are actually creations of the mind, somehow released into the physical world.

But if there is a possibility that magic works, it is necessary to ask by what mechanism. It is worthless to observe that the mind *seems* to influence the world: we need to know how.

Magicians have their own theories:

What powerful operation the Imagination hath ... So quick and swift a Runner and Messenger is the Imagination that it doth not onely fly out of one house into another, out of one streete into another, but also most swiftly passeth from City and Country into another; so that by the Imagination onely of one person, the Pestilence may come into some whole City or Country, and kill many thousands of men . . . Neither let any think that I speak this as a fable.

This hath suddenly happened to many who have followed the process of their Imagination, so that they have attained to great honour and Riches.

Object. But some may Object that fortune, strength and industry hath helped them and promoted such men; also that some have worne herbs, rootes and stones &c. by reason of the virtue whereof they could not be overcome nor wounded.

Answ. I say that all these things are consorts and helpers with the Imagination, which is the chiefe and general ruler over all things . . .[178]

This thesis, put forward by Paracelsus in the sixteenth century, has been supported by occult practitioners ever since. Almost every technique of the Western Esoteric Tradition is based on the belief that imagination is the key to controlling reality. Éliphas Lévi attempted to explain why in the Introduction to his *History of Magic*:

A particular phenomenon occurs when the brain is congested or overcharged by Astral Light; sight is turned inward, instead of outward; night falls on the external and real world, while fantastic brilliance shines on the world of dreams; even the physical eyes experience a slight quivering and turn up inside the lids. The soul then perceives by means of images the reflection of its impressions and thoughts. This is to say that the analogy subsisting between idea and form attracts in the Astral Light a reflection representing that form, configuration being the essence of the vital light; it is the universal imagination, of which each of us appropriates a lesser or greater part according to our grade of sensibility and memory.[179]

This is not a particularly easy passage, but it does at least introduce the term *Astral Light* and the concept of a 'universal imagination', both of which are vital to the understanding of magic.

The Astral Light – a term generally synonymous with the more familiar *Astral Plane* – has been used by magicians for centuries to describe the world of the visual imagination. But the usage embodies a different perception of imagination to that held by orthodox psychology. In two previous books,[180] I attempted to explain esoteric thought on the subject using the diagram below.

Mental world   Self   Physical world

This showed subjective and objective worlds as a continuum with our conscious awareness – labelled *Self* in the diagram – centred somewhere between them. Magicians would, however, label the diagram a little differently, preferring the usage in the diagram below.

Astral world   Self   Physical world

While the change in heading is minor, it is by no means trivial, since it suggests there is an inner, finer, intangible aspect of physical reality, a mind-side of matter, which we can (and do) sense by the act of visualization. In other words, what we see by looking inwards is just as much a part of physical reality as the environment we perceive while looking outwards. What we are sensing with inner vision is, to use another of Lévi's interesting terms, the 'imagination of matter'.

This is not an exclusively occult concept. Something very similar lies at the root of Jungian psychology in the theory of the collective unconscious, which Jung himself explained in these words:

> The hypothesis of a collective unconscious belongs to the class of ideas that people at first find strange but soon come to possess and use as familiar conceptions. This has been the case with the concept of the unconscious in general . . .
>
> At first the concept of the unconscious was limited to denoting the state of repressed or forgotten contents. Even with Freud, who makes the unconscious – at least metaphorically – take the stage as the acting subject, it is really nothing but the gathering place of forgotten and repressed contents and has a functional significance thanks only to these. For Freud, accordingly, the unconscious is of an exclusively personal nature, although he was aware of its archaic and mythological thought-forms.
>
> A more or less superficial layer of the unconscious is undoubtedly personal. I call it the *personal unconscious*. But this personal unconscious rests on a deeper layer, which does not derive from personal experience and is not a personal acquisition but is inborn. I have chosen the term 'collective' because this part of the unconscious is not individual but universal; in contrast to the personal psyche, it has contents and modes of behaviour that are more or less the same everywhere and in all individuals. It is, in other words, identical in all men and thus

constitutes a common psychic substrata of a supra-personal nature which is present in every one of us.[181]

Although Jung frequently referred to the collective unconscious as the *objective* unconscious, concern over his academic reputation ensured he did not push this too far. He was careful to suggest that the collective unconscious might be no more than a reflection of the basic structure of the physical brain. It was therefore 'collective' only in the sense of *common to all*, not in the sense that there might be a *single* collective unconscious 'out there' which individual humans somehow shared.

In his least academic work, however, the mask slips as he tells the story of a depressed patient, once healed but fast sliding into a relapse:

At that time I had to deliver a lecture in B. I returned to my hotel around midnight. I sat with some friends for a while after the lecture, then went to bed, but I lay awake for a long time. At about two o'clock – I must have just fallen asleep – I awoke with a start, and had the feeling that someone had come into the room; I even had the impression that the door had been hastily opened. I instantly turned on the light, but there was nothing. Someone might have mistaken the door, I thought, and I looked into the corridor. But it was still as death. 'Odd,' I thought, 'someone did come into the room!' Then I tried to recall exactly what had happened and it occurred to me that I had been awakened by a feeling of dull pain, as though something had struck my forehead and then the back of my skull. The following day I received a telegram saying that my patient had committed suicide. He had shot himself. Later I learned that the bullet had come to rest in the back wall of the skull.

This experience was a genuine synchronistic phenomenon such as is quite often observed in connection with an archetypal situation – in this case, death. By means of a relativisation of time and space in the unconscious it could well be that I had perceived something which in reality was taking place elsewhere. The collective unconscious is common to all; it is the foundation of what the ancients called the 'sympathy of all things'. In this case the unconscious had knowledge of my patient's condition. All that evening, in fact, I had felt curiously restive and nervous, very much in contrast to my usual mood.[182]

However strongly we evoke the basic structure of the physical brain, there is, of course, no way in which this can explain the experience Jung is describing. Clearly, by linking his curious knowledge of his patient's suicide with the collective unconscious, Jung is suggesting the collective unconscious itself is *singular*, a unique sea of common experience shared by all. Small wonder that Jung so often spoke of it as 'objective' – as defined by his experience, it could be nothing else.

But it is probably true to say that while Jung's followers accept the term 'objective', they tend to use it only to describe psychic contents which are not generated by the individual. They do not, by and large, suggest such contents are objective in the same way that the physical world is objective. Magicians go further. Their world of the imagination is thought to be objective in exactly the same way that the physical world is objective. Indeed, it is seen as the ultimate *foundation* of physical manifestation, without which the physical world could not exist at all.

The difficulty with this notion is, of course, the observable fact that anyone can control the content of his or her imagination by a simple act of will. Should I ask you to visualize the Eiffel Tower or Mickey Mouse, you could probably do so without problems. Since we know it is impossible to influence the physical world this way, does it not indicate that the 'pictures' in your imagination are purely subjective?

Magicians answer this objection by insisting that

the Astral Light, or Astral Plane – their world by the imagination – is almost infinitely plastic by nature. That is to say, it is far more malleable than the physical world and consequently shapes itself to any influence. This characteristic means that much of what is experienced when one 'enters' the Astral (e.g. sinks into a daydream) is subjective in origin, but the 'material' from which it is created, the essence of the Plane itself, is objective. Furthermore, if you can train yourself to 'travel' within the Astral without imposing personal influence, you will enter an environment that is wholly objective, as real and, in a curious way, as 'physical' as the familiar world of matter.

According to this thesis, the Self in the diagrams on page 219 is a Janus-headed entity capable of looking two ways at once: into the physical world in one 'direction', into the Astral Plane in another. The reality tone of each is largely a matter of concentration and focus. When, for example, you are absorbed in playing soccer or completing a commando assault course, your awareness of the world inside your head (the Astral Plane) is non-existent. By contrast, perception of external reality dims should you become involved in a gripping fantasy. When you dream, it disappears altogether.

(Focus also seems to be what makes the difference between a fleeting daydream and a full-blown trance experience. Occultists hold they are both aspects of the Astral Light, differing areas of a single spectrum. This has led to the conviction that the full-blown trances of early shamanism – which sometimes involve loss of conscious control – are unnecessary to achieve magical results. A trained imagination, exercised in the full waking state, will do the trick just as well.)

All of which is very well as theory, but is it true? Do we have any evidence to suggest the world of the imagination, so long considered the most ephemeral of human experiences, is actually an objective reality? The unsettling answer is yes.

The anthropologist Michael Harner is now an experienced shaman involved in investigating shamanic techniques and teaching shamanic practice. How he found the shamanic way is a fascinating story with elements of importance to our present study. In 1959, Harner was invited by the American Museum of Natural History to undertake a field study of the Conibo Indians, a forest people living in the Ucayali River region of the Peruvian Amazon. The study itself took place in 1960 and 1961.

After a year living among the Conibo, Harner found his hosts reluctant to discuss their religious beliefs, the supernatural or their magical practices. Eventually he was told that if he really wished to learn, he would have to take the sacred shamanic drink made from the 'soul vine' *ayahuasca*. He was, however, warned that this could lead to a very frightening experience.

According to Lyall Watson, who sampled *ayahuasca* in Brazil, it is a woody vine which contains a number of alkaloids with hallucinogenic properties – one of which has been called 'telepatin' because it seems to turn those around you to glass, so that you can see through their bodies and read their minds. Harner experienced something rather different when he took it, however.

A Conibo elder named Tomás collected enough *ayahuasca* and *cawa* leaves to fill a fifteen-gallon pot and boiled them all afternoon until only about a quart of dark green liquid was left. This he bottled and left to cool.

As night fell, the Indians muzzled their dogs and instructed the children of the village to be quiet since any intrusive sounds could send mad a person who has drunk *ayahuasca*. In the firelight, Harner was offered a gourd cup containing about a third of the bottle of liquid. He felt, he says, like Socrates accepting the hemlock, but drank it down.[183]

Lying on a bamboo platform under the thatched roof of the communal house, he became aware of faint traceries of light which burst into brilliant colours, then the distant sound of a waterfall which grew increasingly strong until it filled his ears.

Overhead the faint lines became brighter and gradually interlaced to form a canopy resembling a geometric mosaic of stained glass. The bright violet hues formed an ever-expanding roof above me. Within this celestial cavern, I heard the sound of water grow louder and I could see dim figures engaged in shadowy movements. As my eyes seemed to adjust to the gloom, the moving scene resolved itself into something resembling a huge fun house, a supernatural carnival of demons. In the centre, presiding over the activities and looking directly at me, was a gigantic, grinning crocodilian head, from whose cavernous jaws gushed a torrential flood of water.[184]

Visions of two strange boats followed, combining to form a sort of Viking longship with a square sail. He became conscious of singing, the most beautiful he had ever heard. He saw bird-headed people on the longship, like the gods of Ancient Egypt.

As predicted, the experience became frightening. Harner felt as if his soul was being drawn from his body to be carried away on the boat. As this happened, a sort of numbness crept through him, as if he were turning to stone. It required an enormous effort to keep his heart beating and he became convinced he was going to die.

As the conviction of death increased, he found he

was in communication with giant reptilian dragon creatures, shiny and black with short pterodactyl-like wings and huge whale bodies. They had, they explained, come from Outer Space and had flown to Earth to escape an enemy. It was they who had created the myriad of terrestrial life-forms in order to hide themselves. Thus they now lived in everything, including humanity and could communicate from the depths of the human mind.

Only moments from death, Harner managed to ask the Indians for medicine and they hurried to prepare an antidote which eased his condition, but did not stop the visions. He seemed to travel beyond the galaxy and conversed with grinning demons.

Harner's experience ended in sleep and when he awoke, the visions had ended. Despite his scientific training, he found himself taking them seriously – so seriously that he considered himself in grave danger because the dragon creatures had revealed information reserved for those about to die. He began to tell anyone who would listen, on the premise that sharing the information might make it less dangerous to him.

Among those he told were two American evangelists who were staying at a nearby missionary station. As he described his vision, they were struck by the similarity of its elements with the vision of St John the Divine as expressed in the New Testament Book of Revelation. Two passages in particular stood out for them. The first was:

> And the serpent cast out of his mouth water as a flood after the woman, that he might cause her to be carried away of the flood.[185]

This fragment, they thought, was close to Harner's experience of the 'grinning crocodilian head' which had also gushed water. The second passage, beginning with verse 7 of Chapter 12, was even closer:

> And there was war in heaven: Michael and his angels fought against the dragon; and the dragon fought and his angels.
>
> And prevailed not; neither was their place found any more in heaven.
>
> And the great dragon was cast out, that old serpent, called the Devil, and Satan, which deceiveth the whole world: he was cast out into the earth, and his angels were cast out with him.[186]

The missionaries were impressed by the fact that a drink of witch-doctor brew could help an atheistic anthropologist experience the same sort of revelation as one of the great saints. But there was, of course, the possibility of a rational explanation. Most people in our Western culture are exposed to biblical material in childhood, even where their upbringing is not overtly 'religious'. It seems entirely likely that Harner had absorbed some of the compelling imagery of Revelation and used it to create his own narcotically induced trance fantasy.

Lyall Watson somewhere suggests that Harner himself accepted this explanation for a time. If so, he did not hold to it for long. He was still experiencing unpleasant side-effects from taking the *ayahuasca* brew and so decided to seek out an expert on its effects, an old blind shaman who had used it many times to visit the spirit world. What happened when he did so was as weird as anything he had seen in his visions.

> I went to his hut ... and described my visions to him segment by segment. At first I told him only the highlights; thus, when I came to the dragon-like creatures, I skipped their arrival from space and only said, 'There were these giant black animals, something like great bats,

longer than the length of this house, who said that they
were the true masters of the world.' . . .

He stared up toward me with his sightless eyes and said
with a grin, 'Oh, they're always saying that. But they are
only the masters of Outer Darkness.' He waved his hand
casually towards the sky.

Harner was, in his own words, stunned. It was obvious
from his conversation that the world he had visited
was well known to the blind shaman from personal
experience. But this meant it could not be a fantasy
Harner had created using elements from Revelation or
any other source. It had to be an area of objective
reality open to exploration by those who took the drug.

This personal revelation would come as no surprise
to practising magicians who quickly find that pathworkings – their own drugless explorations of the
Astral Plane – show aspects that have to be objective
since they arise again and again in the reports of
different 'travellers' once specific 'areas' of the Plane
are reached. This is particularly noticeable in the
Qabalistic system where pathworkings associated
with the Tree of Life and the Major Arcana of the Tarot
contain so many objective elements that they are used
as convenient landmarks for newcomers.

22

THE PHYSICS OF SORCERY

Primitive shamans thought of the Otherworld they visited – what magicians would now call the Astral Plane – as a place apart. Even modern shamans tend to use the term *non-ordinary reality* to describe it,[187] as if it were somehow different from the world in which one eats fish and chips or takes a bus to the office.

I have my own reasons for believing that the Astral world of the visual imagination is actually a part of our familiar universe, forming a continuum with it, as in the diagrams on page 219, with the dividing lines not nearly so clear-cut as one might suppose.

Several years ago, I was engaged in a ritual magical operation in the company of a psychic who had no experience of magical theory or practice. The operation was almost entirely astral – that is to say, except for a few preliminary gestures, it was carried out in my imagination – a technique not uncommon for this type of work. No words were spoken aloud, nor was the other person involved made aware at any time of what I was attempting.

Despite this, when I came to the preparation of the place of working, using the Pentagram Ritual described earlier, she asked at once if I had 'called anything up'. Still without giving any indication of what I was doing, I asked the reason for her question. She told me she was aware of four vast figures which had suddenly appeared at the cardinal quarters of the room.

When I asked her to describe them, she admitted – with some embarrassment – that they looked like the traditional description of archangels. Pressed for details, she was able to describe accurately, including colourings and backgrounds, the telesmatic figures I had been visualizing at the relevant point of the ceremony.

It is, of course, possible that telepathy was involved here. Qualitative research, although less widely publicized than Rhine's statistical approach, has shown conclusively – and as long ago as the 1880s – that some subjects can receive good approximations of pictures aimed mentally towards them.[188] It has even been demonstrated that the content of a sleeping subject's dreams can be influenced in this way.

But to evoke telepathy as an explanation of my companion's ability to see my imagined angels really explains nothing, since the mechanism of telepathy is itself unknown. Besides, our 'magical' experience differed in nature from any telepathic sender/receiver experiment. In such experiments, the action (for both sender and receiver) is entirely inward: a mental image is 'sent' and mental impressions 'received'. In the case I have been describing, I was consciously attempting to visualize the figures as if they existed in the real, objective world . . . which is precisely where my companion saw them.[189] Furthermore, her description of the figures was wholly accurate and highly detailed. This is extremely rare in telepathic experiments; and the chances against experiencing it four times in succession are astronomical. It seems far more reasonable to assume any mental images somehow 'appeared' in the physical world, at least strongly enough for my companion to perceive them.

This curious 'objectivity' of an imagined image is completely in line with W. E. Butler's description of magical training in which small objects, like the head of a rose, are visualized so vividly that they become real not only to the operator, but others may eventually be persuaded to see them as well. It also underlies Madame Alexandra David-Neel's experiment in *tulpa* creation, described earlier, where her little monk eventually became visible to others in her camp.

The 'spirits' evoked to visible appearance for the examiners of the Golden Dawn would have been done so as the result of visualization, since visualization was the approved method of evocation in that organization. Whatever the essential nature of spirits, it is clear that many of them have an imaginary aspect, so that here again we have an indication that a visualized image can take on a certain 'tangibility' in the world of matter. Sometimes, indeed, this tangibility is literal, as when Madame David-Neel was aware of a tactile sensation when she reached out for the fearsome Tibetan deity which had accompanied her visiting painter.

Perhaps it can actually become dangerous. *Something* savaged the conspirators at Jena and, given their culture and beliefs, we may be assured their minds were filled with imaginings of the most horrific demons. Earlier, we made the tentative suggestion that magic might be a system designed to create hallucinations. It may be that such 'hallucinations' can become far more solid than science believes.

(I might mention in parenthesis one further example which may be of relevance to the present thesis. A colleague of mine was involved in the use of 'magic

squares' taken from the Abra-Melin system of conjuration. Briefly, each square is associated with a particular
'demon' believed to have specific abilities. A psychic
– the same woman who had shown herself capable of
seeing my angelic visualizations – was able accurately
to describe several entities linked to the Abra-Melin
squares, even though neither my colleague nor I were
aware of their nature at the time. Her descriptions
tallied with the traditional associations which were
checked out following the experiment.

While this procedure leaves a great deal to be desired
in terms of controls and scientific method, the results
have interesting implications if taken at face value.
One must wonder, for example, whether the little
'demons' seen by the psychic were totally independent, pre-existent natural entities or permanent *tulpas*
established by generations of magicians visualizing the
same associations with the same squares.[190]

The notion, which has arisen again and again in the
present work, that visualized images can somehow
appear as part of the physical world, leaves the world
of the imagination theoretically subject to investigation by the discipline of physics. That is to say, if
visualized images are, or can become, fully objective
then they must be composed of matter – albeit
possibly an unusual type of matter – just like everything else.

Here, however, we run into an immediate problem
since the very concept of 'matter' is more or less
outdated in modern physics, except as an intellectual
convenience. In the early years of the twentieth
century, Einstein showed matter could be viewed as an
expression of energy. Heisenberg went on to demonstrate, with his famous Uncertainty Principle, that
there was no ultimate solidity in matter at all – the

entire manifest universe was founded on nothing more than a statistical probability.

As a result, physicists have long since abandoned the Victorian approach to matter (which suggested that, given time, the whole universe could be weighed and measured) in favour of the investigation of particles, sub-atomic 'packets' of energy which sometimes behave almost as oddly as the physicists themselves.

By 1931, the problems of the new physics had become acute. In an attempt to reconcile certain difficulties arising from an attempt to unify Einstein's relativity theory with Schrödinger's wave mechanics, Paul Dirac of Cambridge proposed that space was not really empty at all, but filled with negative electrons – this is, electrons displaying negative energy and mass. What he was talking about was the substance of ghosts, something which existed but was, by definition, virtually impossible to detect. Had he not been a Nobel Prize-winning physicist, it is doubtful that the scientific community would have taken so outlandish a theory seriously.

Dirac labelled this negative particle the anti-electron and predicted it would be extremely short-lived, since there was a tendency for it to be annihilated in collision with a positive electron.

When first propounded, this theory sounded so outlandish that Neils Bohr suggested it might be used to fascinate elephants in order to facilitate their humane capture. Nonetheless, within a year of publication, cosmic ray tracks in the bubble-chamber of the California Institute of Technology convinced the physicist Carl D. Anderson that he had stumbled on a new type of electron which he called a *positron*. The particle turned out to be identical in every way to Dirac's predicted anti-electron.

It was the opening of the floodgates. Within a relatively short period of years, physicists discovered anti-particles corresponding with every known particle. Eventually Dr Edward Teller, the scientist who, more than any other, made the hydrogen bomb possible, was constructing a broad theory of anti-matter, a whole negative universe which, if it came into contact with our (positive) cosmos would result in a gigantic explosion. The concept was discussed within the scientific community, then introduced to the general public by the mischievous Dr Harold P. Furth in the November 1956 edition of the *New Yorker*:

> Well up beyond the tropostrata
> There is a region stark and stellar
> Where, on a streak of anti-matter,
> Lived Dr Edward Anti-Teller
>
> Remote from Fusion's origin,
> He lived unguessed and unawares
> With all his anti-kith and kin,
> And kept macassars on his chairs.
>
> One morning, idling by the sea,
> He spied a tin of monstrous girth
> That bore three letters: A.E.C.
> Out stepped a visitor from Earth.
>
> Then, shouting gladly o'er the sands,
> Met two who in their alien ways
> Were like lentils. Their right hands
> Clasped . . . the rest was gamma rays.

It was a magnificent exposition of the anti-matter theory which showed, though no one pointed it out at the time, that immaterial entities like spirits and certain of the effects of magic were no more unlikely than the world the physicists were actively investigating. The question was, 'Could it be the *same* world?'

There is no suggestion at all that spirits, or the rolling billows of the Astral Light, are actually composed of anti-matter. Whatever else magicians may experience, it is not instant annihilation from contact with their stock-in-trade. But if anti-particles do not fit the bill, there may be other, less dangerous particles which do. An early hint of their existence came at the 1932 Copenhagen Conference on Nuclear Physics.

There, contrary to their public image of sober-sided academics, the scientists mounted a playlet based (very loosely!) on Goethe's *Faust* during which Mephistopheles declared:

> Beware, beware, of Reason and of Science,
> Man's highest powers, unholy in alliance.
> You'll let yourself, through dazzling witchcraft yield
> To weird temptations of the quantum field.

At which point Gretchen entered singing:

> My rest-mass is zero
> My charge is the same
> You are my hero
> *Neutrino's* my name!

Faust was played by Wolfgang Pauli, one of the foremost nuclear physicists in the world.[191] He was the focus of the humour on account of his prediction, two years earlier, of a new particle, the neutrino, with very curious properties . . . or, rather, lack of them.

It was, Pauli suggested, the most elusive of all particles, having virtually no characteristics by which it could be detected. It had neither mass, electric charge, nor magnetic field. It was not subject to gravity, nor influenced by the electrical or magnetic fields of any other particles with which it came in contact. Accordingly, a neutrino could pass through any solid body – even a solid body as large as a planet – as if it were empty space. The only thing that could stop it was a head-on collision with another neutrino: and the chances against that happening were estimated at ten thousand million to one.

Long though these odds were, it seemed there were enough neutrinos about to ensure the occasional collision actually did occur, so that in 1956 the scientists F. Reines and C. Cowan eventually detected one at the Atomic Energy Commission's nuclear reactor on the Savannah River. However Faustian his idea, Pauli was proven justified: neutrinos definitely existed.

They do not, however, exist in the way that many other known particles exist. They resemble nothing more closely than the building-blocks of ghosts in their lack of gross physical characteristics. This resemblance was not lost on scientists themselves, who began to speculate on the existence of other particles which, if they did not actually define ghosts, might at least provide the more respectable 'missing link' between matter and mind.

Since it is the fundamental thesis of magic that a link between matter and mind is an experiential fact, such scientific speculation must be of considerable interest to every thoughtful magician. Nowhere has it been more clearly expressed than in the work of the eminent astronomer V. A. Firsoff, who suggested in 1967 that mind was a 'universal entity or interaction' of the same order as electricity or gravitation. In other words, mind was neither an illusion nor something apart from the physical universe, but an aspect of it, exactly as our spectrum diagrams on page 219, predict.

Firsoff went on to speculate that, within this model, there had to exist a 'modulus of transformation' perhaps similar, and certainly analogous, to Einstein's famous energy/matter transformation, $e = mc^2$. In such a transformation, Firsoff argued, 'mind-stuff' could be equated with other entities of the physical world.

As Pauli had done more than thirty years earlier, Firsoff predicted the existence of a new particle, the *mindon*, as the elementary aspect of 'mind-stuff'. Mindon properties would be very similar to those of the already confirmed neutrino.

Firsoff's insights into the nature of an entity composed of mindons – or, for that matter, neutrinos – are fascinating to anyone with an interest in paranormal research or the mysteries of magic. The physical universe of planets, asteroids and meteors would scarcely exist, appearing at best as 'thin patches of mist'. Even suns would be only barely visible, in relation to their own neutrino emissions.

He felt the brain of such an entity might deduce our existence only from secondary effects and would find confirmation difficult since humanity would naturally elude such (neutrino/mindon) instruments at the entity's disposal.

But this latter conclusion obviously relates only to our physical bodies which, as a matter of experience, comprise only part of the total human being. The mindon entity would surely be aware of the human psyche (itself composed of mindons, according to Firsoff's own theory) and might, if it managed to communicate, accept the psyche's perception of itself as having a physical body.

At this level, one might envisage the growth of an essentially religious belief structure, in which the 'immaterial' body was one of the mysteries of existence.

Firsoff has pointed out that our physical universe is no 'truer' than that of the neutrino, only rather more familiar. We now know that neutrinos exist, but exist in a different kind of space and are governed by different laws. Einstein's calculations show that the speed of light is an absolute in the physical universe: it is simply impossible for anything to travel faster. Except, Firsoff suggests, neutrinos which, since they are not subject to electro-magnetic or gravitational fields, may not be bound by any speed limits either. They may, in fact, have their own, different, time.

Despite the fact that these ideas emanate from a scientist and not from a magician, they have a haunting familiarity for every occultist. Projectors of the astral body – believed by many to consist of 'mind-stuff' – are familiar with the phenomenon of instantaneous travel, time distortion and the illusory quality of the physical world.

Says Firsoff:

> From our . . . analysis of mental entities, it appears that they have no definite locus in so-called 'physical' or, better, gravi-electromagnetic, space, in which respect they resemble a neutrino or, for that matter, a fast electron. This already suggests a special kind of mental space governed by different laws, which is further corroborated by the parapsychological experiments made at Duke University and elsewhere . . .

Paracelsus or Lévi could not have put it better.

CHAPTER
23

FORGOTTEN SECRET

Colin Wilson opened one of his most extraordinary works[192] with the words:

> Primitive man believed the world was full of unseen forces: the *orenda* (spirit force) of the American Indians, the *huaca* of the ancient Peruvians. The Age of Reason said that these forces had only ever existed in man's imagination . . .

Any analysis of magic compels agreement with the conclusions of the Age of Reason. Occult forces *have* only ever existed in humanity's imagination. But behind this statement lies a forgotten secret – the actual nature of imagination.

There is substantial evidence, much of which has already been presented in this book, for the thesis that the human mind can directly influence objective, physical reality. Magic, as practised for 40,000 years or more, appears to comprise a body of techniques aimed at systemizing this influence and placing it under conscious control. Almost without exception, the techniques involve the use of the visual imagination.

But if the imagination can act on what we have long called the 'objective' world, then it would seem reasonable to suggest imagination shares that same objectivity and exists, as Firsoff says, in the same way as gravitation or electricity. Occultists postulate a continuum, with the experienced world of imagination an objective part of nature, albeit one which can be influenced so easily that its essential nature can easily be thought subjective. Control of the imagination, say the magicians, is everything. Anything done there, in proper order, will eventually reflect on our more familiar physical environment.

This is difficult stuff for the modern mind to comprehend because it is so alien to our present way of thinking. According to one theory, our ancestors – and perhaps some present-day primitives – may have found it easier, since the reality of the imagination was, to them, a matter of direct experience.

The theory was published in the middle 1970s[193] by Dr Julian Jaynes who argued that consciousness itself is a very recent evolutionary development, no more than a few thousand years old and consequently something which has arisen well within historical times. Lacking consciousness, the individual was unable to withdraw inwards, experience what we recognize as subjective states, create pictures in the mind. This whole world of introspection simply did not exist. And since, according to Jaynes, it did not come into being much before 1000 BC, there should be some indications in ancient literature that humanity then did not think as we do now . . . indeed, hardly thought at all.

To support this theory, Jaynes embarked on an analysis of ancient literature and was satisfied he had found the evidence he was looking for. In the *Iliad*, for example, Homer's characters show no sign of reflection or any awareness whatsoever of inner states. They were individuals of action and in their actions they were the puppets of the gods.

It is difficult to argue with this. Classical literature is chock-a-block with divine interventions and it is rare indeed for any mere mortal to defy the archetypal orders. But Jaynes, as a twentieth-century scientist, does not accept that the gods are supernatural beings. He believes that what were thought of as messages from on high were actually right-brain hallucinations communicated across the rainbow bridge of the *corpus callosum* to the awareness seated in the left-brain hemisphere.

Consequently, early humanity lived in a world where tangible experience and hallucination inter-mingled almost every waking moment *and where one was indistinguishable from the other*. Thus, when 'the gods' directed a particular course of action, there was no argument and precious little resistance: it was simply carried out. Humanity lived in a magical world where illusion was inextricably interwoven with real-ity, where one was just as likely to meet an elf as an elephant and a left turn at a sacred grove could carry you to fairyland.

If Jaynes is correct, it was in this world that shamanic techniques were first developed. Particularly observant individuals must have come to realize that certain experiences and environments were more *controllable* than others, more malleable, more plas-tic; and that when control was exerted effectively, a sort of 'knock-on' effect occurred, influencing other matters which were far more difficult to handle directly.

But it is important to point out that Jaynes' notion of right-brain hallucination is an orthodox scientist's interpretation of the evidence. The shamans them-selves would have seen the situation differently. For them, the fairylands and gods were always real, other worlds and alien beings which were a matter of everyday experience. And as the evolutionary shift in humanity's mentation occurred – approximately three thousand years ago, according to Jaynes – what really came about was a change of *perception*. We began, inexorably, to lose the special 'sight' that had for so long permitted us easy access to other worlds and easy communication with spirit beings.

The 'sight' did not disappear completely. Rather it changed character, becoming nebulous and inward. It seemed less real and eventually, in the fullness of time, it came to be considered *as* less real.

Oddly, there is substantial evidence for another, far less controversial, change in human perception at about the time Jaynes argues that we stopped experiencing gods and spirits as external. This was a change in the perception of colour. In 1887, the scholarly historian and Orientalist Max Müller quoted classical sources[194] to support the thesis that our present range of colour perception is far more recent than people imagine. Aristotle and Xenophanes were aware of a spectrum of only three colours: red, yellow and purple. Democritus knew of only four . . . but two of these were black and white. Homer's compelling phrase, 'the wine-dark sea', actually makes no sense at all unless the writer's perception was very different from our own.

Against this background, it seems reasonable to suggest that prehistoric and early historical humanity perceived the world differently to the way we do today; and it would be chauvinistic to claim their perception was any less valid than our own.

From the viewpoint of modern magical practice, today's occultist would, of course, claim that the ancients had a direct, objective perception of the (equally objective) Astral Plane. Their sensory apparatus, or possibly the structure of their brains, enabled them to explore its environment and communicate with its inhabitants in a way no longer possible today.

This easy ability did not, of course, disappear in an instant. It is much more likely that it faded gradually and erratically, so that certain individuals retained the 'sight' while others did not. Such individuals would have become shamans, specialists in a talent that was once the common possession of humanity. As time went on, even the shamans must have found the exercise of their talent more difficult and would have had to stimulate it with essentially artificial techniques like drumming, dancing and drugs.

From this, it can be seen that certain states – now usually referred to as 'trance' – actually represent a regression to the primaeval form of perception. It is a regression which may open doorways not, as modern scientists believe, on subjective states, but on objective dimensions all too familiar to our distant ancestors.

The primeval perception was so vivid that its reality was never questioned. Today, only trance can generate the same degree of 'reality tone'. But it is easily forgotten that the only difference between trance and the exercise of imagination is the apparent objectivity of the experience. Trance visions tend to present themselves as 'real' and 'objective' (even if we are perfectly convinced they are not) while imagination, which is generally less vivid, does not. Yet the two are no more than different aspects of the same spectrum. Even outside of magical practice and paranormal phenomena, the objective nature of imagination can be clearly demonstrated. Nikola Tesla, the inventor of alternating current, showed himself capable of building machinery in his imagination, setting it to work, then leaving it to run for several weeks before dismantling it to discover the degree of wear on its component parts.

Despite this, the lack of inherent reality tone has led to a gradual devaluation of imagination until, within the body of our own culture, it is perceived as the ultimate yardstick of unreality. When a friend claims to have seen a ghost, we say it was 'only' his imagination and dismiss his report as worthless. Even psychosomatic illness carries a pejorative 'only imagination' label in the public perception, as if this somehow made the pain less real.

Historically, the devaluation has gone to extremes. Nowhere is this so evident than in the case of Franz Anton Mesmer, who gave his name to the technique of mesmerism, now often thought of (incorrectly) as synonymous with hypnosis.

Mesmer was born to wealthy parents in Switzerland in 1734. At the age of thirty-two, he obtained his degree at the University of Vienna with a Latin thesis on *The Influence of the Planets on the Human Body*. It was not, despite the title, entirely astrological. Mesmer postulated a sort of universal ether or fluid energy[195] subject to tides caused by the movements of the planets. It was these tides, he believed, which maintained human health. Where there was a blockage in the energy, sickness resulted.

A Jesuit professor interested in Mesmer's theories discovered it was possible to cure stomach cramps by the application of a magnet and suggested to Mesmer that the magnet was actually influencing his 'etheric fluid' in its circulation through the body. Mesmer experimented and found this seemed to be true.

By this time, Mesmer had embarked on his career as

a physician, using what were, in their day, orthodox medical techniques like the administration of antimony and leeching. One day while bleeding a patient, he observed that as he approached closer to the patient the blood-flow increased, while it decreased when he moved away. He came to the conclusion that his own body was acting like a magnet on the blood of the patient. In 1775, he published a pamphlet on his discoveries in which he coined the term 'animal magnetism'.

His theories impressed potential patients far more than his medical colleagues who, by and large, considered him a quack and satirized him savagely. Nonetheless, he got results; and when he managed to cure a member of the aristocracy of chronic spasms, his fame spread.

Mesmer considered that 'animal magnetism' and the more familiar metallic variety were one and the same, and consequently devised some spectacular apparatus to amplify and conduct the energy. He created an enormous wooden tub, half filled with iron filings and water into which were sunk jars containing magnets and water. From these jars emerged L-shaped metal rods to conduct the magnetism into Mesmer's patients.

Treatment sessions were often theatrical. Patients would sit holding the rods in a dim light while a hidden orchestra played emotional music. Then, at the critical moment, Mesmer himself would appear, dressed in spectacular robes and holding a magnetic wand. It was not unusual for patients to fall into convulsions. Nor was it unusual for them to emerge from these fits cured.

Criticism continued to grow. It was increasingly suggested that Mesmer was using 'magnetic passes' as an excuse to caress his female patients in intimate places. Eventually he had a call from the Morality Police. Mesmer fled Vienna for Paris where he established a practice that proved equally successful. The King offered him a pension, he taught his methods to scores of enthusiastic pupils, and his followers established a 'magnetic company' with funds in excess of 350,000 golden louis.

The State Medical College was noticeably less enthusiastic and set up a Commission of Inquiry in 1784. The good doctors watched the antics of the magnetizers and their patients, and eventually reported there was nothing in Mesmer's results that could not be explained by imagination. It was a striking testament to the devaluation of imagination that this was all that was required to ruin Mesmer, who ended his days in Prussia, having abandoned the practice of medicine for several years.

The incredible thing about this case was that after early incredulity, no one – not even the medical establishment – doubted the validity of Mesmer's cures. Only the reality of his method was in question. And having dismissed his method as imaginary, it never occurred to the members of the Medical College Commission to recommend that if imagination alone had shown such amazing curative powers, then imaginative techniques should become part of the physician's armoury.

This blindness to the results obtained by the application of imagination has dogged the medical profession ever since, although there is some indication that the prejudice may now be breaking down under the weight of substantial evidence that manipulation of the imagination is capable of curing the incurable.

Outside of medicine, however, the power of the imagination remains beyond the pale of scientific investigation. It continues to be the sole prerogative of the shaman and the magician, whose results, like those of Mesmer, are airily dismissed.

24

SPIRIT WOLF

If Dr Jaynes is correct, the woman who crawled into the Altamira cave to paint her pictures may not have been conscious in the way that we are. But she had an awareness of another world, a world which her shamanic counterparts in the wilds of modern Esalen would call 'non-ordinary reality'. It is important to remember that this vivid and objective Otherworld was the same area of reality we now experience as the world of our imagination. The only difference in Ice Age times was that it would have been far easier to see it as an aspect of physical reality. In doing so, our Cro-Magnon woman considered this world so important that she ignored the savage pressures of a brutal existence to capture its images on the cavern wall.

Perhaps she only wanted to commemorate it, although this is frankly unlikely. Perhaps she created the images in order to educate others, although this too is unlikely – awareness of the Otherworld was more accessible then than it is now. Perhaps she wished to control it, in the hope of improving the lot of her tribe or herself. Or perhaps she was simply acting under orders, as Homer's characters acted under orders from 'the gods', or modern mediums sometimes act under orders from their 'spirit guides'.

Either way, the likelihood is that this ancient artist

was engaged in an act of magic, a manipulation of her mental processes in order to influence events in the mundane world. This would not have been the crude hunting-magic postulated by the anthropologists, but something far more subtle and wide-ranging. Since the entities with which she communicated were what we would now call archetypal, it may even have been concerned with the evolution of the human race. Certainly such entities, masquerading as angels, hidden masters, human ancestors or God Almighty, frequently claim the evolution of the human race to be their prime concern.

The two aspects of magical practice – communication with spirits and manipulation of outer events through inward disciplines – are closely inter-linked. There is substantial, even overwhelming, evidence that many magical techniques were originally dictated by bodiless intelligences. Indeed, there is one school of thought that holds all magical practice ultimately derives from Otherworld information.

But whatever about information, the Ice Age shamans certainly derived personal power from their experience of the Otherworld. Cave paintings show masked and antlered human figures. All of Ice Age humanity dressed in hides and furs, but this was something different: an attempt to mimic the animal itself. It was a mundane manifestation of an Other-world adventure, an indication that the sorcerer had met and befriended his or her power animal.

Michael Harner writes:

The connectedness between humans and the animal world is very basic in shamanism, with the shaman utilizing his knowledge and methods to participate in the power of that world. Through his guardian spirit or power animal, the shaman connects with the power of the animal world, the mammals, birds, fish and other beings. The shaman has to have a particular guardian in order to do his work, and his guardian helps him in certain special ways.[196]

Power animals are a particularly interesting aspect of shamanism since the tribal myths of humanity have almost universally tended to attribute certain characteristics to whole animal species – coyotes were seen as essential mischievous, serpents wise, lions brave and so on. This led to the personification of a species in a single individual. Indian mythologies throughout the Americas are filled with references to the adventures of Coyote, Raven, Bear, Wolf, Eagle, Snake and many others, each one standing for an entire genus. It was these individuals, the guardian spirits of their breed, with whom the shaman sought to make contact.

The choice of spirit was never arbitrary, for it was believed that a link with a particular animal was already there, forged by the nature of the shaman, even though the shaman might not be aware of it. Thus the spirit would often make itself known, in visions or dreams, before the shaman practised those techniques which called it to him.

Often these techniques involved dance. After several minutes of preliminaries, the shaman would begin to *dance her animal*, a sort of freeform movement in which she would attempt intuitively to feel the presence, nature and emotions of her animal guardian. Once she sensed the spirit, she would typically begin to mimic its movements in her dance, thus increasing the linkage. When the animal appeared, she would make it welcome and invite it to remain within her body.

This calling of the beasts, creatures of myth and mind-stuff, had many benefits. Harner says:

Shamans have long felt that the power of the guardian or tutelary spirit make one resistant to illness. The reason is simple: it provides a *power-full* body that resists the intrusion of external forces. . .

A power animal or guardian spirit, as I first learned among the Jivaro, not only increases one's physical energy and ability to resist contagious disease, but also increases one's mental alertness and self-confidence. The power even makes it difficult for one to lie.[197]

This shamanic linkage with power animals was almost certainly the foundation of the tribal totems of pre-history, where whole groupings of humanity felt themselves to be under the protection of a specific spirit animal. Tribal shamans would maintain the special relationship with Coyote or Bear, but the entire tribe would benefit.

When the shaman entered non-ordinary reality to dance the animal, he or she would often become temporarily possessed by it, so that the dance was no longer mime or pretence, but the manifestation of the (imaginary) spirit form in a physical human body. This led naturally on to the concept of *were* animals and lycanthropy, the belief – which to many tribes was a matter of simple experience – that certain individuals could shape-shift and *become* the animal concerned. Since a popular totem was the wolf, ubiquitous throughout Europe, it is scarcely surprising that the tradition of the werewolf has survived to the present day.

As a tradition it has always been extraordinarily widespread. Danish, Gothic, Old Norman, Serbian, Slovak, Russian, Greek, Romanian, French, German, Slavic . . . indeed every Indo-European language with-out exception had its own word for, and myth of, the werewolf. Although the roots were prehistoric, wolf

totems were a part of Graeco-Roman minority wor-
ship: Virgil drew on the practice to make his claim that
the first werewolf was Moeris, husband of the Fate
Goddess from whom he learned the secrets of magic
and necromancy.

The tradition strengthened in the early Middle Ages
with the spread of the wolf clans who worshipped their
totemic gods in a manner that would not have been
entirely out of place in the Ice Age.

The religious origins of the werewolf tradition are
indicated by the term lycanthropy itself which derives
from Apollo Lycaeus, the god worshipped in Socrates'
Lyceum. But as the years went by, the practice of
totemic shape-shifting became, in the so-called
civilized communities at least, increasingly occult and
feared. About AD 1000, the term werewolf became
synonymous with 'outlaw'. Soon those suspected of
the practice were hunted down for persecution, as in
the case of the werewolf captured in 1598 by the
Inquisition, who claimed he was possessed by a
demon. He seems to have been tortured to death,
forced to drink huge quantities of water until his
stomach ruptured.

Some scholars[198] have suggested that the entirely
negative werewolf tradition was the result of Christian
persecution of the old wolf clans and ecclesiastical
distortion of their true nature. While this may well
have been an element in the process, it is also true to
say that, stripped of its shamanic safeguards, the
calling of the beasts can sometimes lead to frightening
results, as the travel writer W. B. Seabrook reported.

Prior to World War Two, Seabrook was in a flat
overlooking Times Square in New York as part of a
small group which included a career diplomat and a
Russian émigré he called Magda. They were engaged

in a curious experiment with the Chinese *I Ching*.

The *I Ching*, sometimes claimed to be the oldest book in the world, is a work based on the subdivision of phenomena into negative and positive forces called *yin* and *yang*, the current state of which is read through the development of six-lined figures known as hexagrams.

The hexagrams have a long, disreputable history in that they sprang from a very ancient form of fortune-telling: the Tortoise-Shell Oracle. In China, from a time dating back into prehistory, tortoise-shells were heated until they cracked and the patterns interpreted as indicators of the future.

In time the cracks became stylized into three-lined figures, known as trigrams which were composed of broken (yin) and unbroken (yang) lines. Diviners eventually began to study trigram patterns in their own right, divorced from the original tortoise-shell rituals.

Some time prior to 1150 BC (the actual date is uncertain), a provincial noble named Wen fell foul of the Emperor, who had him thrown into prison. Wen turned to intellectual pursuits to fill his days and began to assign definitive meanings to the trigrams already widely in use for divination. But he broke with tradition by combining them into six-lined figures (hexagrams) and adding his own brief commentary, called a Judgement, to each.

On his release, Wen led a rebellion which eventually overthrew the Emperor, but died before he could seize the throne. His son, the Duke of Chou, consolidated the victory and founded a new dynasty. Scholars have awarded Wen the posthumous title of King.

The Duke of Chou finished his father's work by adding his own commentaries on the individual lines

1 Creative	2 Receptive	3 Difficulty at Beginning	4 Youthful Folly
5 Waiting for Nourishment	6 Conflict	7 The Army	8 Holding Together
9 Taming Power of the Small	10 Treading	11 Peace	12 Standstill
13 Fellowship with Men	14 Possession in Great Measure	15 Modesty	16 Enthusiasm
17 Following	18 Work on what has been Spoiled	19 Approach	20 Contemplation
21 Biting Through	22 Grace	23 Splitting Apart	24 Turning Point
25 Unexpected	26 Taming Power of the Great	27 Providing Nourishment	28 Preponderance of the Great
29 Abysmal	30 Clinging Fire	31 Influence	32 Duration
33 Retreat	34 Power of the Great	35 Progress	36 Darkening of the Light
37 The Family	38 Opposition	39 Obstruction	40 Deliverance
41 Decrease	42 Increase	43 Breakthrough	44 Coming to Meet
45 Gathering Together	46 Pushing Upward	47 Exhaustion	48 The Well
49 Revolution	50 The Cauldron	51 The Arousing	52 Keeping Still
53 Gradual Progress	54 Marrying Maiden	55 Abundance	56 The Wanderer
57 The Gentle	58 The Joyous	59 Dispersion	60 Limitation
61 Inner Truth	62 Preponderance of the Small	63 After Completion	64 Before Completion

I Ching *hexagrams*.

of the hexagrams. The completed work became known as the 'Changes of Chou' (*Chou I*) or, more simply, the 'Book of Changes' (*I Ching*).

Today's version of the book contains a total of sixty-four hexagrams, each of which has a different interpretation (see previous page). But each line of each hexagram is also capable of interpretation. This is, however, only done when it is thought the lines contain so much 'tension' that they are about to change into their opposites. Once they do so, they produce a new hexagram which is interpreted in the context of the original. The oracle is capable of delivering more than four thousand answers and is generally used as a system of divination. Seabrook's party were, however, using it differently, as something called an 'astral doorway'.

Astral doorways are special symbols which, when properly manipulated, allow access to those areas of the visual imagination where its objectivity is most apparent. In many ways they are the keys to a modern shamanic journey. By using them, a practitioner may make contact with, for example, the spirits of the Element of Fire, or the powers of a particular Path on the Qabalistic Tree of Life.[199]

The best-known doorways in the Western Esoteric Tradition are the geometric Tattva symbols used in the Golden Dawn, and the Major Arcana of the ubiquitous Tarot pack. But the *I Ching* hexagrams can also be used as doorways. The technique is to create a hexagram in exactly the same way it would be drawn for divination, then visualize it on a closed wooden door. This picture is held in the mind until the door opens of its own accord, at which point the practitioner 'steps through' by an act of imagination into the visionary picture revealed beyond.

In the flat above Times Square, it was the Russian émigré Magda who decided to use the *I Ching* doorway. The hexagram she drew was No. 49, which carries the following interpretation:

Ko/Revolution (Molting)

above TUI THE JOYOUS, LAKE
below LI THE CLINGING, FIRE

> The Chinese character for this hexagram means in its original sense an animal's pelt, which is changed in the course of the year by molting. From this the word is carried over to apply to the 'moltings' in political life, the great revolutions connected with changes of governments.
> The two trigrams making up the hexagram are . . . the two daughters, Li and Tui . . . here the younger daughter is above. The influences are in actual conflict and the forces combat each other like fire and water (lake), each trying to destroy the other. Hence the idea of revolution.[200]

The use of the hexagram as a doorway seems to have enabled Magda to tap into a primitive stratum of her objective imagination, for after a moment she was able to tell her companions that she was lying naked 'except for a fur coat' in the snow, then that it was moonlight and she was running through the snow at great speed.

Seabrook recalls that her face took on a feral appearance and she began to show indications of aggression and distress. Oblivious to her surroundings, she howled like a wolf. When the men attempted to wake her, she snarled, snapped and bit at them fiercely. She was physically a strong woman and it was quite a time before they could overpower her and get her out of trance. She had been temporarily possessed by a spirit wolf (or possibly by the spirit

Wolf) exactly like the primitive shamans who followed the wolf totem.

One of the most interesting aspects of this little case-study is that neither Magda nor her companions were magicians. (Seabrook claimed to be a cynic about esoteric matters, although it is obvious from many of his books that the occult held a real fascination for him).[201] No one present knew what to expect and all, according to Seabrook, were astonished by what did actually occur.

In such circumstances, it seems clear that even an untrained novice can stumble into the world of the objective imagination by the mechanical application of relatively simple techniques. This is quite a disturbing realization, but not, perhaps, quite so disturbing as certain other factors which will emerge as we continue our analysis of magic. In particular, some of the evidence appears to point towards the possibility that even if we take great care to avoid contact with the Otherworld, this is no guarantee at all that the Otherworld will leave us alone.

25

INTRUSIONS

What are we to make of our magicians?

There are clear links between the experiment carried out by Benvenuto Cellini at the Collosseum and the disastrous ritual at Jena almost two hundred years later.

Cellini was not himself an occultist, but rather an adventurer filled with interest in life and prepared to try anything once. He was also a product of his culture and his time. He believed in magic in the same way that people today believe in the ozone layer: they may not have seen it or become aware of its effects, but they accept without question that it is there.

His Sicilian priest would have gone even further. As an initiate of the religious mysteries, he would have been possessed of a mindset which included a great many fundamentalist visualizations. His head contained the seraphim and cherubim . . . and a whole infernal hierarchy of devils. Chances are it was the devils which claimed most of his attention. In the sixteenth century, angels seemed remote, but the influence of Satan was obvious and widespread. Besides, as Cellini himself obviously suspected, demons were more useful. They could be commanded in the name of Jesus and would not be averse to doing dirty work, like bringing a man a woman for his pleasure – or finding treasure in a vineyard.

By 1715, the cultural picture had changed very little, if at all. German peasants like Gessner and Zenner accepted the reality of magic without question, as did almost all of their contemporaries. Their world, like Cellini's, was populated by spirits and devils. If this seems odd to us today, it is as well to remember such a worldview has been universally accepted throughout most of history. It was only in Victorian times that it began to break down; and then only in some parts of the world. The vast majority of humanity has always believed as Gessner did, as Cellini did. In context, it is our modern viewpoint that is odd.

The mental disposition of the conspirators would have been further reinforced by the grimoires they used. The black books were, without exception, filled with dark imagery. Sometimes these images were graphic and crude but evocative. More often they were the result of verbal descriptions; and all the more potent for that, since words can have a far more powerful influence on the human mind than any picture.

The *Lesser Key of Solomon the King*, one of the most popular grimoires, describes Baal, demon King of the East, as appearing with a human head, the head of a toad or the head of a cat . . . and sometimes all three at once. Valefor, an infernal duke, appears as a three-headed lion. Amon is a serpent-headed wolf who vomits flame. Sytry has a leopard's head and griffin's wings. Morax is a human-headed bull. And so on. It is almost a relief to read only that Ronobe, a great marquis and earl, 'appears in monstrous form'.

Such descriptions sound silly to modern ears, but that is because our culture has taught us, by and large, not to believe in demons. If we did, a fire-breathing wolf with the head of a serpent would be a very frightening prospect indeed. Certainly it frightened the old-time magicians, who went to enormous pains to ensure the spirits they evoked looked pleasant. The first conjuration of *The Lemegeton*, for example, opens with the words:

> I exorcise and command thee, O Spirit, by Him who spake it and was done, by the Most Holy and glorious Names ADONAI, EL, ELOHIM, ELOHE, ZEBAOTH, ELION, ESCHERCE, JAH, TETRAGRAMMATON, SADAI: do thou forthwith appear and shew thyself unto me, here before this circle, in a fair and human shape, without any deformity or horror . . .[202]

If, as now seems likely, we accept that spirits are, in some instances at least, the projected creations of the human mind, then the ancient grimoires were without doubt recipe books for some of the most fearsome *tulpas* ever released to plague unsuspecting humanity. And released they were, for while ceremonial magic contained numerous safety procedures, not all ceremonial magicians were as careful as they might have been. Some, like Cellini and his colleagues, left the circle of protection before all the evoked spirits had been licensed to depart. Some, like Weber, drew the circle on the ceiling where it could do little good.

The results of such carelessness were not always academic. Over and over we find evidence that the content of the human mind can escape to appear in the real world. Nor is this appearance always as nebulous as readers of Madame David-Neel might be led to believe. While touching the *tulpa* generated by her artist friend only caused a slight sensation, other projections seem to have taken on a real degree of solidity. This is clear from the works of many occultists, including Dion Fortune who wrote:

> I had received serious injury from someone . . . and I was
> sorely tempted to retaliate. Lying on my bed resting one
> afternoon, I was brooding over my resentment and while
> so brooding, drifted towards the borders of sleep. There
> came to my mind the thought of casting off all restraint
> and going berserk. The ancient Nordic myths rose before
> me and I thought of Fenris, the wolf-horror of the North.
> Immediately I felt a curious drawing-out sensation from
> my solar plexus, and there materialised beside me on the
> bed a large wolf. It was a well-materialised ectoplasmic
> form . . . it was grey and colourless and . . . it had weight.
> I could distinctly feel its back pressing against me as it lay
> beside me on the bed as a large dog might.[203]

The extrusion snarled at her but, ever practical, she
drove an elbow into its 'hairy ectoplasmic ribs' and
told it to behave. The wolf got off the bed and turned
into a dog. 'Then the northern corner of the room
appeared to fade away and the creature went out
through the gap.'

It is clear that the wolf was a full-scale extrusion and
not simply a personal illusion, for despite its disappear-
ance 'through the gap', others in the house reported
being watched by feral eyes. Dion Fortune took the
matter under advisement from her esoteric superiors –
she was only a trainee magician at the time – and
consciously extruded the beast again in order to
reabsorb it properly.

Since not everyone is prepared to trust the reports
of occultists, it is interesting to discover similar
experiences discussed by writers who have never
waved a wand or evoked a spirit in their lives. In one
of his most fascinating books,[204] the research psychologist Stan Gooch describes something very similar to
Dion Fortune's extrusion – a personal encounter with
a succubus, traditionally considered a female demon
intent on intercourse with mortal men:

I was ... lying in a bed in the early morning, awake but drowsy, with daylight already broken ... when, with a strong sense of disbelief, I became aware of another person in bed with me. For a moment I totally dismissed the idea. Then she – it was a she – moved a little closer, pressing against me more urgently ...

I somehow knew that this was a 'psychic entity'. I knew it was not a real person who had got into my room by normal means ... Without opening my eyes, I realized that the 'person' in bed with me – in front of me, I should stress – was a composite of various girls I had known ... including my ex-wife, but with other elements, not drawn from my memories in any sense ... It was its own creature, but seemed, as it were, to be using part of my own experience in order to present itself to me.

On the first occasion my conscious interest in the situation got the better of me and the succubus gradually faded away. On subsequent occasions, however, the presence of the entity was maintained until finally we actually made love ...

I can only say that the experience is totally satisfying ... From some points of view, the sex is actually more satisfying than that with a real woman ...

Gooch's book develops the thesis, somewhat similar to our own, that the unconscious mind has an inherent ability to externalize itself in the form of poltergeist phenomena, incubi, succubi and various other forms once thought of as spirit or demonic. His personal experience is supported by historical and, more importantly, contemporary case-studies, including those of a well-known actress and a former detective sergeant of the Metropolitan Police.

There was nothing ethereal or nebulous about the 'spirits' encountered by these people. Gooch's own succubus was (or at least became) sufficiently solid for him to enjoy physical intercourse with her. The actress was attacked by an entity in the night which manifested such violence that it left her with a bloody mouth. Martyn Pryer, the detective sergeant, described one of his experiences in these words:

> With a massive 'whoosh' which I heard quite clearly, I was seized from behind by a man-like entity. It pinioned my legs with its legs, my arms with its arms, and began breathing heavily in my ear. I was fully conscious, but could not move a muscle.

If a projected entity could do this to a hefty policeman in the present day, it is, perhaps, not entirely outlandish to suggest that even more violent exteriorizations may have committed murder at Jena. Zenner's body, in particular, presents evidence to support some fascinating speculation: it was not only covered in huge weals and scratches, but there were many individual burns on the face and neck. One cannot help but wonder if he encountered some 'demon' similar to Amon, the serpent-headed wolf who vomits flame. For if Amon does not exist in his own right in the depths of some alien dimension, he certainly existed in the grimoires of the time and in the minds of those who used them.

This, as we have seen, is the critical factor. If it can be imagined by the human mind, it can be projected by the human mind into the workaday world. All that is really needed is prolonged, obsessive concentration, like that of Madame David-Neel's Tibetan artist. There is no doubt at all that in those chill pre-Christmas days, the conspirators at Jena concentrated obsessively on the notion of demonic spirits who could point the way to treasure. Their visualizations were reinforced by the descriptions in Weber's grimoires and fuelled by greed. Worse, they engaged in an operation of magic, a system, as we have seen, specifically designed to actualize such mental constructs. Worse still, they did so without reference to the proper safeguards. They became, over the critical period, that most dangerous of all species, the bungling amateur; and they paid a fearsome price.

Éliphas Lévi, who disliked 'phenomena', was more cautious. We may be assured he followed the magical instructions to the letter so that his *tulpa* of Apollonius materialized safely. The worst that happened to Lévi was a bit of a fright and a paralyzed arm, from both of which he quickly recovered.

John Dee and Edward Kelley were more fortunate still. Their 'spirits' remained controllable throughout the long series of experiments, possibly because they were careful to evoke them into a 'shewstone' and thus limit their ability to do damage. One scarcely knows what to make of the experience of Crowley and Neuburg. Crowley behaved with incredible stupidity for a trained magician, but seems to have gotten away with it. Neuburg, a relatively innocent victim of a much stronger personality, had an experience worthy of a horror movie, but came away with little enough permanent damage.

In his examination of exteriorization phenomena, Stan Gooch wrote:

> One of the clear conclusions of this survey is not simply that incubi, succubi and poltergeists are real, but that these phenomena are aspects of the human mind, not independent supernatural entities. Such a conclusion must, nevertheless, be seen in its wider context.

To Gooch, the wider context is that modern psychology is 'itself nothing more than an elaborate psychological defence mechanism against them [exteriorizations]'. This is an intriguing thought, but it is far from being the most important conclusion one might draw. Far more fundamental, surely, is the realization that our most widely accepted psychological models of the human mind are not merely limited, but downright misleading.

There is a famous proposition of logic concerning the colour of crows. It suggests that if you wish to demonstrate that not all crows are black, you are not required to show *all* crows are white. All you need to support your case is to produce a *single* white crow.

If the human mind is a subjective entity, mysteriously linked to the body, but otherwise divorced from physical reality, then it must, by definition, lack the means directly to influence matter. Yet we know, from Grey Walter's experiments and a great deal of other evidence, that it does not lack such means. This gives us our white crow. The human mind cannot be a subjective entity, as we have for so long been led to believe.

This does not, of course, negate every insight of contemporary psychology, but it does call for a new and fundamentally, different model of the psyche. This model must be sufficiently elastic to encompass evidence suggesting that mind forms a continuum with matter and, in certain circumstances, manifests itself far more like a place than a state.

Against this background, the whole testimony of magical practice – itself one of the oldest and most persistent of all human preoccupations – points towards interaction between both aspects of the continuum. It is well enough accepted that physical events can influence the mind. Magic insists the reverse is also true.

All psychological theories are no more than attempts to systemize empirical experience. To date, the empirical experience of magical practitioners (whether they see themselves as such or not) has been roundly ignored in the formulation of contemporary models. This is hardly surprising. The phenomena we have been examining are rare. *Tulpas*, however strong the evidence for their existence, do not appear every day, otherwise our cupboards would be chock-a-block with childhood nightmares. Synchronistic incidents are few and far between, otherwise they would not be noteworthy. Even successful magical operations do not happen all that frequently, for bringing them about requires intensive training and substantial effort. In these circumstances, it is hardly surprising that science has marched on, stolidly ignoring the evidence of magic. Magicians and occultists of all ages share a portion of the blame: they are typically secretive and not much given to investigation of how or why their methods work.

The situation as a whole is, however, unfortunate. Parapsychology is an uneasy science, for its laboratory techniques have (so far) yielded only small, emotionally unsatisfying results, like the deviations from chance expectation shown in Rhine's card-calling experiments. The most striking examples of psi phenomena – the violent poltergeists, the accurate prophecies, the wailing ghosts – have all (so far) refused to manifest to order under test conditions.

Yet creating such spectacular manifestations is just what magic is all about; and for that reason, if no other, deserves to be investigated far more fully.

The results of such an investigation may prove surprising, for if our suspicion that there is something to magicians' claims should prove correct, then we will have to revise more than our model of the human mind. Our model of physical reality will have to be revised as well.

This does not quite mean a return to what are now disparagingly called primitive belief systems. If our ancestors saw the world as populated by spirits and abutting fairyland, we can no longer say they were entirely wrong. But they were not entirely right either. What is needed is a far more subtle model; and one that is sufficiently flexible to answer some very difficult problems.

If, for example, it is possible to think a spirit (*tulpa*) into existence and for that spirit to show self-awareness, intelligence and knowledge, are we then safe in saying *all* spirits are *tulpas*? It seems unlikely, for we are aware of at least one spirit which was not 'thought up' in the manner of David-Neel's little monk – the 'spirit' within our own head. Do we then have a mix of 'natural' and 'artificial' spirits walking the world? And if we do, how can we differentiate one from the other? Philip, the 'ghost' created by the Toronto group, was so successful in mimicking the 'real thing' that his creators began to wonder if they might not have called up a deceased human accidentally.

Nor does magic begin and end with spirits, despite the attention we have paid to this type of magical phenomenon. There remains the problem of direct magical influence on what we have, until now, happily called 'objective reality'. Specifically, our model will have to tell us why, if wishing can make it so, wishing does not *always* – indeed not usually – make it so.

It may be that the starting-point for the development of a new model of reality will be the ancient magic of shamanic practice, now a far more fashionable focus of attention than it used to be. In the world of the shaman there has always been an 'imagination of matter' accessible via the imagination of the human mind. This is why certain sites were magical or holy: their inner continuum contained treasures of especial value. If the scientists can ever be persuaded to take this viewpoint seriously, even as a working hypothesis, we may yet open up wonders the like of which have gone undreamed of even by the most creative of our technicians.

And if there is a crying need for some genuine scientific investigation of magical techniques, there is an equally urgent need for the reappearance of a species now sadly close to extinction, the magical philosopher. The great names of the occult arts – Paracelsus, Cagliostro, even poor, deluded Dr Dee – were all prepared to speculate on how the effects of their chosen system came about. We may find their speculations naive today, but at least they tried. Modern magicians, almost without exception, are prepared to practise their art without the least attempt to find out how or why things work; or at best to accept without inquiry the theories of antiquity or the doctrines passed to them by disembodied entities whose very nature they have not even taken the trouble to understand.

NOTES

Chapter 1: The Cave-Art Mystery

1. It is likely, though not absolutely certain, that the figure was female.

2. Its financial characteristics, as an investment, tax haven or hedge against inflation, remain secondary, even in the most materialistic communities.

Chapter 2: Trance

3. As quoted by Rosalind Miles in *The Women's History of the World*, Paladin Books, London, 1989.

4. And quite possibly a great deal earlier.

5. The pronoun is a literary convenience. Shamans can be male or female. Given the matriarchal structure of prehistoric cultures, it is likely that Ice Age representatives of the profession were female. Today, in a majority of cultures, the shaman tends to be male.

Chapter 3: Shamanic Journey

6. From *Black Elk Speaks* by John. G. Neigardt, quoted by Nevill Drury in *The Elements of Shamanism*, Element Books, 1989.

7. Quoted by Nevill Drury in *The Elements of Shamanism*, Element Books, 1989.

8. From *The Way of the Shaman* by Michael Harner, Bantam Books, New York, 1986.

Chapter 4: Shamanic Sorcery

9. Quoted by Ernest de Martino in *Magic, Primitive and Modern*, Tom Stacey Ltd, 1972.

10. The whole incident is described by Trilles in *La sorcellerie chez les non-civilisés*, forming part of an analytical report on religious ethnology issued in 1914.

11. Quoted from Trilles' *Les Pygmées de l'Afrique Équatoriale* by Ernest de Martino in his *Magic, Primitive and Modern*.

12. Recounted in Grimble's *A Pattern of Islands*.

13. Quoted in *The Psychomental Complex of the Tungus*.

14. Quoted from *Among the Zulu and Amatongos* by D. Leslie, Edinburgh, 1875.

15. The story is told in Trilles' *Les Pygmées de la Forêt Equatoriale*, Paris, 1932.

16. Quoted from *The Chukchee, The Jessup North Pacific Expedition*. Vol. III.

17. I have bowdlerized his account by deleting the habitual quotation marks with which he encloses the word spirits and removed several references which leave the reader in no doubt about the cynicism engendered by his observations.

18. Publications of the Folk-lore Society, XV, 1884.

19. Although most of them hunt, which requires both.

Chapter 5: Modern Magic

20. Writing in the *Grolier Electronic Encyclopedia*.

21. 'Step on a crack, break your mother's back' according to the children's rhyme.

22. In *Highways of the Mind: The Art and History of Pathworking*, Aquarian Press, Wellingborough, 1987.

23. Ibid.

24. My own, I blush to report, among them.

25. Or uneducated individuals for that matter.

Chapter 6: Occult Practice

26. Literally 'black books', these were ancient, probably medieval, textbooks on magic.

27. A disc, made from wood or metal, inscribed on both sides and used for the control of spirits.

28. Saint-Sulpice was a seminary for secular priests who were not required to take a vow of celibacy.

29. This is the modern rendering. In Lévi's day, the more usual form was Kabbala, or sometimes Cabbala.

30. They have done rather better since his death. All Lévi's major works are still in print and avidly read by our present generation of occultists.

31. The glyph, two interlaced equilateral triangles, is identical to the *Megan David*, or Star of David, found, among other places, on the flag of modern Israel.

32. A contemporary of Christ, Apollonius was a Pythagorean initiate believed to exercise miraculous powers.

33. The quotes are from Lévi's own account of the operation in *Transcendental Magic: Its Dogma and Ritual.*

Chapter 7: Ritual at Jena

34. Which forms the basis of the present chapter.

35. In the (presumably substantial) number of cases where the dog did not die, it was considered naturally immune.

36. Belief in luck pennies endures in rural Ireland where I live, although with a slightly different definition. Here the 'luck penny' is a sum of money (no longer a literal penny) returned to the purchaser of livestock as a gesture supposed to bring luck to both participants in the deal.

37. And, apparently, his mandragore, for this would surely have been an ideal opportunity to test it.

38. The evocation of one's Guardian Angel according to the Abra-Melin system of magic, for example, calls for six months of stringent preparation.

Chapter 8: Enochian Magic

39. Even that curious modern work, *The Ceremonial Magician*, written under the pseudonym Chevalier, only purports to describe the outcome of an operation of Abra-Melin magic. When it comes to the crunch, we are left wondering if the man's Holy Guardian Angel actually did appear after all the trouble he took to invoke it.

40. Near Avignon in 1310.

41. Delightfully, Dee was issued with the code name 007.

42. He predicted Elizabeth's accession to the throne while she was still in jail, thus earning her lifelong admiration.

43. Also known as Edward Talbot.

44. In the original, Dee's name was denoted by the Greek letter *delta*. I have made the small change for the sake of clarity.

45. Quoted by John Symonds in his biography of Aleister Crowley, *The Great Beast*, Mayflower Books, London, 1973.

46. He habitually wore a skull-cap to hide the evidence of his conviction.

47. Jane Dee was many years younger than her husband and considerably more pretty than Mrs Kelley.

48. Including W. B. Yeats, Florence Farr, Sax Rohmer and Algernon Blackwood.

49. Crowley was bisexual and soon initiated Neuburg into a homosexual relationship.

50. Sometimes associated with skin problems, according to Crowley's own *Liber 777*.

51. 'Almighty and Ever-Living God.'

52. The words used are a mixture of Hebrew godnames and Qabalistic phrases.

53. Quoted in translation from volume four of Israel Regardie's *The Golden Dawn*, Aries Press, Chicago, 1940.

54. This is a reference to Gematria, a Qabalistic sub-system whereby numbers are substituted for letters in an individual name, then totalled to provide a final code. The best-known example of Gematria appears in the biblical Book of Revelation, where the Anti-Christ is numbered as 'six hundred, three score and six' – exactly double the number of Neuburg's demon.

55. See *The Magical Dilemma of Victor Neuburg* by Jean Overton Fuller, W. H. Allen, London, 1965.

Chapter 9: Inner Workings

56. In *Ritual Magic in England, 1887 to the Present Day*, Neville Spearman, London, 1970.

57. In its fullest form 'The science and art of creating changes of consciousness in accordance with the Will'. This was itself a reworking of Crowley's 'Magic is the science and art of creating change in accordance with the Will', a definition so wide that, as had been pointed out, it would have covered the drinking of a cup of tea.

58. An umbrella term which covers the occult practice, ancient and modern, of Europe, the Americas, Australia and the Middle and Near East.

59. The fearsome oaths to which he objected were finally abandoned as a general aspect of magical training by the middle of 1960s.

60. Quoted from volume one of Israel Regardie's *The Golden Dawn*, Aries Press, Chicago, 1937.

61. As an invocation in the morning and a banishing in the evening.

62. Magicians often say astral.

63. Robert Wang's useful little book, *The Secret Temple* (Samuel Weiser, New York, 1980), describes pillars, altar, banners, diagrams, tablets and such furnishings as lamp and censer – all prerequisites of a purely personal temple workplace. Magical Orders and similar groups will frequently construct substantially more elaborate temples.

64. The reference is to an earlier exercise in the course.

65. Now more respectably called out-of-body experience.

66. Energy centres believed by almost all occultists to exist within the human body or aura.

67. Quoted from *The Magician: His Training and Work*, Aquarian Press, 1963.

68. Ibid

Chapter 10: The Nature of Spirits

69. Quoted from *Magical Ritual Methods*, Helios Books, 1969.

70. Quoted from *Ritual Magic in England, 1887 to the Present Day*, Neville Spearman, London, 1970.

71. Quoted from *The Middle Pillar*, Aries Press, Chicago, 1945.

72. At least until the 1960s.

73. Quoted from Dion Fortune's *Psychic Self-Defence*, Aquarian Press, 1981.

74. Years ago, as a court reporter, I heard psychiatric evidence at an inquest on a schizophrenic who had killed himself on what he believed to be the instructions of spirit voices.

75. In his autobiography, *Memories, Dreams, Reflections*, Collins, London, 1963.

76. The case is quoted by Colin Wilson in *Mysteries*, Panther Books, London, 1979.

77. See Dr Prince's article, 'The Mother of Doris', in the *Proceedings of the American Society for Psychical Research*, New York, 1923.

78. The ranking of indwelling personae is intriguing since a majority of grimoires insist that the spirit kingdom is arranged in hierarchies, angelic and/or infernal, reinforcing the apparent connection between the 'spirits' of magic and the multiple personalities of psychiatry.

79. See *Sybil* by Flora Rheta Schreiber, Henry Regnery, New York, 1973.

80. See *When Rabbit Howls*, a biography written by the various personalities inhabiting the body of Truddi Chase, Pan Books, London, 1988.

81. At least I hope not, having been a practitioner of magical evocation myself in the past.

82. Who sooner or later find life so uncomfortable that they will typically seek psychiatric help or suicide.

Chapter 11: Creating a Ghost

83. See, for example, his *Astra and Flondrix*, Pantheon Books, New York, 1976.
84. *The Greythorn Woman*, Doubleday, New York and Collins, London, 1979.

85. Illustrated by an example from a slightly different field. Tibetan medical theory suggests that rotting meat is infested by tiny invisible demons which can cause illness ... a fascinating expression of Western bacteria theory within a different cultural context.

86. Aquarian Press, 1985.

Chapter 12: Spirits Visible

87. When Aleister Crowley claimed to have achieved it. See *The Great Beast* by John Symonds, Mayflower Books, London, 1973.

88. Quoted from *The Complete Golden Dawn System of Magic* by Israel Regardie, Falcon Press, Arizona, 1984.

89. Quoted from *The Magician: His Training and Work*, Aquarian Press, 1963.

90. Florence Farr, an initiate of the Golden Dawn.

91. Quoted from *Ritual Magic in England, 1887 to the Present Day*, Neville Spearman, London, 1970.

92. A pseudonym. While the entertainer concerned is, so far as I am aware, now retired from the stage, I doubt he would approve of my revealing his trade secrets too openly.

93. Quoted from *Magic and Mystery in Tibet* by Alexandra David-Neel, Souvenir Press, London, 1967.

94. Ibid.

95. Ibid.

96. Ibid.

97. One wonders in passing whether this begins to explain the historical link between magic and the bard; not to mention Robert Graves' curious assertion that the nearest thing to a magician has always been a poet.

Chapter 13: Spirit Knowledge

98. Quoted from the King James Edition.

99. Quoted from *Fifty Years a Medium* by Estelle Roberts, Corgi Books, London, 1969.

100. From *The Reincarnation Workbook*, Aquarian Press, 1989.

101. Methods of uncovering what appear to be memories of past lives.

102. A pseudonym used by Bloxham when the case became public.

103. Lady of the house.

104. *More Lives Than One*? Pan Books, 1977, from which the foregoing extract was quoted.

105. For a fuller outline of this intrinsically fascinating case, see Ian Wilson's *The After Death Experience*, Corgi, 1989.

106. From the *New Scientist*, 20 August 1970, as quoted by Arthur Koestler in *The Roots of Coincidence*, Hutchinson, London, 1972.

Chapter 14: Spirit Action

107. In his *Poltergeist: A Study in Destructive Haunting*, New English Library, London, 1981.

108. Which stood on the site of the present Zouche Manor.

109. All names in this case-study are fictitious in order to preserve the privacy of those involved, but the essential facts are reported without distortion.

110. Two of her children did, however, find her in a heap at the bottom.

111. Quoted from *Poltergeist: A Study in Destructive Haunting* by Colin Wilson, New English Library, London, 1981.

112. For a much fuller exposition of Batcheldor's important work than this brief précis, see my book *Mindreach*, Aquarian Press, Wellingborough, 1985.

113. From Batcheldor's original article as quoted in *Mindreach*.

114. Quoted from *Mindreach*.

115. From Jung's *Collected Letters*, Vol. I, as quoted by Colin Wilson in *Afterlife*, Grafton Books, 1987.

Chapter 15: Occult Anatomy

116. Quoted from *The Divine Pymander of Hermes Trismegistus*, Shrine of Wisdom, London, 1923.

117. Although not all modern astrologers would subscribe to it.

118. Quoted from *The Art of True Healing*, Helios Books, 1966.

119. Ibid.

120. And possibly plants and animals as well.

121. In *Awareness*, Berkley, New York, 1968.

122. Metal electrodes carrying high frequency charges tend to be dangerous, and can sometimes be lethal.

123. Quoted from *Psychic Discoveries Behind the Iron Curtain* by Sheila Ostrander and Lynn Schroeder, Bantam Books, New York, 1971.

124. Quoted from the private papers of an esoteric school in the author's possession.

125. Notably those along the midline.

126. Relaxation, simple breathing exercises and, in some cases, sonic vibrations also play a part.

Chapter 16: Magical Influence

127. See, among various other sources, *Peace, Love and*

Healing by Bernie Siegel, Rider, London, 1990.

128. *Liber 777* available as *777 and Other Qabalistic Writings of Aleister Crowley*, Samuel Weiser, USA, 1987.

129. Quoted from *The Art of True Healing*, by Israel Regardie, Helios Books, 1966.

130. An exercise in the stimulation of the central astro-mental centres.

131. Quoted from *The Art of True Healing*.

132. Quoted from *Magick in Theory and Practice* by The Master Therion, undated edition privately published by the author.

133. Ibid.

134. Quoted from *The Complete Magic Curriculum of the Secret Order G:B:G:* by Louis T. Culling, Llewellyn, USA, 1969.

135. Quoted from *Magic for the Aquarian Age* by Marian Green, Aquarian Press, Wellingborough, 1984.

136. Quoted from *The Power of Your Subconscious Mind* by Joseph Murphy, Prentice-Hall, New Jersey, 1987.

137. Quoted from *Psychogenesis* by J. E. Addington, Dodd, Mead & Co., New York, 1977.

138. Ibid.

139. Quoted from *Your Maximum Mind* by Herbert Benson, Random House, New York, 1987.

Chapter 17: Synchronicity

140. Quoted by Arthur Koestler in *The Roots of Coincidence*, Hutchinson, London, 1972. The studies were Koestler's own translation from Kammerer's *Das Gesetz der Serie*, published in 1919 but unavailable in English.

141. Ibid.

142. A Swiss version of the British 'April Fool'.

143. Quoted from *Synchronicity: An Acausal Connecting Principle* by C. G. Jung, Routledge and Kegan Paul, London, 1972.

144. Ibid.

145. Ibid.

146. See *The Roots of Coincidence*.

147. Difficult, but not quite impossible. *The Jupiter Effect* by John Gribbin and Stephen Plagemann (Fontana/Collins, London, 1977) argues the possibility that Jupiter's gravitational field may be among the factors involved in earthquakes. This is, however, a far cry from traditional astrology which looks on Jupiter, by and large, as the harbinger of good fortune.

148. Quoted from *The Cosmic Clocks* by Michel Gauquelin, Paladin Books, St Albans, 1973.

149. To complicate the picture even further, Gauquelin eventually discovered there actually *was* a clear statistical relationship between certain horoscope positions and human personality characteristics. The positions were *not* those of traditional astrology and in effect formed a completely new, statistically verified system of 'astrology' – which has been roundly ignored by astrologers ever since.

150. Quoted from *Synchronicity: An Acausal Connecting Principle*.

151. Lest the thesis, so baldly presented, seems too farfetched for serious consideration, let me emphasize that at this point I am not at all concerned by how magic works – that little problem will be dealt with later. All I want to show at this stage is that the familiar elements of magical practice are present, albeit quite unwittingly, in many instances of synchronistic coincidence.

152. From *The Structure and Dynamics of the Psyche*, Collected Works, Vol. VIII, Hull, London, 1960.

153. *Experimental Magic*, Aquarian Press, Wellingborough, 1973.

154. And was asked to become Honorary President of the British Society of Synchronicists for my pains!

Chapter 18: Alchemy

155. Britain's Royal Family employs a homoeopathic physician.

156. Quoted from *Psychology and Alchemy* by C. G. Jung, Routledge and Kegan Paul, London, 1980.

157. Ibid.

158. Ibid.

159. Or sometimes silver.

160. Price apparently created silver by mixing a white powder with mercury, borax and nitre, then stirring the heated mixture with an iron rod. The same operation using a red powder produced gold. Following his suicide, by drinking prussic acid, the assumption was that he had introduced the precious metals into his mixtures through the hollow stirring rod.

161. Quoted from *Man, Myth and Magic*, by Hans Biedermann, Purnell, London, undated.

Chapter 19: Impossible Objects

162. Quoted from *The Turin Shroud* by Ian Wilson, Penguin Books, 1979.

163. The published findings suggest a date of AD 1325, plus or minus sixty-five years to allow for the imprecision of the carbon dating method.

164. Quoted from *The Turin Shroud*.

165. For a fuller exposition of this interesting theory, see Tort's paper in the *Journal of the Society for Psychical Research*, Vol. 56, No. 818, January 1990.

166. One instance of a 'ghost' at a window turned out to be the photographic imprint of the house occupant on the glass. The 'snapshot' occurred naturally while she was watching a thunderstorm.

Chapter 20: Witch-Doctors

167. A pseudonym.

168. Perhaps not coincidentally, the time between treatment – of any sort – and result has remained constant at three weeks, exactly the time it took for Jean Manchester's warts to disappear.

169. From *Sylva Sylvarum* by Francis Bacon, quoted by J. Finley Hurley in *Sorcery*, Routledge and Kegan Paul, London, 1985.

170. Quoted from the *Grolier Electronic Encyclopedia*.

171. And also how unwise it can be to believe everything you read in the papers.

172. In *Sorcery*, where he quotes Evans' findings.

173. Genuine drugs show this decline effect as well, prompting one physician to advise, 'You should treat as many patients as possible with the new drugs while they still have the power to heal.'

174. Published in the journal *Circulation* in 1958.

175. Shortcomings in Rhine's original experiments have been corrected by the host of parapsychologists who attempted to duplicate his work in subsequent years. With the loopholes closed, statistical evidence of telepathy continues to present itself.

176. It may be as well to mention I had Léonie's permission for the experimentation, although she had no prior warning of when it was likely to take place.

177. Ochorovicz remarked unkindly that this was due to the strain of thinking.

Chapter 21: Astral Plane

178. Quoted from *The Archidoxes of Magic* by Paracelsus, facsimile of the 1656 edition published by Askin, London, 1975.

179. Quoted from *The History of Magic* by Éliphas Lévi, Rider, London, 1922.

180. *Astral Doorways* and *The Astral Projection Workbook*, both published by Aquarian Press, Wellingborough.

181. Quoted from *Four Archetypes* by C. G. Jung, Routledge and Kegan Paul, London, 1972.

182. Quoted from *Memories, Dreams, Reflections* by C. G. Jung, Collins/Fontana, London, 1971.

183. In *The Way of the Shaman* by Michael Harner, Bantam Books, New York, 1986.

184. Ibid.

185. Quoted from the King James Edition.

186. Ibid.

Chapter 22: The Physics of Sorcery

187. When they do not simply consider it as a state of consciousness.

188. For a synopsis of the research, see *The Roots of Coincidence* by Arthur Koestler, Hutchinson, London, 1972.

189. Although it is fair to say she was never tempted to confuse them with physical objects.

190. For a fuller exposition of the Abra-Melin system, see *The Book of the Sacred Magic of Abra-Melin the Mage*, S. L. MacGregor Mathers trans., Aquarian Press, Wellingborough.

191. And the scientist, you will recall, who collaborated with Carl Jung to develop the theory of synchronicity.

Chapter 23: Forgotten Secret

192. *The Occult*, Grafton Books, 1989.

193. In *The Origin of Consciousness in the Breakdown of the Bicameral Mind*, Houghton Mifflin, 1976.

194. In *The Science of Thought*, Scribner, New York.

195. Not unlike the Chinese concept of universal *ch'i* or the Hindu *prana*.

Chapter 24: Spirit Wolf

196. Quoted from *The Way of the Shaman*, Bantam Books, New York, 1986.

197. Ibid.

198. Notably Barbara G. Walker.

199. For much fuller exposition, see my own *Astral Doorways*, Aquarian Press, Wellingborough.

200. Quoted from the Richard Wilhelm translation of the *I Ching*, rendered into English by Cary F. Baynes, Routledge & Kegan Paul, London, 1969.

201. See, for example, his *Voodoo Island*, Four Square Books, London, 1966.

Chapter 25: Intrusions

202. Quoted from *The Book of Ceremonial Magic* by Arthur Edward Waite, University Books, New York, 1961.

203. Quoted from *Psychic Self-Defence* by Dion Fortune, Aquarian Press, Wellingborough, 1981.

204. *Creatures from Inner Space* by Stan Gooch, Rider, 1984.